Copyright © 2019
All rights reserved

This book or any portion thereof may not be reproduced or used in any manner whatsoever without permission.

For more information about this book and others, please visit www.enlivenculture.co.uk

Acknowledgements

This book is published by Enliven Press, for Didcot Writers.

Didcot Writers opened international submissions for this volume in January 2019, and received over fifty works, of which thirty-one were selected for publication, from thirty authors. Submissions were judged anonymously by members of Didcot Writers.

We are very grateful for the time given by our judging team:
- Angus Broadbent
- Sarah Byrne
- Zoe Chater
- Emma Crees
- Sheila Davie
- Maggie Elliott
- Linda Francis
- Margaret Gallop
- Tracy Hewitson
- Rachel Waters
- Kathryn Wills

We would like to thank our editors, Alice Little and Mike Evis, for making each of the stories accepted the best it could be. We would also like to thank our proofreader, Rose Little.

To find out about future opportunities for publication, local writing events, workshops, competitions, and everything else we do, visit **bit.ly/didcotwriters**.

First Contact

Edited by Alice Little and Mike Evis

Contents

Staring at the Sun, by MM Lewis — 9

Playing Bach on the Equator, by Rose Little — 15

Introvert, Extrovert, by Zoe Chater — 22

Condolences, by Angus Broadbent — 30

Oh, What a Night, by Lavonne Roberts — 43

Her First Lead, by Mike Evis — 47

Take My Hand, by Alice Little — 62

The Ultimate Joink's Exploration of Planet Beautiful, by Margaret Gallop — 68

Grandmother knows best, by Oliver Bussell — 77

Unexpected Turns, by Abigail B Vint — 83

The New Term, by Rachel Waters — 97

The Right Choice, by Emma Crees — 101

Making Contact, by David Rudd — 108

Reaping and Sowing, by Sarah Byrne — 116

People I Know, by David McVey — 128

Night Without End, by Stewart Greene — 135

Handmade by Rosa, by Tony Lawrence — 139

Exoskeleton, by Grant Waters — 150

Serving Tea to God, by Marina Favila — 156

Pandemonium, by Kathryn Wills — 168

Swarmer, by James Debenham	*173*
The Dressmaker, by Deborah Freeman	*183*
A Moment in Time, by Thomas Redjeb	*194*
Found and Lost, by Clare Marsh	*198*
Time's Corner, by John Ludlam	*204*
Bridal Veil and Visions in Red, by Shirley Muir	*218*
Absent Friends and New Acquaintances, by David Perlmutter	*225*
Gift of the Sky God, by Arthur Carey	*228*
Home Improvements, by Georgia Hilton	*232*
Seeing is believing, by David Binelli	*238*
La Petite France, by Mike Evis	*243*
About the Authors	*261*

Staring at the Sun

by MM Lewis

Don't look up. Keep Calm and Carry On. That had been the government advice. Some mastermind at the Home Office had decided it was time to use the posters that had become so popular during the Recession. Now something more ominous than the threat of financial catastrophe hung over people.

Don't look up. Of course everyone looked up. Jacob Freeman always left the curtains closed when he got ready in the morning though, resisting the itch to see if it was still there.

'Why don't you open the curtains now?' Jacob said, standing in the doorway.

Diane's lined face was sad, as ever these days. 'It's a bright, fresh morning,' he continued. 'There's no sense being in denial.' Diane's mouth twisted into a smile. 'It'll be there, whether you open the curtains or not. It's not going anywhere. We might as well get some daylight.'

'Do you have to go?' Diane asked.

Jacob chewed it over for a moment.

'I have to see a patient. I would consider her psychologically vulnerable.'

'That's more important than us?' Diane looked down, considered, and said with difficulty, 'I'm afraid. They keep looking at me.'

'Of course it's not more important than you. But I have to work. I have to pay the mortgage.'

'The world's ending! Don't worry about the mortgage.'

'Diane, the world is not ending. Stay indoors if you need to. I'll not be late home. You're rational enough to know there's nothing there. If there was really anything in the sky it would have had a devastating effect on the Earth's atmosphere and tides. It's a mass hallucination. End of.'

Diane laughed.

Jacob grasped her hands gently and looked in her eyes. 'Tell me you'll be OK.'

'You know I will be,' she said, but she did not meet his eyes. 'Do you really have to work today? It was nice when you only worked three days a week.' Jacob had reduced his hours to spend more time with Diane and her shattered nerves. Three days a week just about paid enough, but it was hard. And now he found himself working full time anyway, trying to contain the situation.

'I've got a responsibility to my patients. This has tipped so many of them off the edge. And there is nothing up there, no monsters, no alien invasion and certainly no God watching over us, there's just us.' He stopped, and looking at Diane's face realised his tone had become harsh. He stroked her cheek and spoke quietly, 'So we're going to have to look out for each other.'

He knew very well his words sounded hollow. He looked away as Diane's eyes locked on his.

Jacob left, and as he looked back, spotted her peering through a gap in the curtains. He couldn't help but see that the sky still burned, even though that was not what Diane saw. Diane had told him she saw eyes, watching.

*

As Jacob drove to work, he listened to Radio 4 for reassurance; it was not reassuring. John Humphrys was interviewing the Home Secretary.

'Is that the best you can do?' Humphrys said. 'Keep Calm and Carry On: really? What is this? You must know. Is this a first contact event with an alien civilisation?'

'We don't believe so. We've been monitoring the situation in the sky. There have been unprecedented levels of cooperation between the greatest minds of all nations on this, and all are agreed, nothing has physically changed up there. Nothing.'

'What do you see?'

'I'm not here to talk about what I see. There is nothing there. It's been scientifically proven.'

'So you do see something! What is it?'

'That's not relevant here, it's a personal matter.'

'The public deserve to know your state of mind.'

'My state of mind is totally focussed on being Home Secretary, John.'

'Really? You don't fear what you see? Well, I see a host of angels with flaming swords. And I'm an atheist! What do you think is really there?'

'It's a mass hallucination.'

'A mass hallucination that is different for everyone? Come on. You haven't got a clue what's going on, have you?'

'That's rather an unhelpful way of putting it. Our emergency planners and analysts are on top of this and have determined there is no clear and present danger, except from panic. My message is that people need to keep working, keep paying the bills, keep buying. Carry on with normal life and this will work out.'

'But how will it work out? And what are you doing about the thing in the sky? Many councils have even published contingency plans for zombies, for God's sake. You say it's been scientifically proven there is nothing up there. But you haven't shown us any convincing proof!'

And so they argued.

As Jacob drove on, the streets he passed through were filthy, so many people had given up. Rubbish was piling up, rats and dogs ran freely. At least there were fewer cars on the roads as more and more people stayed at home. People felt like they were on notice. Analysing himself, Jacob was throwing himself into his work. It was too hot in the car, he was sweating. Of course the flames weren't real, but then why did they feel so hot?

His first patient today, Elise Ridley, was a young woman who had at one point been on suicide watch, and before that was self-harming. She had divorced parents who both needed their careers more than each other, who found family life too difficult – like his own parents. Jacob had wanted to fix them, like he wanted to fix everyone.

The patient wore a sleeveless vest, and Jacob was glad to see there were no signs of recent scarring or drug use on her arms.

Her nail varnish was chipped, she picked at it when they talked. Her hair hadn't been washed for several days, and although she wore make-up, he suspected it was more to cover up how tired she looked, rather than for adornment.

Jacob went through his process. Pleasantries to make the patient feel at ease, questions to draw her out, probing questions to clarify, open questions to help the young woman come to her own conclusions. Last time she had opened up about her family background that left her needing to find meaning through her work, but the problem was that her work, teaching in a secondary school, was so difficult. Elise lived with depression, the pressure she was under fed it, but the alertness she needed in work precluded a lot of potential drug treatments. Her live-in boyfriend, a crane operator, was no help. He lived in computer games.

'He sees an armada of spaceships,' Elise said. 'Star Destroyers, Tie Fighters, from Star Wars. Poor Glyn, he's afraid to go up in his crane now. He's taken two weeks off work in the hope all this will blow over. I wish I could share his optimism.'

'And what do you see?' The key point. Whatever she saw had triggered a new episode of depression. She hadn't been able to face work, or leave the house, apart from this appointment, for two weeks.

'I don't know.'

'Elise, if you don't tell me, then I can't help you.'

She twisted her necklace around her fingers and looked around, and at the window. The blinds were closed.

'I mean I don't know. I haven't looked.'

'How can you not look up at all?'

'I stay in most of the time. Eyes to the ground, the rest.'

'Why not look up. Aren't you curious?'

'I'm afraid.'

'You can't face something if you don't look at it.'

The session ended without any agreement. They arranged another appointment for a week's time.

Jacob opened the blind an inch and peeked out. The sky was still on fire, even though the online weather report showed it was a cold fresh morning. He went back to the positive anchors: his desk, his framed qualifications, his orderly stationery. Limited comfort when the sky was burning.

Jacob picked up the phone. He had five minutes until his next appointment, a fifty-year-old man who saw himself in the sky, which had only fed his borderline egomania. Jacob called Diane. The borderline egomaniac could wait, even though he wouldn't understand.

On the other end of the phone Diane sounded frightened. She was still at home.

'It's the eyes,' Diane said. 'They've got closer.'

'You think the world's ending.'

'Jacob for God's sake, open your office blinds. Look out of the window.'

Jacob looked outside, and to his horror, the flames were closer. He had even started to feel the heat through the glass.

'Diane, I'm coming home.'

As he left the office, he spoke to the receptionist. 'Katie,' he said, 'tell the egomaniac he'll have to reschedule.'

'It'll do him good,' she said.

Jacob kept his eyes on the rubbish-strewn pavement, then on the road when he drove, but the flames were low enough now that everything had an orange tinge, and he felt the heat rising in the car. The route was diverted because of rioting, then the traffic just stopped. The road was blocked by abandoned cars, scattered like discarded toys. Jacob could smell ashes now, the heat was so close he was sweating uncontrollably and he wondered how long it would be until his exposed skin started to blister. He got out of the car and walked purposefully, avoiding eye contact with any of the increasingly desperate people in their own private hells, some looking skyward while others looked at the ground. Some stumbled around with eyes closed, or even blindfolded. One poor wretch had blinded himself.

Jacob's mobile rang. Not now. He clicked to cut the call off.

Walking on, he gritted his teeth. He was only a few miles from home. He felt the heat on his skin now, saw it start to swell. He could smell his own flesh cooking. He had to get home.

*

Jacob found the curtains drawn when he reached the house. Diane's hands trembled as she poured him a whisky. He looked down at his blistered, shaking hands.

'What happened?' Jacob asked.

'I looked. I couldn't stop myself. It's got worse. There are mouths now, as well as the eyes. They won't stop talking. They say terrible things. What is it all about?' Diane asked. 'Why do we all see something different? If we at least saw the same thing, the same fears, maybe we could all face them together. But this? All of us are alone.'

Jacob nodded, and necked his whisky, then checked his voicemail. It was a young woman's voice, distant, as if she was speaking from another world.

'I'm sitting here on the beach of the Thames,' she said. God. It was Elise Ridley. That lost young woman. 'I guess the world is ending, looking at the people, they're so afraid. They're just running into the river. But I don't see it. The sky is just the sky. I can see the sun in a break in white clouds. And there's nothing to fear. And I think I'm the most alone person in the world.'

Jacob's face crumbled with despair and Diane grasped his hand.

'You can't fix it all Jacob. You never could. Not even us. But bless you for trying.'

Jacob switched the phone off and poured himself another whisky, as he felt himself burning, saw the smoke, smelled his flesh cooking. He closed his eyes; the noise in the background did not matter to him anymore.

Playing Bach on the Equator

by Rose Little

When Grace arrived at Naranda School, a hundred miles north of Nairobi and a stone's throw from the equator, her spirits rose as soon as she spotted the upright piano in its oak case, pushed to a corner of the stage. There weren't many pianos in upcountry Kenya in the 1970s. Although confident with teenage students, she was shy, especially with men, and only felt truly at ease when she was playing; but Mr Kamau, the deputy head, was steering her away and they left the hall.

'I expect you'd like to see your house and settle in,' said Mr Kamau, bringing her tour of the school to an end. He had met her at Naivasha railway station for the drive up to the school and had given her dinner. Now he courteously refrained from checking his watch. 'I like to look in on the students at prep,' he remarked casually.

'Yes, of course,' said Grace. 'I expect they'd go off to the village, would they, or go back to the dorms if you weren't there?'

Mr Kamau laughed. 'No, they are very good students. Very studious. It is important to them.'

Grace was embarrassed at her gaffe. 'I see,' she said. 'That's excellent.'

'Secondary education is expensive. They do not want to fail and disappoint their families.'

'No.' Inspired by her recent reading she ventured, 'Are all the students Kikuyus?'

'Many are,' he replied, 'but we have several different tribes here – Luos and Kalenjins, Masai…' and Mr Kamau mentioned another name that Grace didn't catch: there was so much to take in. She thought regretfully of the piano in its corner and wondered if she could slip back. She was longing to try it out and she knew that once her fingers touched the keys she would feel at home in this strange environment. But Mr Kamau led her along the path to the row of English-looking bungalows opposite the school and pushed open a door. It was in two halves, like a stable door, and they stood in the freshly painted kitchen of the bungalow that would be her home for the next two and a half years.

'You have plenty of neighbours here,' he said, his voice full of enthusiasm, his smile never wavering. He indicated the row of identical bungalows either side of hers. 'But I'm afraid the teachers have gone out tonight with some of our students – to the school in Thompson's Falls. Their English class has put on a play.' He beamed. *This must be a highlight of the social calendar,* thought Grace, murmuring appreciatively. So, her mother had been right, there wasn't much going on here. She began to miss her friend Janet even more than on the journey out.

'I'll leave you to get unpacked,' Mr Kamau was saying, 'and we'll see you at the staff meeting tomorrow morning, nine o'clock.'

Grace said goodbye and manufactured what she hoped was a convincing answering smile as he turned away: what a long day! First the flight with East African Airways – it had been smooth enough but she had not flown before, in spite of Freddie Laker and his student deals to the USA. She saw the chequerboard of English fields passing further away below her and her stomach dropped. Then they were above the clouds, and the sunshine reflected on the white blanket below. She stopped feeling scared: the illusion of the safety net steadied her nerves. Conscientiously, Grace read the recommended book about the Kikuyu people, *Facing Mount Kenya,* till she finally dozed off, but the eight-hour flight seemed long and she woke up grumpy.

When she arrived in Nairobi, the scarlet bougainvillea everywhere consoled her, greeting her with a blaze of beauty. She took a taxi to the railway station, opening her window to benefit from the breeze and narrowing her eyes against the glare. Thank goodness Naranda was eight thousand feet up and consequently much cooler. In the streets the women carried baskets and were dressed in cotton tops and skirts in orange and purple and red. The men mostly wore trousers and open-necked shirts left untucked.

In the train Grace shared a carriage with two Kenyan businessmen in opposite corners who were leaning forward and talking in low voices, speaking in English, she noted. She was relieved they did not pay her any attention. She felt shy of them and didn't want to have to make conversation. The countryside rolled by as she watched – it was disappointingly dull and brown. The men occasionally glanced at the reserved English girl who stared out of the window, no doubt stunned by the grandeur of the scenery as they dropped down the escarpment into the Rift Valley on their way to Naivasha.

Standing in her kitchen Grace blinked and returned to the present. She felt overtired and agitated. If only Janet had been accepted too, they could have shared all this as they had shared everything in boarding school, and afterwards at university.

Kenya had seemed fascinating when the newly returned expatriate gave them a talk in their final year. He was an enthusiastic speaker, showing slides of his safari in the Masai Mara with lion cubs playing and gazelles leaping, as well as shots of his Kenyan students standing round the school flagpole in dazzling sunshine. He told anecdotes about the people he had met and he peppered it all with quirky local knowledge. She and Janet both applied but Janet was unsuccessful. She planned to write to Janet about everything; she must buy some aerograms.

Meanwhile she had her house to explore. She walked across the kitchen to the sitting room and through some french windows into the garden. She could smell the wood smoke from the village just down the hill from the school: people were stoking their fires on their smallholdings or *shambas*. She was pleased to have remembered the word, but felt suddenly doubtful about the life she had chosen – she couldn't speak the local Kikuyu language, would she fit in here?

Grace thought of the people in their simple huts below and felt almost guilty, her house with its electricity and plumbing was a palace by comparison. Over the hedge at the back of her little lawn stretched green fields of young maize, very soothing to her eyes, and gradually her chaotic thoughts drifted away in the still of the evening. The sun was going down fast, and there was that lovely hush that comes when work is over and it's not yet twilight.

Grace became restless and her thoughts returned to the neglected piano: she would go and play it tonight, as tomorrow it would be new people, lessons to give, information to take in – she would be starting work. Her heart turned over with excitement, this was really *it*. She felt renewed, full of energy, and quickly putting on her cardigan she left the house for the school.

No one was about. The students, she could see through the lighted classroom windows, were all bent over their desks at prep, brown heads and black, girls and boys. The light was failing and the businesslike feel of the school changed to uncertainty in the dimness. She thought she could remember her way to the hall but was it a wise thing to do, wandering about at dusk? What if she was challenged by the caretaker?

She found the main corridor, gloomy and deserted at this hour. She wasn't going to give up. After playing, she felt sure, she would be able to sleep in an unfamiliar bed and face the challenge of her first day.

Grace opened a door at the end of the corridor and found herself immediately in the school hall. She was taken aback to see a small light shining on the stage and to hear someone already playing. But the lure of the music emboldened her and she stepped into the room, listening entranced: it was her favourite Chopin nocturne, the one in E flat major. As a child she had come home from school to hear her piano-teacher mother playing it and that had been the start of her love affair with music.

Grace made no sound but the pianist somehow became aware of her. He stopped in the middle of a bar and turned round. He was fair-haired, compactly built and healthy looking, with a steady, frank expression.

'Hi,' he said, 'come on in!' and he stood up. He was obviously an American, friendly and reassuring, probably a Peace Corps volunteer. The temperature had dropped when the sun set but he didn't seem to mind, for he wore only shorts and a short-sleeved shirt. As there was no avoiding it she walked towards him down the length of the dim hall, across the rough concrete floor. He stepped forward to meet her and held out his hand.

'Spencer Adams, I teach Math,' he said, 'and I'm Acting Head of Science.'

'Grace Harmer,' she replied, shaking his hand, his firm grip meeting her cool and nervous one.

'You must be the new science teacher – I hope someone welcomed you, showed you around?'

'Yes, Mr Kamau was very kind. Won't you go on playing?'

'Oh… that's alright.'

He looked back at her in the half light. She imagined what he saw: a tall, self-possessed young woman with long dark hair to her waist, tapering to a point down her back. She wore a summer dress of filmy material under her cardigan, cool and shimmering green.

'Have you been teaching long?' he asked.

'No, I've come straight from university.' She looked at him anxiously. 'Of course I've done a term's teaching practice.'

Spencer nodded. 'You'll find the teaching here a breeze, the students are very respectful – and smart!'

'I hope they'll like me!'

'Why wouldn't they?'

They were walking back into the circle of light.

'It gets dark very suddenly here,' Grace observed, talking to cover her anxiety.

'Regular all year round, come six o'clock sun's below the horizon. You don't get any twilight. Sunup's worth watching though.'

'Are you up at that time?'

'Six o'clock? Sure.' Spencer smiled at her.

'I was worried the caretaker would wonder what I was doing, prowling around after dark,' Grace confided.

'You mean the watchman? You wouldn't be challenged by him. He would know you're a teacher. *Wazungu* round here are always teachers.'

'*Wazungu?*'

'It's a Swahili word, the plural of *muzungu* – you're a *muzungu*, so am I, a white person.'

Spencer had noticed her stray glances towards the upright on the stage.

'Do you want to play?' he asked her.

She was a little self-conscious but she really needed to touch that keyboard. She sat down on the piano stool. Her fingers fumbled for a moment – would he like more Chopin? But after that nocturne she felt Bach was the only possible choice, and she decided on the adagio from Concerto No 5. The sublimity of Bach's architecture put her mind into order as she played, until each layer of the day's impressions, delight and doubt, was calmed and she felt in control again.

She came to the end and looked round at Spencer.

'Mmm,' he said. 'Mmm.' He seemed to return from a distance. He was gazing at her intently and she realised that he had been moved. She smiled to herself a little as she looked down and closed the piano lid.

'We-ell… I guess I'll see you tomorrow, Grace,' he said. 'I've got some marking to do right now, but there's the staff meeting in the morning. I'll introduce you to a bunch of people.'

Grace was sorry not to go on talking to Spencer but it seemed he had nothing further to say to her. She stood up. 'That would be great!' she said. And he nodded and led the way out.

Grace allowed herself to be conducted from the hall and returned to the front of the school in a kind of dream. The buildings were well lit now as the lamps had come on, and in a few steps she was back at her front door. Spencer waved as he set off for his own house and she was alone with her thoughts once more. There were no lights on next door and there was nothing for it but to go to bed. But she had been comforted, taken up, and the world felt less strange. She began to hum to herself.

As she was falling asleep, the music she and Spencer had shared continued to sound in her head, a soothing backdrop to the scenes of the day that replayed themselves in radiant colours. She would start work tomorrow and her new life would begin. In the classroom the students would look up at her expectantly, and lion cubs would tumble and gazelles leap in the Masai Mara.

Grace smiled and slept.

Introvert, Extrovert

by Zoe Chater

Dr Penny Greenwald had no intention of making small talk with strangers today, thank you very much. She was sitting quietly on the platform at Congleton railway station, her headphones providing a backdrop of nineties indie, making absolutely no eye contact with anyone. Her face was, as usual, firmly buried in an obscurely titled book. Today's choice was *Quantum: A Guide For The Perplexed*, by Jim Al-Khalili.

Everything about Penny said, 'Leave me alone, I am not in a chit-chat mood.' She was, therefore, understandably narked when she was tapped on the shoulder and assaulted with an 'Oh, wow, I've read that one!', delivered loudly and animatedly by a tall, sweaty woman, fifty or so to judge from her eyes, but with the acne of a teenager, grinning inanely and gesturing at her to remove her headphones. 'Have you listened to his *Life Scientific* podcast?'

*

Bernie Harkness was already feeling better. This trip was going to be good for her, she could feel it in her bones. The sun was starting to peep through the clouds, giving her skin that involuntary tingle of pleasure. She hadn't even boarded her train, yet her mind was starting to buzz, to delight in the thrill of being off-timetable.

This break was all about taking risks, getting comfortable with being uncomfortable. Bernie was heading into Manchester to spend a week learning the basics of amateur urban photography. She would start each day with an hour of class, in a structured environment along with other people who were all there to learn the same thing. There would probably be some kind of get-to-know-each-other activity with clear rules to follow. This was her favourite kind of socialising.

Then, later, she would hit the city streets of the Northern quarter, China Town and the stunning Victoria Station, observing, trying to catch the beauty in the bustle of people. Surrounded by hundreds of strangers, she would be able to practise her strategies, try to start conversations, and when it all flopped she wouldn't have to see them again. 'The goal, actually, is to be rejected,' her therapist had said. 'Rejected, over and over, until it starts to feel safe to fail.' That was the plan. Fail, like she always had, but without the high stakes, the terrible consequences. And hopefully, gradually, to get used to the crippling embarrassment that would come afterwards.

Now though, before her journey had even started, here she was sharing a near-empty platform with this smart-looking young woman with a cool intellectual vibe. She was reading a physics book of all things. It felt like fate. She was surely destined to be Bernie's companion for the journey, and her first risk of the week. Perhaps she would tell her to sod off. Or perhaps they would become friends. Either way, Bernie knew they were meant to meet.

'Are you heading into Manchester, too?'

*

Having not answered the first question, Penny was perplexed as to why this odd individual was asking yet another. Yes, she too was Manchester-bound, heading to university late, as she had spent the morning at home reading a student's thesis draft. She had a horrible thought that this would put them in each other's company for the next forty minutes. It was now past the point where she could continue to ignore the woman without looking overtly rude, so she reluctantly removed one, just one, earbud, and looked up from her book with a weary smile. This was met with an immediate, explosively cheery reply:

'I'm Bernie! Great to meet you!'

It transpired very quickly that they would both be in the quiet coach, and when they boarded the train Penny's bad luck continued: they were sharing a table. By the time the train was moving, it was abundantly clear that Bernie was not going to take the hint. Too late in the morning for the commuter rush, the carriage had hardly anyone else in it, so there was no one to save her by complaining about Bernie's incessant, shrill rambling. So, Penny finally and reluctantly put away her book and headphones and braced herself for conversation. It was a shame, her favourite Alanis Morissette song had just come on.

*

Bernie was elated to be sharing a carriage with this highly studious young woman, Penny. It turned out she had read all the Carlo Rovelli books too. She couldn't wait to ask her for her thoughts on Bell's theorem and entanglement; Bernie had always found the idea that two photons could be intimately and instantly linked across endless space sort of romantic. However, she had been told that such conversations are better suited after introducing lighter topics like the weather and saying things like, 'So, what do you do?' Penny did seem a little tired, so perhaps she would save her quantum questions for later.

Even so, Bernie felt good to be in such stimulating company. It was freeing to be with somebody new, and in a different place. She hadn't told any colleagues where she was going. 'A break,' she'd said, that was all. The photography course had been her therapist's idea, and the first thing she'd planned to do during her time off. Things had all got too much at work recently, and Ade, her line manager, had sent her to Occupational Health, following three 'incidents' that he described as 'problematic'. After a short chat and some unexpected ugly-crying, Bernie had been swiftly signed off with 'stress' and sent to therapy. And now here she was, gallivanting off on a train journey to the city to work on her 'people skills', 'stability', and 'robustness'. Bernie tried to put all these hot words away and focus instead on her fascinating travel companion, and the giddy feeling brewing inside her from having no one to answer to.

*

There were a few reasons 'Hand in my Pocket' was Penny's favourite. *Jagged Little Pill* had been a defining album for her growing up, and there was a sad but beautiful nostalgia to recalling that time. Mostly though, this song felt like it was written to describe her. She recalled taking a quiz years ago in General Studies, a secondary school class with about as much specificity in its syllabus as in its name. This particular lesson had been about careers and personality, and some of the questions in the quiz had been geared around extroversion and introversion. Most kids in her class had identified strongly one way or the other, many before even seeing the questions, but Penny had fallen firmly in the middle. Moreover, her ticks hadn't formed a straight line down the centre, that middle ground which was 'neither strongly agree nor strongly disagree'. Instead, they had swung from one side to the other, making a zig-zag.

Penny felt that this summed her up very well. It wasn't that she was neither shy nor loud, neither social nor isolated, a kind of balanced in-between state. No, Penny felt like she was absolutely an extrovert, and absolutely an introvert: a two-state system, a kind of Schrödinger's cat of social outgoingness. As an undergraduate, half of her had delighted in sitting in her cosy student room or her regular corner of the library, reading and drinking coffee, and not speaking to another human for days; half of her had blossomed playing argument table tennis until 4am over whiskey with fellow philosophy students. At times she wanted to disappear completely, and at other times yearned desperately to be seen, to be heard, to be understood. It was as though she had one hand shoved right down inside her pocket and the other was reaching out to shake, to greet, waving frantically to whoever would look. It left her feeling both lonely and socially anxious.

And then, one day, someone all but bit the waving hand clean off. No warning. As if she'd been petting a domestic Shorthair that, in one blink, revealed itself to be a tiger. So, for the past few years, Penny stuck with the mantra 'one-hand-in-my-pocket, and-the-other-one-clinging-tightly-to-a-book-I'm-using-as-a-mask-to-cover-my-face-so-you-can't-try-to-talk-to-me'. It served her well, most of the time. It meant she could focus on her research and not be distracted by friendships or dating. However, it did mean that her relationship with her PhD students was colder, and more distant than it probably should be. And there was always the occasional Bernie, that person who had never learned what 'I'm not interested' looked like. Penny never knew what to do with those.

*

The first of these 'incidents' was, in Bernie's view, not really a problem. One of the boys had set the back of her dress on fire with a lighter while she had been clearing away the biology teacher's digestion demonstration. She explained that she had confiscated the lighter, reported the boy and cleaned up the bowl of mulched food she had dropped on the floor in shock, so she didn't really see the issue. Ade had replied that the problem was more to do with her continuing a full day's work with an untreated second degree burn and not consulting the school medic or, in fact, telling anyone she was hurt.

The next incident was something she'd done a few times recently but only once been caught. After overhearing a critical comment from one of the teachers along the lines of 'socially inept moron' and assuming it was about her, she had promptly walked into the storage room and locked herself in it for an hour. Standing there in the dark, she had waited for the shame in her cheeks to cool and her heart rate to slow, while Ade had searched the classrooms, hallways and toilets to track her down. Sadly, on this occasion he had found her, opening the door to reveal her crouched alongside boxes of glass beakers. It had taken some explaining, but Bernie felt this was actually a sensible strategy for managing her anxiety, and wasn't hurting anyone.

The final incident, Bernie had to admit, was perhaps a sign that she was not necessarily as well as she could be. She had woken in the early hours one morning with the realisation that she had forgotten to put out the stopwatches for the GCSE physics practical that morning, and she had, in her tired and panicked state, tried to gain access to the building at 5am to rectify the situation without anyone noticing. She had set off all the alarms, and Fred from maintenance had had to come in to turn everything off again. Highly inconvenient for him, she could see that now.

Almost without realising, Bernie had been saying all of this out loud, and she was beginning to hear how bad it sounded: it was just like Ade had said, 'Not normal behaviour.' Penny's facial expressions seemed to concur with this, she kept looking over at her book and nodding with a pained half-smile; she looked uncomfortable. Still, there was some catharsis in confessing your humiliations to a stranger.

'I'm over-sharing again, aren't I? I'm sorry,' she insisted. What was she doing, telling this stranger her most intimate fears as if they were sisters? It was exactly this kind of behaviour that got her into trouble, her therapist had said. It felt good though, to have someone listen and not worry about the consequences.

*

Penny was unsure whether Bernie had intended to share quite this much of her personal work drama, but Bernie certainly didn't seem embarrassed. Penny wanted to ask her, 'Why on Earth are you telling me all this?' She wanted to tell her it was inappropriate to talk to a complete stranger about one's mental health issues without having been asked. Most of all, she wanted to pretend she needed to use the toilet and move carriage. Instead, she found herself smiling politely and listening and, before long, had become absorbed in Bernie's world. After a while, she started to feel an openness she hadn't felt in a long time, like back when she was an undergraduate and she and another student would start talking about the measurement problem or something over drinks, and hours would go by in free-flowing conversation. It felt good. She wasn't constantly looking for a way out of the conversation anymore. She realised she actually preferred listening to Bernie to reading her book.

'But anyway, the point is, I'm supposed to start taking risks, talking to people, you know. Oil the social cogs or something like that.' Bernie was saying. Suddenly quieter, she added, 'And it's OK if you'd rather not: I'm meant to get rejected sometimes, that's all part of it.'

Bernie had an openness that Penny found naïve, yet refreshingly endearing. She had been awkwardly searching for something profound or comforting to say and was considering quoting one of the Stoics. Or Epicurus perhaps. Something about what you can and can't control, that all pain can be endured, or something. Quoting philosophers usually had a way of closing a conversation, if only because people considered it a bit pretentious. However, as Bernie had finally stopped for breath and seemed to be hoping for a reply, Penny couldn't bring herself to be another 'rejection', and instead wanted to show that she really heard her.

'So, I think I'm getting it: you are hoping to become stronger through, sort of, safe failures? That makes sense. But why photography, is it a hobby of yours?'

*

Penny was smiling and making eye contact now. Bernie knew that was a good sign. Proudly, she raised the shiny new DSLR hanging from her neck.

'No, not at all! This is my first camera! My therapist saw the class advertised online, but it's kind of perfect I think. There's something about the busyness of a city centre, you know? – the frantic scurrying of too many people in a rush to be somewhere… it feels so claustrophobic to me. I get full of jitters and I want to hide, or shrink out of everyone's way. But that's why this is the perfect challenge, I suppose.'

*

Penny knew that feeling. Walking down Oxford Street late at night feeling altogether too big, too visible. Wanting to disappear, to float through the crowds and drift away on the wind. She offered,

'It's pretty normal to feel like that, I think'.

She had no idea under what authority she could talk about what 'normal' looked like. And yet, she felt that it was probably true. The more she learned about Bernie, the more she started to get the overwhelming feeling that she wanted to mother this woman, this stranger almost twice her age; she wanted to reassure her. She wanted her to feel accepted. She could see something in Bernie that she always tried to conceal in herself. She thought back to a time when, as a child, she had been this trusting, open, vulnerable. It was a risky way to live.

'I think everyone finds it scary putting themselves out there. It's not a flaw to feel that way. You just need to find a balance, not let fear run your life.'

As the words fell from Penny's mouth she could taste the hypocrisy in them. Was she not letting fear dictate her own choices? Suddenly, the armour she had been clutching to so tightly all these years felt cowardly.

*

Bernie was transfixed by Penny's sage advice. She seemed to be speaking from experience. How did this young, confident, almost aloof woman gain such wisdom on fear? From experience? She didn't seem afraid of anything.

'So, Penny. Tell me more about you.'

*

Penny slowly brought her hands from deep inside her pockets and lay them on the train table. She closed her eyes, took a deep breath, and decided. She was going to talk about the tiger.

*

As the journey continued, these women searched deeper into each other, uncovering a feeling of connection, not unlike the sensation of looking into a mirror. An eerie familiarity with a spatial inversion. Molecules with opposite handedness. Matter and antimatter. An entangled pair.

'Bernie, I don't know how you can still be such a strong believer in determinism with all you know about quantum physics.'

'I know! Logically, I know I'm compartmentalising, but I don't care.'

By the time the train pulled into Manchester Piccadilly, the quiet coach was illuminated by the joyous sound of two women deeply engaged in a debate about free will, fate and chance, arms flailing and gesticulating, and entering their numbers into each other's phones as they said their goodbyes.

Condolences

by Angus Broadbent

Condolence Book

In loving memory of Maggie Miller, please feel free to leave a message for the family.

Name: *Jacob Wilson*
Address: *14 Longhorn Blvd. Houston, Texas, TX 77052*
Message: *To the family of Maggie Miller, I offer you my most deepest condolences in this troubling time. Words cannot express how much Maggie meant to me. She was a very special person, who I shared lots and lots of happy memories with. I am well and truly going to miss her. Maggie probably never told y'all much about me, but that's alright, I guess some things are better left unsaid. I'm sorry I haven't the time to say howdy to y'all, but if I don't leave now, I'm surely going to miss my flight back home. Thank you for such a delightful wake. God bless. Rest in peace Maggie, I'll always remember you.*

27 Station Road
Kingston upon Thames
London, KT1 3BK

Wednesday 23rd May 2018
Dear Mr Wilson
I hope you don't mind me reaching out to you like this, my name is Gracie and I'm the daughter of Maggie Miller. I've just been reading through the condolence book from the wake and I stumbled across your message. I'd like to thank you for your kind words, they were touching and a joy to read.

   I must say though, I am rather baffled as to why you came all the way from Texas to come to my mum's funeral! You must have really been close to her if you were willing to make such a long journey. It's a shame that I didn't get the chance to meet you, I'm intrigued to know how you knew my mum. Unfortunately, Mum didn't tell me anything about you, or anyone from Texas for that matter. As far as I'm aware, Mum lived her whole life without ever leaving the country! She was pretty stubborn when it came to holidays, insisting that we take our holidays a little closer to home, ie, within the UK. Devon was a particular favourite of hers. I just thought that she loved England so much she couldn't bear to leave, that or she was terrified of flying.

Since her passing, I've come to realise that there was a side of Mum that I never got to know. We were close, Mum and me, but there is so much that I don't know about her. She loved her secrets; certain subjects were never to be spoken about. She never told me anything about my dad, even his name, and although I've been fine all this time without a dad, I'm curious to know where I came from, or rather who I came from. I suppose I'll never find out now though, as that's one secret she took with her to the grave.

Mr Wilson, I'll be honest, I have no idea who you are, or how you knew my mum, but I'd love to find out. It's possible that you may have some of the answers I am looking for. Anything, absolutely anything you tell me, might help me better understand my mum.

I really hope to hear from you soon.
Yours sincerely,
Gracie Miller

14 Longhorn Blvd.
Houston, Texas, TX 77052

June 17, 2018
To Gracie,
I sure am glad to be hearing from you, bless your heart. It truly saddened me to hear of Maggie's passing, I only wish I could have found out sooner as I could have made proper arrangements. But you can bet that as soon as I did find out, there wasn't a snowball's chance in hell I was going to miss it.

I booked a last-minute flight, which of course, to my annoyance, was delayed. So, I do apologise for my tardiness, I did get there in time for the wake though. It warmed my heart to see so many people there. Every one of them all had such nice stories to share about Maggie. And can I also say, the catering was outstanding. Why, there were more cucumber sandwiches than you could shake a stick at, and I ain't never eaten so many scones in all my life. I still don't quite know the proper way to say scone though, nobody would give me a straight answer. How would you say it? Scone like an ice cream cone? Or scone like gone?

I met your mom way back, she was eighteen and I was twenty-one, I think it must've been 1997 if my memory serves me correctly. We both worked at a summer camp down by San Antonio: *Camp Stevens for Boys*. I had some of the best days of my life in that there camp. Your mom was a horseback instructor. And me? Well, I taught archery. I'd been going to this camp for years and years; they'll take you on when you're young as heck. You know, I think I could've been as young as six when I first went there. It's a kind of family ritual as well, you see: my pa went to camp when he was younger, and his pa went before him. Why, if I had any kids of my own, then I'd sure enough be sending them to camp too, without a shadow of a doubt. Come to think of it, I'd say that's one of the major differences between us Yanks and you Brits, not one of y'all ever went to summer camp. If you were to go ahead and ask any American if they'd ever been to camp, I can guarantee that they did, why I'd even be willing to bet money on it!

So anyways, back to your mom. Like I told you, I'd been going to this camp all my life, we was like one big family that you only get to see for only a couple of months a year. When I turned twenty-one, I volunteered to be a counsellor, the pay was damn awful, but you didn't do it for the money. It felt good to give a little back to someplace that gave so much to me. That year was the first year they decided to hire staff from other countries. We had all kinds of different folks coming over to our humble part of Texas, we had people from New Zealand, Australia, South Africa, why I think there could've been someone from Germany. The main bulk of these newcomers came from Britain, which is how your mom ended up in my neck of the woods. I can remember the day we went to pick everyone up from San Antonio airport, your mom was the first one off of the plane and first one to make it through to the arrivals hall. She was wearing this stiff pantsuit, and I can remember thinking to myself, 'Why in goddamn hell would anyone want to sit for twenty-four hours on an airplane in such uncomfortable get-up.' Must've been that someone didn't give her the memo there was going to be hundred-degree heat in Texas. She looked so hot and miserable, I felt awful sorry for her. Boy, she didn't know what was in store for her!

We spent a summer together in a Texan summer camp, and that's all there is to it. Thank you again for taking the time to write to me, I really do appreciate it.

Kind regards,
Jacob Wilson

27 Station Road
Kingston upon Thames
London, KT1 3BK

Tuesday 3rd July 2018
Dear Mr Wilson,
Thanks for writing back. I'm glad my letter reached you alright, I wasn't sure how long it would take to get to you, I've never posted anything to another country before. The chap at the post office told me it could take between one and four weeks, he wasn't particularly helpful. Hopefully this letter will get to you nearer to one week than four.

It's a shame you were unable to attend the funeral service, it was a beautiful celebration of Mum's life. It's OK though, I forgive you and I'm sure Mum would have too, international flights can be so temperamental. The only time I've ever flown in a plane was when I flew out on my own for my Auntie Jacqui's wedding, when I was thirteen. The flight was delayed due to 'adverse weather conditions', I was absolutely livid! Why couldn't they just fly the plane round the bad weather, or even above or below it?

We held the funeral service in the chapel of Mum's old school. It's a gorgeous old building that sits right on the top of a hill. It's got an incredible dome: the inside's decorated with a stunning mosaic of angels, cherubim and seraphim. Mum used to tell me stories about how she had to walk up the steep hill every day after breakfast for morning prayers. She told me that the nuns would always tell her off and whack her with a ruler for staring up at the dome instead of bowing her head. Mum hated that school, but she loved the chapel and, although she didn't have the best memories of her time there, it felt right to hold the funeral in one of her favourite buildings. It's a miracle that we managed to get the place booked, somebody cancelled their wedding last minute and we snapped up the spot. (Very lucky indeed! Well, not so lucky for the poor couple who had to cancel two weeks before their wedding, but lucky for us.)

Inside the building is pretty standard for an English place of worship: dusty pews, shiny chandeliers, candles, etc. But there are three defining features that I think make the building rather unique. First, there is an enormous organ, it's huge! Far bigger than you would ever expect to be inside such a modest building, it takes up an entire wall all by itself. I never much cared for organs before the funeral. This one was special though; I was in awe of its majesty. And you wouldn't believe the range of sounds that thing can create! Deep brassy tones from the pipes of the bass notes to sweet florid melodies of the upper register. I bumped into the organist during the wake, apparently, he's been the resident organist there for the last thirty years, and he actually remembered teaching piano to my mum for a short period. Well, that's what he told me, but I think he was just trying to be nice; the man was at least seventy, I'd be surprised if he could remember who his current students were, let alone one from thirty years ago!

The second thing I feel is worth mentioning is the magnificent stained-glass window on the south facing wall of the chapel. The window depicts the story of the Creation and right slap bang in the middle, there's a kangaroo. A kangaroo! I bet you've never seen a kangaroo on a stained-glass window before! OK, so this feature probably isn't the most interesting,

I just like kangaroos, Mum did too, they were her favourite.

Third, I need to tell you again about the dome because it really is stunning, I wish I'd taken photos. Next time you get the chance you should google Wantworth Catholic School Chapel and you'll see what I mean. In case you don't get the chance, let me try describing it. Looking from directly underneath the dome, you'll see a layered circle, the innermost layer is the spire on the top, it's not a big spire but it's circled in windows so light pours down from the centre of the dome. The next layer out from there is a deep blue ring, sapphire blue I would call it, and every now and then there's the occasional gold mosaic tile, interspersed with the blue ones, that makes the dome sparkle and shimmer. In the outer layer are the angels, hovering gracefully in a circle, each one of them holding a different instrument with their wings unfurled. Then, just below, there is another set of windows that let in light and fill the dome with sunlight from all directions.

So, now that I've set the scene for you, let's press on to the service itself. Mum was brought in to the hymn, 'The Lord is My Shepherd'. It's a fine hymn, it wasn't my first choice, but Auntie Jacqui had the final say on the music. I was of the opinion that it would be better if we played some music that Mum actually liked, something along the lines of Pink Floyd or Queen. Whereas Auntie Jacqui, for some reason, didn't think it would be very respectful if we had Mum carried in to Queen's, 'Tie Your Mother Down'. Personally, I think Mum would have found it hilarious. I'm not too fond of 'The Lord is My Shepherd', it was made famous by this British television comedy, *The Vicar of Dibley*. I'd probably say the hymn is more famous for being the theme tune for that show rather than for just being a pleasant hymn. I did voice my concerns to Auntie Jacqui, and she said she didn't even think that many people had watched the show, so we'd be fine. We were not fine! I had several pensioners corner me in the wake, all of them saying, 'Oh, the service was lovely, but did you really have to bring her in to a television theme tune?'

Auntie Jacqui did, however, let me choose the flowers. I went for a mixture of tulips and daffodils. They're cheerful flowers, daffodils are a sign of spring and rebirth while tulips can mean a lot of things depending on the colour – I decided on yellow and purple. Yellow represents joy and happiness and purple is a sign of royalty. Of course, Mum wasn't royal by any means, but she had a very privileged upbringing that she had to give up when I was born. Her *very* religious parents had a big fall out with her over having a 'bastard' child and choosing to bring me up on her own. They disowned her, it's tragic really. Nana came to the funeral, but Granddad downright refused, Auntie Jacqui begged him to reconsider but he said, 'I only have one daughter, my other has been dead to me for years, what difference does it make now if she's actually gone.' He's a cold-hearted, spiteful old man, I've only met him once and he wouldn't even look me in the eye, it's like I didn't exist to him. It was no real loss that he didn't come to the funeral.

One of the school's nuns led the service, she didn't know Mum, and Mum wasn't a religious person anyway, not since she left school at least. She did an amazing job though, she brought the whole service together. She was so confident and so sure of her faith that if I had spent any amount of time with her, I'd probably start believing in God too. I don't though, I'm an atheist. I don't believe Mum is in heaven, or in any afterlife for that matter. She's nowhere, one moment she was here, and the next she wasn't. But that's OK, I always think that being dead must be a little bit like a dreamless sleep: nothing happens, but nothing needs to happen. I wonder, do you believe in heaven, Mr Wilson? From what I've heard of Texas, it's a very religious part of America. I have been picturing you as a man of God.

I have a strong feeling that there's more to you and my Mum than you're letting on. I wonder if you might be able to elaborate a bit on your relationship with her, rather than how you met. You must have been closer than you've said, to be willing to make the journey all the way from Texas just for her funeral.

Yours faithfully,
Gracie

P.S. If we are going to continue our correspondence, perhaps you would rather we email or video call? My email address is graciemills98@cosmail.com if you want to email me.

Subject: Howdy Gracie
Jacob Wilson <jacobwilson11@outtook.com>
16/07/2018 02:12
To Gracie,
I think that it'd be a swell idea if we switched to email. It sure was nice though, to get your letter in the mail, it makes a nice change from all the other crap that turns up in my mailbox. Tell you what I'm going to do though, when you reply to this email, I'm not going to read it straight away, instead I'm going to print it out, put it in an envelope, and put that in my mailbox. It may sound a little crazy to you, but I always thought that there was something wholesome about getting a nice letter from somebody. But for convenience's sake, emails are fine, I suppose.

It's hard for me to talk about your mom, stuff ended badly between us and it still hurts me a little inside when I've got to remember it. I didn't mention this in my last letter as I didn't quite know how to say this, but, your mom and I were in love. I do suppose your mother's love life may be an embarrassing subject for you to read about, so I can completely understand if you don't want to hear no more about it.

It was awful kind of you to try describing the ceremony to me. I did do an internet search for that domed building you were talking about, and you were absolutely correct – that is one fancy looking dome they got there. You seemed mighty fixated on the inside of the dome, whereas I, on the other hand, am much more partial to the outside of it. I like the way the copper of the dome has been worn down and eroded by the elements. I did some research into the building and I found out that the dome used to be kind of a green colour, cause of the way the copper had reacted to the acidity of the rain over the years, but they replaced it with fresh plating a couple of years back now.

I realise that I, in fact, do not know a whole lot about you, Gracie, and, well, I've been fixin' to ask you if you could tell me a little about yourself. Just simple things, mind you, such as your profession, and where you live. I also realise that I ain't actually told you all that much about myself either, so here goes. I'm forty-two years old and I'm unwed, I was married to a lady back in my mid-twenties, but things didn't work out for us, so we got a divorce. I guess I would say that the whole divorce situation put me off of relationships ever since. Well, that and the whole situation with your mother, I never do seem to have much luck with women.

As you can tell by my mailing address, I live in Houston, Texas, in the downtown area of the city. I live in a small house, around 500 yards away from Minute Maid Park, which is the stadium where the Astros play at. They're our city's baseball team, I go see them as much as I can. I work in property development and I own a lot of property over in the hills to the west of San Antonio, we mostly buy up land and build ranches on them, a lot of Texans want to retire to a ranch in the country so there's a big market for that kind of thing. Right now, I've had to take some time off of work for health reasons, Doctors aren't at all sure what's the matter with me yet, but they've told me to take it easy for a while.

I remember Maggie telling me a little about her pa, your grandpa, and he sure sounded like a piece of work to me. Why, I wouldn't trust that man any further than I could throw him, so it doesn't surprise me that he didn't have the guts to turn up to his own daughter's funeral. You mentioned in your letter that your mom raised you by herself, it's awful to think that my Maggie might've been struggling as a single mother, boy, do I wish she had told me about it. I'm not sure how I could've helped but I would've done whatever I could.

Kind regards,
Jacob Wilson
Go Astros!

Re: Howdy Gracie
Gracie Miller <graciemills98@cosmail.com>
07/17/2018 06:04
Hi Jacob,

I completely agree with your stance on letters, I like receiving them too. There's something raw and organic about having words written down on pen and paper, words that are intended for you and you alone. It is, as you say, wholesome.

You don't need to worry about embarrassing me by telling me what went on with you and Mum, I'm twenty years old now, I'm not a child anymore. Mum's love life has always been a mystery: like I mentioned previously, she liked to keep secrets.

So, you want to know a little about me? I don't see why not, although there isn't that much for me to tell. I'm twenty years old and I live in a town called Kingston upon Thames, it's technically a part of London, but it's nowhere near the city centre where all the cool landmarks are. I finished college two years ago with pretty good A-levels (they're what our big exams are called in the UK) and was looking at going to study Physics at Birmingham University. They offered me a place and everything, but I decided to put all that on hold when I found out about Mum's cancer. I found her unconscious in her bed one morning and called an ambulance for her, I've never been so scared in all my life, it was horrible seeing her like that. Things only went downhill from there; she was diagnosed with stage four cervical cancer. It was so advanced that it had spread to her liver. She had all the chemo and radiotherapy, but the doctors knew they would never be able to rid her of it, only prolong her life a little bit. Everything's been at a standstill ever since, I'm trying to get things back on track; I'm due to start University in Birmingham at the end of September.

I'm not sad about Mum dying, not anymore; now I'm just angry. This shouldn't have happened, things shouldn't have got this bad. If Mum had had her smear test when they wrote to her, doctors would have been able to detect any early signs of the cancer and treat it before it was too late. It sounds horrible but I do blame Mum for what happened to her, this was entirely preventable if caught early enough, and it was entirely her fault that they didn't know until it was too late.

Listen, Jacob, I've been doing a lot of thinking recently, mostly about the time you and Mum were together, and the years following that. You say that you were at summer camp with Mum in 1997, well I was born in June 1998. This might sound a little barmy to you, but do you think that there's any chance, any possibility at all, that you might be my dad? It's crazy, I know, it's just that I have been thinking about it a lot and I just can't see any other possibility. You're the only man I've ever known my mum to have been with romantically.

   What do you think?

   Gracie

Re: Howdy Gracie
Gracie Miller <graciemills98@cosmail.com>
28/07/2018 7:11
Hi Jacob,
It's been a little over a week since my last email and I'm a little worried that I might have scared you and made you not want to talk to me anymore. I'm really sorry if I did, you probably aren't even my dad anyway, please just forgot I said anything. I would hate for us to fall out over something so silly.

   Please reply,

   Gracie

27 Station Road
Kingston upon Thames
London, KT1 3BK

30th August 2018
Dear Jacob,
Since you won't reply to my emails, I'm writing you this letter instead.

   If the idea that you might be my dad is such a horrible notion that you can't even bring yourself to reply to me anymore then so be it. You know what? Maybe it's a good thing that you were never a part of my life in the first place. I've lasted twenty years without a dad and I can certainly keep on going without one now.

   Have a great life,

   Gracie

Subject: Gracie please
Jacob Wilson <jacobwilson11@outtook.com>
16/09/2018 02:26

Gracie, please forgive me for not replying to you. Ever since my last email to you I've been unable to access my emails or get a chance to read my mail. I'm afraid that the worst possible result came back from the tests the doctors were doing on me. I've got prostate cancer, and it's bad, real bad. My doctor tells me nothing but bad news and I'm feeling worse and worse every day. They've told me there's nothing more they can do for me and have let me go back home to enjoy what little time I may have left.

I've always wanted to be a father, and while the idea that you could be my daughter may sound crazy, I want to believe it's true. There was a time when your mom and I talked about having a life together, kids and all. I even proposed to her and we were mighty close to actually getting married in Las Vegas. After she returned home from camp, I never heard from Maggie again. I tried and tried to get hold of her, but I guessed she wanted nothing to do with me. She broke my heart. It would make sense to me that she found out that she was pregnant not long after getting back home. After the unfortunate events with her parents I guess she couldn't forgive me for what happened. I wish I could've been there for you, Gracie, I really do.
Jacob

Re: Gracie Please
Gracie Miller <graciemills98@cosmail.com>
09/16/2018 07:55

If things are as bad as they sound, I need to see you face to face. I've booked the next flight to Houston. See you soon.
G

Condolence Book

Jacob shall never be forgotten. His memory will live on forever in our hearts.

Name: *Gracie Miller*
Address: *27 Station Road, Kingston upon Thames, KT1 3BK*
Message: *Jacob passed before I got the chance to really know him. I only wish we had met sooner and that I had had the opportunity to learn what kind of a man he was, what kind of a father he might have been. Despite being in my life for the briefest of moments, the void he has left will be impossible to fill. I think of all the moments we never had, I think of all the memories we never shared, and I think of all the love that never had the chance to grow. I will forever be thinking of my dad who never was.*

Oh, What a Night

by Lavonne Roberts

What are the odds of the two of us, both hailing from Texas, being in Manhattan?

I got myself into this big mess because I had a spell of writer's block. Zilch. Zero. Nada. Not a word could I get down on the page. So I hit the bottle, and that's how we met. It's an unoriginal story, meeting in a bar. But the way he made contact was unnerving, a virtual staredown. All to the tune of 'Oh, What a Night'.

I see him looking at me. Well, out of the corner of his eye, anyway. I'm uncomfortable with the attention, especially in front of so many people. I sip my martini slowly, and the frozen heat warms me all the way to my bone marrow. It's five degrees outside, and the chill has highjacked my composure. I lean over like a cat to a bowl and sip my magic elixir. Not willing to lose a drop trumps manners. The fireplace is hissing and popping, competing for my attention. The ceilings are tall, the rooms are expansive, and the chandeliers sparkle, but I think he's too close to the heat to notice the chill, towering above the mantelpiece. I can see the fire reflecting in his cold glassy eyes.

I feel him boring a hole through me like I'm responsible for something monstrous, or is he just over-confident? Ladies stare at him when they walk past. I'm a tsunami of contradictions, gregarious with most, shy with some, soft and feminine, defensively harsh when shaken or afraid, but with him I'm defenceless. There's a sense of urgency about him as if he needs to possess something I can't give him. I think he's trying to tell me something. It's like he's speaking to me through the music: 'Oh, What a Night' is into its second verse.

Avoiding his eyes, I stare down at the Persian carpet. I look around the bar. Red Moroccan tea glasses with gold trim cast a soft lens on a room of imbibing patrons. There's a buzz that rises and falls like the tide under a full moon. Old white men read the *Wall Street Journal* and sip bourbon in the corners of the room, relics of an exclusive old boys' club. The pomp is palpable, the money feels close, the conversation is privileged.

A man grazes my shoulder as he leans across me to speak to the bartender. 'You don't mind if I order do you?' Of course I mind. He's so close that I can smell the beer on his breath. 'Not at all,' I say, as he barks out an order for two beers and then winks at me like we're in cahoots. He turns like he wants to whisper something in my ear, but a woman shouts out, 'Marty,' and he retreats with an impish look on his face. Then I'm alone again. Almost.

He's still staring. I can feel the sadness in his eyes – almost a vacantness. He doesn't even blink. Why did I come here again? I knew he'd be here. He's always bloody here. It's my fault. When I look into my glass, I can see his reflection in the liquid – as long as it's at least half full. So I order another.

I can feel him judging me. The crowd is thinning. A couple of strangers have paired off. The woman has Marty's thigh clenched between hers. She keeps squeezing his leg with her hands like she's trying to extract toothpaste and he laughs louder each time. The bartender is starting to clean up.

What? Now he can read my mind? I order my third martini, or is it my fourth? He knows why I can't write, but I'm not buying his telepathic psychobabble. It's not like he can explain himself. He looks at me tenderly, as if he understands why I am haunted by melancholic memories. Forgetting allows me to live, but he asserts that remembering will allow me to live. I already know what he's going to say. 'If I try and remember my childhood, I'll go mad,' I say.

I sip the liquid slowly. It feels like molten silver filling a mould as it slides down into my deepest corners. 'My days have lost their shape. Past and present commingle,' I say, looking him squarely in the eye. He doesn't even blink. Nothing makes sense. Rage rises from the pieces of my broken narrative. He waits for me to speak. I tell him about my mentally ill mother and how she abused my four brothers and me. He tells me about being shot. He understands pain – he understands me, I think. I don't trust anything I can't nail down cognitively but he's different. It's as if I'm hypnotised.

I am possessed with a past I can't recall entirely. Memories arrive in fragments which can't be organised. I put my hand up for another martini because thinking about my chronic childhood amnesia makes me sad. He's so kind. He neither looks away, nor tries to trivialise my feelings with empty words.

We are lost to each other, separated by our silences because neither of us wants to remember the pain. Nothing can clear my psychic inheritance or give me back my innocence. Maybe he can. His charm and magnetism amount to a kind of moral authority. I don't just believe in him, I trust him.

We live in a place where rage is currency and running away is commonplace.

'I chose to amputate my mother, and in doing so I was left with a phantom limb I could neither grasp nor let go of,' I confide in him.

'Phantom limbs indeed. The world is a slaughterhouse,' he says. The vodka has filled in cracks where previously winds whistled through my grief; now I'm warm.

'I'm afraid to stay,' I tell him. 'Staying in one place reminds me that where I came from no longer exists.' Thoughts come to me, as transparent as the last of my drink. 'We don't choose the body we are born into, nor do we control the laws of physics or the seemingly infinite causes and reactions that shape a life,' I say. He looks at me with a sense of wonder.

'What did you say?' asks the bartender, with one eyebrow raised.

I look around to see if he's speaking to someone else. Before I can answer, he adds, 'It's just you and me.'

I wonder why the stranger behind the bar making my martinis can't he see we're not alone. I look above him at the object of my attention.

'Stay with me,' he says with his eyes, but I get up to leave. I hesitate. One last glance. Face to face. Deep brown melancholy eyes. Haunting. Glass eyes. I can see the outlines of his skull.

His huge horns jut out and then turn upwards. They span as long as I am tall. Taxidermy at its finest.

Her First Lead

by Mike Evis

Duncan spotted the bottle, the one labelled paracetamol that wasn't paracetamol, a fraction of a second before the police officer did. Christ, why hadn't he flushed it down the loo, instead of leaving it there? But it was too late. Like a hawk seeking its prey, she swooped on it. Silently, he swore. But what the hell did it matter now? What did anything matter?
 'Are these yours, sir?'
 If she opened the bottle….
 'I've never seen them before.'
 'Funny that, sir, when they're on your mantelpiece.'
 She unscrewed the lid, peered inside.
 'They're rather large for paracetamol. Odd colour too. Are they – were they the young lady's?'
 'Must've been,' he shrugged. 'You know what the young are like.'
 Her expression was unreadable.
 'And she was very young, wasn't she, sir?'
 He couldn't be sure if there was a twitch in her eyebrow as she spoke.
 'Let's go through to the bedroom.'
 No, no, he wanted to say, not there, I can't. But like a dog following its owner, he tamely slouched behind her, heart thumping, sweating profusely, knowing what it was he didn't want to see.

*

He was sitting at his desk. The sweat and the fear he felt were all too real, as was his racing heart, but nothing else was. It had been a flashback. It wasn't happening. It was all in the past. Six years ago. A shiver went through him as he ran a tissue across his forehead; his heartbeat calmed, and he let out a sigh. He pushed his hands through his unruly grey hair. Would he ever be rid of these memories?

It had been difficult, with weeks, months gone in a haze, a whole summer and autumn lost to the bottle. That, on top of what had happened with the girl: they'd had to let him go. He'd been tossed aside by that pompous ass of a department head, dismissed with those weasel words, 'Sorry old man, if it were up to me… but my hands are tied.'

Eventually he'd dragged himself out of the mess he was in and found a new position at a different university. One of his new colleagues had shown him to his office: it had a sad, uncared-for feel about it. There was a large dent in the door, marks on the walls, scratches all over his desk, and the drawers wouldn't lock.

'You've got the wrong place,' Duncan had said.

Instead of an answer, he shrugged, giving Duncan a long cool look.

'I mean, clearly this can't be my office, it's nowhere near big enough. And the view–' But the man was gone.

He consoled himself: at least he was working again. And he was confident he'd soon be promoted back to his old level – and assigned a larger office. So he'd never bothered to unpack all his books, and still they stood, boxes piled on the grey carpet, unshelved, partly obscuring the grimy windows looking out on the incinerator chimney.

To his annoyance, they'd never corrected their blunder, despite regular protests. He couldn't push things too far though, because he knew this was his last chance. He couldn't waste it. He had to be careful: no more booze, no drugs – he had to be squeaky clean. Above all – and he sighed heavily – there couldn't be a hint of impropriety with his students.

Yet, when he walked across the campus, and saw the new students arriving, the girls lying on the grass in that Indian summer, bare legs glistening invitingly in the sun, he couldn't help feeling that old urge come over him.

It had been a minor lapse of judgement, what happened six years ago, that was all. It was no use going over that again.

His office door swung open, bringing him back to the present. He looked up to see a girl – one of the new intake, he thought – standing there, a folder across her chest. Her black eyes shone with defiance and for a moment he sensed something else in the frank stare she gave him, something he couldn't put his finger on, as if her eyes could see into the shadowy recesses of his very soul. Then it was over, and he breathed again, taking in – as if drinking whiskey after a long abstinence – her perfect smooth skin, the tightness of her black and white leggings, and the curve of her mouth, oozing with lipstick, and he felt desire creep over him. How could he resist, how could he control himself?

Without asking, she sat down on the hard wooden chair opposite, leaning forward. He couldn't stop staring at her cleavage where it vanished into her top, seeing a bead of sweat run down from her neck, imagining his hands… stop it, stop it, he thought. This is where it all goes wrong.

He wiped his hand across his brow and she smiled. With that smile he felt all the pain of the past few years melt away.

*

Running her finger down the menu, Justine felt a rising sense of panic that couldn't be quelled by the subdued lighting and the melodic sound of a piano playing in the corner. She should have known Suzy would suggest an overpriced place like this. She put the menu down.

'Decided already?' asked Suzy. 'I'm finding it so difficult to choose.'

Justine picked the menu up again.

'So,' said Suzy, her oversized glasses emphasising her thin, birdlike head. 'I thought you had an interview at the Chronicle? Certain to get it, you said.'

Twisting her glass several times, she finally settled it down on the bistro table, concentrating her gaze on Justine.

'I didn't get it,' said Justine, her voice scarcely audible.

Suzy clicked her fingers, summoning a nearby waiter.

'I'll have another – large glass of the 2018,' she said.

Christ, had she seen the price of the wine? Maybe if Justine stuck to water – tap water, if they weren't too posh for that –

she could cover her share. And if she had a starter instead of a main....

Needing distraction, she took up the menu to hide behind but Suzy pushed it away.

'So what went wrong at the Chronicle?'

'Nothing,' said Justine, her voice sunk to a sullen whisper. 'They're just not taking many people, that's all.'

'And you got the job at the Post?'

'Yeah.'

'Well, that's great news!'

'Is it?'

'Come on, the Chronicle is so last century. And it's so dull. You've only got to see the headlines–'

'Not like the ones in the Post then. JAIL THE BARMY JUDGES? CRUSH THE TRAITORS?'

'I know, great aren't they?'

'It's not the sort of paper I want to write for.'

'Why not? It's entertaining.'

'When there are so many real issues–'

'Boring. People don't want to read that. They're not interested, I'm not interested. People want punchy stories that grab you. That's what I want to read. I haven't got time for anything else.'

'Even if it's all lies?'

'You need to lighten up. It's only a bit of fun.'

'Suzy, I wanted to make a difference. I wanted to expose wrongdoing. That's why I went into journalism.'

'The Post had a story last week about some dodgy American preacher–'

'You don't understand.'

'You're still a journalist, Justine. Just a different paper, that's all.'

'Yeah.'

*

But it wasn't the same. She thought over and over again about the interview at the Chronicle – and the aftermath, when the sole woman on the panel led her out of the room, stopping in the corridor outside, next to the miles of peeling grey paint and unlagged pipework that stretched into the distance. The woman's eyes were warm, surrounded by crow's feet. Lightly, she touched Justine on the shoulder.

'I can see you have a real passion for what we do, but look, do you have other avenues you're exploring?'

Justine was taken aback. Her face must have told all.

'You mean…?'

'It's just, we get a lot of applications. Hundreds in fact. From really qualified candidates. And we'd like to have strong female candidates like yourself on board but, thing is, don't get your hopes up too much.'

She looked over her shoulder as they walked down the corridor.

'I probably shouldn't tell you this but we're only taking on one trainee. You've got to understand, our budget's really tight. You know what it's like now. We simply don't have the resources for more.'

Justine nodded, her head drooping as she felt her dreams vanishing in the harshness of the fluorescent lights overhead.

'But that's why I want to work here,' said Justine. 'You're not like other papers.'

'If it were up to me….'

They had walked to the reception area now. Outside, red London buses crawled past, jostling with taxis and delivery vans. Inside, the noise from the street was muffled, silence only broken by the regular sound of the receptionist picking up the phone endlessly saying 'Chronicle–'

The calm atmosphere was a million miles from how Justine felt.

'Try applying–' she lowered her voice '–to the Post. They're taking lots of trainees this year. They're bound to snap you up.'

'But I don't want to work there. I hate the Post. I hate everything they stand for.'

The woman blinked.

'You can always approach us again in a few years.'

*

'How you finding it here?' asked Amy, her new colleague. If Justine thought how to describe her, it would all be in 'b' words

– blonde, brassy, and bossy. Her long hair darkened into black streaks the closer it got to her head. But she was friendly and helpful and cheerful.

'Fact checking's… different. But I can put up with it for a while, it's not like I'll be doing it forever.'

'You going travelling or something then?'

'What do you mean?'

'That's the only way out. Three bloody years I've done this lousy job. There's no way out. The lowest of the low, Jus, that's what we are, no mistake.'

'But – they told me–'

'Told you what?'

'Well, at interview they said this was a stopgap. Six months, a year at most and they'd move me up to be a reporter.'

'And you believed them?' She laughed. 'This is the Post. They'll tell you anything. Face facts, girl: you ain't going anywhere.'

'But I want to be a journalist.'

'Here? At this rag? Come off it.' She waved her hand dismissively. Conversation over. 'Got anything on that dodgy TV presenter yet?'

Her dreams were lying shattered into pieces, like a pane of glass fallen from one of the steel and concrete skyscrapers looming outside the windows. She was imprisoned behind the rows and rows of desks and partitions that stretched away on all sides. Like the leaden London sky, they oppressed her, emphasising her sheer insignificance. But she had to believe there was a way through, that if she worked hard and kept at it, she'd make it as a reporter yet. Whatever Amy said.

'Cheer up,' Amy grimaced. 'Could be worse. At least we get paid, unlike the work experience bunch. And we don't have to make people tea or coffee.'

She glanced back at her screen.

'Hello, I've got a cabinet minister here. Maybe not for much longer if he carries on like this. Hours of fun.'

A sense of failure hung round Justine's neck. Shame and regret, guilt too, dripped off her. She should have stuck to her guns and kept her principles intact. Instead she had this: the reality of working at the Post.

When the Tube train, on her way to work, stopped close to the Chronicle offices, she couldn't stop thinking of the future that might have been, a future that became more distant with every passing day, the present blotting it out with the overbearing reality of working for the Post.

It was two stops to the Post from there, but it might as well have been a million miles. Trudging up the steps to the broad plaza, she felt alienated from the hordes striding across the square, her every step begrudged. She didn't want to be there, didn't want to do this job. And the brazen, shiny, steel and concrete Post building mocked her with its size and strength, its corridors wide and smelling of newness, unlike the twisty old passages of the Chronicle, with its grimy 1960s building, its offices worn and peeling, its carpets threadbare, coated with long-dried chewing gum.

Her shame would be complete when she entered the sterile stainless steel reception area and swiped her card to let her through the door. Perhaps it would have been bearable if she'd got a job as a journalist there, but she hadn't. And from what Amy said, she never would.

The only comfort was the forbidden object in her bag – she touched it lightly to reassure herself – today's copy of the Chronicle. It wasn't exactly banned, but any sign of liberal views, causes or ideas were frowned on here. This was her way of making a stand.

When the job offer had come, though she'd been thinking about it for days, she still wasn't sure. Turn it down and that would be that for a career in journalism. Take it, and abandon her principles? But perhaps she'd already made her decision at the interview, when they asked her which paper she read and she quickly answered, 'The Post.' A two word lie, and she'd surprised and betrayed herself.

'Anything on the judge?' Amy asked, and Justine realised she'd been staring hard at her screen for the last five minutes.

'Only a thirty-year-old speeding fine.'

Amy sucked her pen thoughtfully. 'Not much use, but tell them about it anyway. Might be usable. I've got something really juicy here: some YouTube kiddies star sharing videos of a sadomasochistic session in his own dungeon.'

*

Amy had gone out for lunch. They couldn't both go at the same time in case someone needed facts urgently checked or something researched. All Justine could hear was the tap tap of fingers on keyboards, a few people talking into phones, and, far off, someone shouting across the office. The gentle hum of machinery filled the huge space.

She stared at the screen, seeing the few sentences, the misspelt words and the bad grammar, comparing the angry Twitter rant with the article the journalist wanted her to check. This wasn't journalism, she thought, but it still had the power to make or break people, to destroy them completely. She sighed. Every day, she could feel her ethics sliding into the abyss. But what choice did she have, if she wanted to work in the media?

'You the new girl?' said a voice behind, making her jump. She turned, the word 'girl' grating on her ears, to see a nearly bald man in his fifties or sixties, standing up close to the back of her chair. His skin was lined and haggard like old leather, a pen sticking out of the corner of his mouth like a substitute cigarette. Girl – no one would have dreamed of calling her that at the Chronicle.

'Yes,' she said, her voice flat with irritation, 'Justine.' She felt annoyed that she hadn't objected.

'Charlie. Charlie Walters. I'd ask the other girl, but she's out – thing is, we're a bit short-staffed. Could you talk to some people? Just a quick word, so we can see if it's worth sending a journalist out?'

Journalist. Meaning she wasn't one. She smarted again, but held herself back.

'Of course,' she smiled, instantly regretting her smooth compliance.

'Probably nothing in it. Should only take a minute or two. God knows why but it seems to be moving up the agenda.'

He dropped a thin folder on her desk.

There were two ways she could deal with this, Justine

thought. She could either sulk about it, getting grumpy because this was a journalist's job and it was perfectly clear they didn't consider her a journalist and never would – or the other way, the way she had to view it – was that it was the closest she was likely to get, and maybe she could turn this to her advantage.

Inside the folder were a few pieces of paper and an envelope with scribbled notes and phone numbers, jotted down in a hurry. There was a newspaper clipping too, several years old now. Intrigued, she began to read the article, enticed by the headline 'Drug Death Girl Scandal: Cover-Up, Protest Parents'. Obviously from some local paper. (And couldn't she have done that, worked for a provincial paper as a reporter – and kept her principles? Instead here she was, a fact checker on a paper she despised, what would she turn into after six months or a year doing this?)

She carried on reading. It was about an eighteen-year-old student, Meredith Jones – unusual first name, she thought – who died of a drugs overdose. What made her sit up and read with more interest was that the overdose happened at her English tutor's flat one night. The verdict was misadventure, but the parents complained that the police hadn't properly investigated.

She felt a stirring within – anticipation, the smell of a good story? That's what the lecturers on her course had talked about. Instinct, the intuition that sometimes led you to something special. She felt excitement too – could this be her first story? Her first lead?

No, of course not. She had to be realistic. The journalists upstairs just wanted her to do their dirty work. They would take it away from her. She felt deflated. Ringing a couple whose daughter had died – it was awkward, even if it was six years ago. But if it led to an opening it might be worth it.

Amy listened patiently, when she returned, as Justine rambled on.

Finally, she interrupted.

'They've handed you the shitty end of the stick. They're always doing that. You can forget any credit, if it leads anywhere. Don't fool yourself.' She shrugged. 'I've told you before: there's no escape.'

Quickly she dialled the number, before hesitation halted her in her tracks. Excitement and trepidation held her fast. The phone rang – and rang. With each ring, she felt more certain no one would answer. She pictured it ringing in some lonely, empty house – where was it they lived anyway? She picked up the newspaper clipping, scanned it: West Wales. Her imagination leapt further, visualising a closed bedroom door, shut up for a year or more, a shrine to their dead daughter inside, photos of her propped up in every corner.

'Who is it?' The woman's voice was abrupt.

'My name is Justine Williams, I'm calling from the Post. In London.'

'Press, are you?'

Her heart jumped and she couldn't answer at first. 'Yes, but I wanted to–'

The line went silent; she heard muffled voices, then a man's voice, louder, unfriendly, came on the line.

'You've got a ruddy nerve. After all those filthy lies you lot printed about our Meredith. Terrible it was. When it was him all along.'

'Mr Jones, that's what I wanted to you talk about.'

'Hanging's not good enough for the likes of him.'

'I understand completely.'

'Understand? How can anyone know what we've gone through? Understand?'

'I'm sorry.'

She could sense her big opportunity slipping away. She had to turn this around, fast. If she could get them to talk, she could still make a journalist. If. It was up to her, she needed to find the right words. She needed to act.

'Look, I know what the papers said. But we want to take a fresh look, tell your story.'

A pause.

'Which paper did you say you're from?'

'The Post.'

Had she gone too far? Charlie asked her to check some facts. Should she really go beyond that, and promise them something she couldn't be sure she could deliver? Heart pounding, the adrenaline drove her on.

The woman's voice came back on the line. 'She'd be twenty-four now.' Her tone was quiet, reflective. 'If she hadn't…. Will you really tell our story?'

'Yes. Of course.' She gulped. Another lie.

'Alright, we'll talk – but you have to tell it our way.'

'Mrs Jones, is it true she was seeing her lecturer?'

'Lecturer? More like lecher. We never knew. Never.'

'And the – I'm sorry, I have to ask you – the drugs?'

'She never touched drugs. Never. Not till him. We'd have known, see. He took our daughter – our beautiful daughter – and…'

Justine heard sobbing.

'I'm sorry, one more thing. The coroner's verdict was misadventure.'

'What did he know? What did any of them know?'

'The CPS didn't bring charges.'

'The police never investigated properly, see. Useless, they were. Soon as they found out he was a university man, that was it.'

'You think there was a cover-up?'

'I know there was. We had a letter, some poor girl he got pregnant. Meredith wasn't the only one. There were lots of others.'

'And what did this letter say?'

'I could hardly bear to read it. She said Meredith was the latest in a long line of goings-on he'd had with his students. He was old enough to be their father. You think you can trust them, the lecturers.'

'This letter, does it give details?'

'Too much detail if you ask me.'

'Could you… possibly send me a copy?'

Minutes ago she'd been worried she would lose her chance at becoming a reporter for good. But now it looked like there were things to follow up, and a story to tell.

'We want justice for Meredith, that's all. And that bastard to face what he's done. Even after all this time.'

Justine sighed.

'I can't promise that'll happen. But–'

'You'll help us, though? I know you will.'

She pursed her lip. The old hacks in the office would promise anything – just get the bloody story, they'd say, nothing else matters. This wasn't the Chronicle way, but then she wasn't working for the Chronicle. Was the Post wearing her down, eroding her sense of ethics?

'You could make such a fuss he'd never work again. Even if we never see him in court, it'd be some sort of justice.'

'You deserve that,' said Justine. 'I'll come and visit. You can tell me your side of the story. This man clearly needs to be stopped.'

'Would you, love?'

Amy was staring at her across the office, open mouthed. As Justine put the phone down, Amy shook her head.

'Aren't you going a bit far? Charlie said to check the facts. When he hears about this… you need to remember you're still on probation.'

A shiver of apprehension went through Justine, but she shook it off. It would be alright. After all, she'd got them a story, hadn't she?

*

But it wasn't alright.

'You said what?'

Charlie leaned over her desk, hands planted on either side of her, imprisoning her, so close she could smell his stale aftershave, and alcohol on his breath.

'But I thought–'

'You're not paid to think. We want the facts checked. That's all. You check things, you tell us about them. You're not a journalist.'

The words, his tone flat and blunt, came like a car slamming into a brick wall at speed.

Justine squirmed out from under his sweaty arms, leaning back as far as she could against her desk.

'I had to say something, they weren't keen to talk at first.'

He gave a loud sigh, drummed his fingers on the wood. Over

the top of her monitor she could see Amy fuming, glaring at Charlie.

'You're a fact checker. How many more times do I need to tell you?'

Amy leaned over, resting her chin on her hands. 'Is that all we are? Without us checking the rubbish you write, researching the facts, you'd be sued into the ground within a week. Do you realise that? Look what Justine's done. She's found several leads, she's got the parents to talk, she's getting somewhere with this story. She's done all the hard work. Isn't that worth something? She's not merely a researcher, for God's sake, she studied journalism. Give her a chance. Why don't you let her look into it a bit more, let her talk to people. From what she's said, this bloke needs exposing.' Amy's face was flushed.

Silence.

It was as if he saw Justine for the first time. He glanced at the myriad scraps of scribbled paper on the desk, the hefty dictionary propped at an angle against her lamp, the notes stuck to the edge of her screen.

'Alright. Dig into this one a bit more. Talk to people, see what you can find. That girl he knocked up – maybe even go and visit this scumbag yourself, see if you can get him to admit to anything. But if there's nothing....' The words hung like a threat.

Then his face and his tone softened. 'Look, don't get your hopes up. Stories – sometimes they're no more than that, just fairy tales that people would like to believe. But real life they ain't. There's only one thing that counts here: does it sell newspapers? Bottom line.'

*

Once it had been so familiar, dressing like this, but as she slipped on leggings, a T-shirt, and a scruffy rucksack, she realised that she never dressed like this during the week anymore. Working in an office, she'd got out of the habit.

It had been easy to slip into the English department common room. She simply followed someone else through the door.

She got a coffee from the machine, looked for a suitable group of students and sat down near them. Lucky it was close to start of term, she wouldn't arouse too much suspicion.

She'd already clocked the noticeboard with its photos of all the students and their names. All she needed to do was to find someone who'd never turned up. There were always some.

She turned to the girl next to her, casually saying, 'I've never seen half the people in those photos.'

'Me neither,' said the girl, her mouth full of biscuit.

'Suppose some of them must have dropped out.'

'Yeah. I knew Lucy.' She pointed to a photo. 'And she left last week,' she said, pointing to a picture of an Asian-looking woman, that Justine had to instantly discount. 'Her too.' She indicated another picture a few rows down. 'She hardly unpacked before she was off. Her parents took her home the next day.'

Justine got up to take a closer look. Kate Dugdale: hair a bit too curly, but she would do, the photo might have been taken some time ago.

'Do you know where I'd find Duncan McAllister's office?' she asked.

'Dunno. You could try the second floor.'

In the ladies she re-applied her lipstick, her mascara. She assessed herself in the mirror, with her skin-tight leggings, the denim jacket, and the Doc Martens. Was it all too obvious, would he see through her?

And what had she become? Was she setting out a honey trap here? Wasn't this the sort of journalism she despised? Had the Post corrupted her so much that she'd thrown all moral considerations away, just to get a story? No, morals didn't come into it, when you looked at what he'd done, he was the corrupt one here. He'd led a young woman to her death: that was all that counted, that justified anything. This way she might find out more. She'd have done the same at the Chronicle.

Walking along the corridor, scanning the names on all the office doors, she felt acutely aware she was an imposter, she shouldn't be here. She told herself her new name for the tenth time: Kate Dugdale, first year student. If she became Kate, sooner or later his words would condemn him. And that was what she needed.

His office was at the far end of a long corridor. Beyond, there was only the grimy fire door, its window overlooking some waste bins and the boiler house. She knocked on the door while making a small adjustment to her leggings, ensuring a strip of midriff was showing between them and her top.

She knocked again more firmly, and without waiting longer she opened the door. He looked up, a middle-aged man with scraggly grey hair, sunk behind his desk, looking furtive. Faced with this harmless looking remnant of a man, she started to wonder what she was doing here, until she noticed the way his eyes, though watery, kept their firm gaze on her, sweeping up and down her body. Meeting his stare, she thought, I know you, I know who you are and what you've done. And if you knew what's in my notebook....

I am going to nail you for what you've done. For poor, dead Meredith, for her grieving parents. For all the other girls you've preyed on.

And you know what else for? For me, for my own career.

She pushed the thought away, and, without asking, sat down on the worn office chair in front of his desk. She leaned forward and could sense him staring at her breasts. What a sleazy old man, she thought, forcing a smile onto her face.

'Professor McAllister? I'm Kate Dugdale. I'm a first year.'

'Kate,' he said, his tongue licking the corner of his mouth as if tasting her name. 'What can I do for you, Kate?'

Take My Hand

by Alice Little

I'm sitting on the beach, my bare toes in the hot sand, thinking about Toby and our first kiss the night before. I remember the feel of his hand in mine as we walked home, and the taste of the salty air as he kissed me. I can't forget the way he held me, as if he'd never let me go. The wind on my neck is like warm breath, I raise my chin and let it whisper under my hair.

'So, what happened?' Cynthia plops down on the sand beside me and hands me a beer she has just fetched from one of the bars along the esplanade.

'We went to Richard's party,' I begin. 'Separately, I mean. We were both invited.'

I look up the beach to the road I walked along to get to Richard's place. Had it only been yesterday? There had been kids playing in the sand, begging their parents to let them stay out longer, and music thrumming from the pier. The seagulls were making a racket and the smell of frying batter hung in the air. It was a totally perfect summer's evening, and anticipation bubbled in my belly.

'Toby was wearing that leather jacket you like so much,' I say. Cynthia grins. We had both liked Toby all year, since the first time we saw him in the campus bar, hair flopping in his eyes, his black T-shirt taut across his chest. But we had been too shy to talk to him. Instead we gossiped, making up what subject he was studying, and envisioning the cool flat he lived in.

'Did you know he's not actually a student? He just works behind the bar,' I reveal.

'All the better,' Cynthia says, 'a man with a job.'

'Richard said he invited him because he knew everyone would have a good time if Toby were there. Apparently, he's good at parties.'

'I can imagine.' Cynthia sips her drink. 'What else did Richard tell you about him?'

'Not much, he introduced us when I started asking questions, then left us to it.' It felt inevitable that we should spend the evening together. It felt like fate. 'I was meant to be staying over. Richard said I could sleep on the sofa to save walking home alone. But then Toby said he could walk me back.'

She'll come with me. That's what he actually said, when Richard was about to fetch me some bedding. I felt strangely proud to be taken under Toby's wing.

Cynthia raises her eyebrows.

'Don't look at me like that!' I protest.

'Why not? You've skipped to the end of the night without even mentioning what happened at the party, I assume it's for a good reason?' she says. I wish I could see her eyes behind her too-large sunglasses.

'It was a party. We chatted, and danced a bit.'

'And flirted?' she winks. She's enjoying this, while I don't really want to think about it. I'm reliving the night before purely for her, hoping she doesn't notice I'm not reacting to her teasing.

'I guess.' I look down at the sand without smiling, and see that the nail varnish on my toes is chipped.

'And then he offered to walk you home? I see where this is going.'

'I knew he meant he wanted to be invited in when we got to mine, but...'

Cynthia laughs. 'It's OK, I would have been fine with that too.'

'It was surreal,' I say. 'We've been talking about him for months – and here he was, taking an interest in little old me.'

'So, what happened?' She's still grinning, eager.

'I was a bit surprised, actually, that Richard didn't check that was OK with me first.' Richard had been too drunk to care who I left with. By that stage in the evening I expect he was only thinking about getting to his own bed. *Whatever*, he said, and shrugged. Toby and I let ourselves out.

'I didn't mean with Richard, I meant with Toby.' Cynthia disregards my disquiet.

'Oh. Right. We left the party, and…'

'You came along the beach?' she prompts. 'How romantic.'

'Yeah,' I say. 'I guess it was.'

'Did you hold hands?' She taps my leg impatiently and I flinch.

Recovering, I nod in answer to her question. It sounds so juvenile when she says it, but at the time it felt reckless and wild. It's such a cliché: moonlit walks on the dunes, tender kisses in the sand. But it wasn't like that; it wasn't as I'd imagined at all.

Toby held out his hand to me as we came round the corner from Richard's street onto the esplanade, and as soon as I took it he started to run. He led me down the slope to the sand, where it was much darker than up on the road. I struggled to keep up, but gave a squeal to show him that I was up for his little adventure. His laugh was a deep, warm chuckle that made my heart flutter.

'So, you kissed, right? Come on, I want all the details.'

The truth is that I wanted him to kiss me, of course I did, it was what Cynthia and I had both wanted for months. Toby and I were at the edge of the land, passing through the lamplight. I willed him to stop, to turn to face me, to lean towards me. I would stand on tiptoe, his arms would encircle me. I had pictured this moment a hundred times.

But now I was there I felt graceless. My cotton dress flapped at my knees as he pulled me along, and I held it down awkwardly with my other hand.

We slowed as we reached the end of the concrete slope and our shoes sank into the sand.

'He joked about going skinny-dipping,' I say, knowing it will make Cynthia giggle.

You don't want to go swimming, do you? I said, not wanting to go near the dark water. He danced around me and toyed with the strap of my dress, laughing. *Why? Are you that keen to take off your clothes?*

'It would have been freezing!' Cynthia says.

'That's what I told him.'

'So, what happened next?'

'That's when he kissed me.'

'Ooh!'

I smile at Cynthia's thrill, rather than at the memory of the kiss itself.

Toby jerked me towards him and pressed his lips to mine, harder than I would have liked, his cold tongue prodding at my teeth. I pulled away.

'And?'

Poor Cynthia, I can't tell her how disappointing it was. 'And then he walked me home,' I say, fiddling with my beer bottle.

'Don't be coy,' she scolds. 'I'd tell you everything if it were me.'

Toby had been at a bit of a loss and, like a child unsure of what to do next, had returned to the previous game and pulled me onwards towards the sea, shouting *Come on!* and tugging my hand.

I could see the white froth of the waves on the shore, deep black stretching above to the horizon. My pumps were full of sand and I was starting to get cold. I hoped maybe he would lend me his jacket.

At the water's edge he went as if to lift me up, but I let out a yelp and he relented, pretending it had been a joke all along. *Alright then, no swimming tonight.*

'We continued on to my place,' I tell Cynthia. She watches me, expectantly.

My slim hand in his large paw, I led him back up the beach to the esplanade, and we walked past the closed bars, one or two firepits still glowing from earlier in the night. His hand was warm, and I kept reminding myself that this was *Toby*, the guy we had daydreamed about all last term, and here he was with *me*. But he wasn't much like the Toby we had invented.

Instead of being confident and suave, or even sweet and kind, he didn't seem comfortable holding hands without it being part of a game and breaking into a run. He tried swinging our arms, which made him laugh his deep guffaw, then he rocked me sideways as we walked so he could drape his arm across my shoulders instead.

I've seen you around campus, he said, as if trying to explain himself. *I thought you were really pretty. But you were always with your friend, and–*

It's just up here, beyond the museum, I interrupted, willing my building to be closer.

I glance up at the museum now, and Cynthia follows my gaze.

The six-foot high metal face that announces the entrance to the outdoor sculpture gallery watched us as we passed.

Are you always this quiet? Maybe he had imagined me differently too.

I didn't know what to say, so confirmed it by not answering.

Outside my building he leaned down to kiss me again and I let him, though the first occasion hadn't been worth repeating. This time was better, he didn't push so hard. But it went on a bit long. And he tasted of stale beer.

His hand was on my waist, his fingers digging into my skin through the thin fabric of my dress. He drew me closer just as I was about to pull away.

'Cynth…' I say.

'Yeah?'

'I don't know. It was strange. I was so flattered by his attention, but then he was different. Not like we'd thought at all.'

As I stood on my doorstep, locked in his arms, all that remained of my nervous excitement was a sour lump growing in the pit of my stomach.

'Maybe you just like the thrill of the chase?'

'Mmm.'

You smell so good, he said, breathing deeply just above my hair.

'Up close he smelled like he'd not washed his clothes,' I tell Cynthia. 'It was gross.'

I shrank away from him, but he held me firmly against his body. I squirmed, surely he'd notice?

I want to hold you forever, he said, kissing the skin next to my eyebrow and leaving it wet. He turned his lips to my ear. *Are you going to invite me in?*

I hadn't thought about it, I lied. I pushed him gently backwards, and after a moment's uncertainty he stepped away from me. Our eyes met. There was a tang of salt in the air.

He watched, curious, as I unlocked the door. *Goodnight*, I said. He looked like a little boy lost in the supermarket. I shut the door quickly behind me.

'That's alright,' Cynthia consoles me cheerily, 'as long as you enjoyed yourself.'

I wasn't sure it was alright, and I knew I hadn't enjoyed myself, but I matched her tone anyway. 'Yeah, I guess I liked him more before I knew him. Last night he was suddenly all over me, and then I wasn't so keen.'

Cynthia laughs. I hadn't meant to be funny.

'You want another beer?'

'Yeah, thanks.'

I dig my toes into the hot sand. The wind on my neck is like warm breath, I raise my chin and let it whisper under my hair. Without meaning to, I recall the feel of Toby's hand in mine as we walked home, and the taste of the salty air as he kissed me. I can't forget the way he held me, as if he'd never let me go.

The Ultimate Joink's Exploration of Planet Beautiful

by Margaret Gallop

High in a lighthouse on the domed island off the west coast of Scotland a young man leaps to his feet with excitement.

'Commander, sir, I've got something.'

'What do you mean you've got something, McTavish?'

'I've got a connection with an extra-terrestrial lifeform, Commander.'

'A what?'

'Our first intimation of extra-terrestrial life, Commander. I thought you would want to be informed.'

'Tosh. There *are* no other lifeforms, McTavish.'

'But sir, our monitoring station, all this equipment, our UNESCO grant. Isn't that why we're here?'

'Are you insinuating, McTavish, that I only came here for the golf?'

'Of course not, sir. But–'

'Oh, let me hear the blasted thing – I thought so, just a blether of crackles.'

'I need more data for the full interstellar translation, sir.'

'You do realise that if we have an intruder I will need to put the British Isles – the world – on full military alert?'

'I think that would be premature, Commander.'

'Exactly. So can I please get on to my appointment at the Royal Troon?'

'Ah, the translation has started. I think it is a young extra-terrestrial, sir, he seems to be falling through space and talking to himself.' I know how that feels, McTavish thought, as footsteps receded down the lighthouse stairs.

The lighthouse door slammed and the sound of a military helicopter drowned out the incoming signal. McTavish watched avidly as the translation gradually emerged.

*

I'm not scared I'm not scared, I'm not scared. I'm not scared, I'm not scared, I'm not scare-ed.

What just happened? Why are they letting me fall? I often fall out of our ship Ultimate Perspective. Then Dad hoiks me in again. It's a game we play. He enjoys it too, doesn't he? Why isn't he coming to fetch me? Are the other members of the spaceship's crew stopping him? How mean! Why would they do that?

I'm not scared, I'm not scared I'm not scare-ed.

They are mean, the joinks, scaring a young joink. *The* young joink I should say. Me. They say 'No more baby joinks. They cause too much trouble.' Huh. They think it's clever to keep repairing themselves with scavenged space junk, forever. I would *like* another little joink to chase round the craft. But they say no, huh!

Still, that makes me very special. I am the last, the final, the most unique, the Ultimate Joink! They should take more care of me.

As for being 'trouble', I suppose I've always pulled the wires out. Perhaps this time I went too far? I can reach higher now. I'm growing, see. I'm the last one to still grow. Perhaps they are angry with me? I know it went dark for a while and they had to use the emergency lighting. But they're good at mending things. They're engineers! If *I* don't keep them entertained, how would they spend their time? Who needs emergency *drills*, when I can cause *real* emergencies?

I thought they liked having me on the survival transport. They did say 'One day you will break something we *can't* repair.' If only I had contact, I would say 'Please let me back. I won't do it again, really I won't.'

Help!

*

'McTavish? You again. I said to only ring in an emergency.'

'Sorry, sir, it is an emergency sir. The creature is asking for help.'

'I don't care what it is saying. I need a location. How can we turn our missiles on it if we don't know where it is?'

'Missiles, sir? It doesn't sound very dangerous to me.'

*

Help, I am falling and falling! I can't see the Ultimate Perspective anymore. What can I do? I know, I have a stupendous idea. I will record my adventure and j-log it to the universe. Some creature may hear me. Or find it later.

Joinks and other lifeforms, wherever you are in the universe, here is my record from deepest space. I am spinning, free of the vessel, free of joink contact. Everywhere around me I see stars glittering. Ah! There, coming into view is a planet many have heard of but few have seen. It is glimmering blue in the surrounding blackness. It is the colour of the Blue Butterfly in the Ultimate Perspective's virtual nature museum.

*

'Ultimate Joink, can you hear me? This is Sergeant McTavish trying to make contact.'

*

What is that crackling?

I am now approaching Planet Beautiful. This planet has its own water, you don't have to mine it, it flows and swirls. It has light that comes straight from the sun by day, and at night this light is sometimes reflected by the shimmering white moon which circles the planet. I love light, it's what joinks live on, what gives us life! The Planet Beautiful is teeming with life. All kinds of creatures you can't even imagine. Not constructed like joinks, but growing and breeding, making little things that grow big.

Planet Beautiful has vast seas that supply water to the land. I can see it clearer now. It is blue and green and muffled with white fluff. The clouds lift the water from the sea back to the land in big cycles. The Two-Legged Ones on Planet Beautiful live off water and air they say, not like us. The planet supplies it for them. Just imagine that: so vulnerable.

I wonder what will happen if I fall into the water? I, your

intrepid reporter will try this on your behalf. I'm a joink and I live on light, what will water do to me? What happens if I am out of reach of the light? Might I run down and stop moving?

I will record my historic journey. It will became a classic in the annals of space discovery and a vital resource for our ship.

So, followers, I'm falling nearer and nearer to the planet's surface. Hey, there's a wind here pulling me round into the planet's orbit. Hang on! Wheeh! I'm spinning. Beneath me is land, sea, land. Now I'm falling, it's hot. Now I'm within the planet's atmosphere. This is what they call gravity. Wowee!

There's going to be a big crash or splash. I think I have some residual wings. Yes, I will try to flare them out a bit. Wahaaa, didn't expect that! I'm looping the loop, but it's slowing me down.

Hey what's that? I am being bumped by some strange bullets. What are they? I'm switching on the info implant in my brain. They have those soft sides and wings. Birds, feathers, it tells me. Why didn't I study the Planet Beautiful more on the craft? Info? They're swifts. Flying together around the world. They have their eyes closed. They are asleep as they fly! No wonder they bumped into me. Wake up swifts, you don't know who's up here!

I'm falling again, flapping awkwardly on my inadequate wings to break my fall. Oh no, a large bird is swooping towards me with big and fully working wings! Ouch. I am not something to eat! Bird, listen to me with your inner mind. You have caught a joink, I'm not tasty or digestible. I'm partly alive and partly made of indestructible substances. Ow! Watch out, bird, my close relatives are machines! I am *not* edible. My brain and my heart *are* organic matter, followers, but I mustn't tell him that, even telepathically.

I think he's carrying me to somewhere he can land, then he'll hold me down with one talon and pick me apart with the other, and eat the juicy bits. I will try to imitate dead prey. I bet he likes things that look wriggly and fresh. I know, I'll create a stink with this methane battery. That didn't work, sea birds obviously like stinky prey. All I know about this planet is from j-tube and they don't convey stinks properly. What does my info implant say? It's a Snowy Owl. Rare species. Amazing – but terrifying. Endangered? He would be if I was a bit bigger. I'm going to biff him on the nose.

*

On the Ultimate Perspective spacecraft a circle of sober joinks, with varying degrees of metal about their persons, were listening to one of their number, Buffalo.

'I can say nothing to excuse my son except that I love him and I request permission and assistance to retrieve him.'

'I regret to say, Buffalo,' said the leader, Mammoth (all joinks are named after extinct or threatened Planet Beautiful animals), 'that your son has proved his delinquency by repeatedly interfering with the ship's systems, and instead of letting himself be called to account, has departed through the recycling chute. He has made his choice.'

'But please, Mammoth, he is still very young.'

Mammoth stood up. 'Your son is a destructive joink. We, who have survived the death of our planet, deplore above all else, destructiveness. Our fathers destroyed the Planet Bountiful. We are sworn to accept our destiny to stay aboard this survival vessel. Your son must be left to his fate.'

*

No. No. I mustn't kick the endangered snowy owl. I can't start my adventure on Planet Beautiful by wiping something out. I must remember that he, snowy owl, broke my fall.

Where *is* he taking me? That rock looks hard. A high rock above what? That must be the curling sea.

*

'I don't believe it, the signal is getting stronger. He's landing on our island!'

The Commander raised a sceptical eyebrow. 'An extra-terrestrial, you say? And he's unarmed?'

'Yes, sir. Harmless. A juvenile. Hasn't got a clue what's going on.'

Unseen by McTavish, the Commander smiled, as if making a joke. 'Then see if you can retrieve him. Unharmed, mind you, we'll want to do tests.'

*

Careful. Ouch! My inorganic bits don't mend, owl.

Oh, he's landing gently, doesn't want to break me. Perhaps he thinks I'm an egg? Where's his nest? Oh, here we go, straight into the middle of a nest full of hungry beaks. Well, I am *not* their next feed. Yes, look away, owl. Wow, you can turn your neck right round! Keep looking away. Get off me, chicks!

Oh, his head is coming back round. I'll hide under this green... er... garment. Yuck, it's wet and dark under here, not good for me. No light. Seaweed, that's what my info says. Never heard of it. I'll scramble down here. Glad of all my limbs.

Ooh, water, in I go!

Totally wet now, but I don't seem to be fizzing or dissolving.

What is that? It has large grab-hands like Dad uses to move about on the outside of the craft. Not magnetic, luckily or I would be straight into the embrace of a... what... a lobster?

Get off, lobster! I do not want to be opened up, thank you. I'm going to kick off from this rock.

I'm swimming! The first joink to swim on Planet Beautiful. I'll make myself into the shape of a sea rocket, yes, my phrase, and speed away!

*

'He's going to be eaten alive, literally. I must get down there,' McTavish said to himself as he rushed down to the beach.

The radio communicator crackled: 'McTavish, come in, McTavish. Where are you now? Are you *en route* to the landing site? Have you got that specimen for me yet?'

'I'm on my way, sir.'

'I want it alive, remember. We must run tests on every aspect of it, first alive and then dead.'

'Dead, sir? It's just a young thing, sir.'

*

Oh no, a giant wave has swept me off into the sea. It's the tide.

Oh, how beautiful. Growing things under water. All different colours. Squiggly things. Fish, gliding past. Dappled light, just enough to keep me running. I could live here in this beautiful sea garden.

But now it's getting colder and darker. The night is falling. Dark, cold. My battery is running low. I must stop recording and conserve…

*

On the spacecraft the Ultimate Perspective, a venerable joink has risen to his feet.

'I must say I enjoyed having a youngster on board. He made me laugh.'

'Delinquent,' said a voice.

'Erm, I would say mischievous, playful, experimental and, dare I say, inventive. We need to raise the designers of the future.' There was a murmur of assent. 'I remember helping him make himself a titanium shell.'

Another joink stood up. 'My name is Saola and I know where he is.'

'You know?' Buffalo rose to his feet. 'Why didn't you tell us?'

'He has landed on Planet Beautiful.'

'What?' roared Mammoth. 'Planet Beautiful is a Designated Nature Reserve.'

'I've picked up his j-log, Buffalo. He is describing his journey to the universe.'

Buffalo rushed across to Saola. 'Thank you Saola! He may yet survive. Thank you.'

'But,' spluttered Mammoth, 'no one is allowed onto Planet Beautiful for fear of contamination.'

'He can go into the decontamination chamber when he returns,' shouted Buffalo. 'But he must survive, we must bring him back!' There was a subdued cheer from the assembly.

'I don't mean *he* might be contaminated,' Mammoth roared, 'I mean Planet Beautiful. We have to take care in a Designated Nature Reserve. Rhino, take the Perspective into orbit around Planet Beautiful. Saola, help Buffalo to prepare a small craft. And sterilise it! And remember: you are not allowed to land.'

*

'OK, McTavish, I'm coming to take over. I'll land the chopper on the beach. You get back to the lighthouse so you can give me the precise co-ordinates.'

*

Erm, sorry, followers, for the break in transmission. The tide has washed me onto this island and a beautiful tall creature is feeding me light. A lighthouse! I am on a beach full of pebbles. I will use my titanium shell and lurk in disguise.

  Wow, the sky is full of colour – the Northern Lights!

  What is that noise?

*

'There he is, Buffalo, I can see him shining on the beach. If he would only fly towards us we could catch him with our magnetic salvage hook. But are his wings strong enough?'

*

'Are you back at your desk yet, McTavish? I don't know where I should be searching. But, I must say, some of these pebbles look nearly as round as golf balls. Where are my clubs? I bet I can get this one into the sea. Did you see that? Marvellous, what a splash! Wow, here's a really wonderful pebble: so shiny. Even when the damn sky is changing colour.'

*

Followers, a strange creature has approached me. It has put me on a pile of pebbles. It has three legs and one is tapping me.

*

'Sorry, sir. Can you come up here, sir?'

  'Let me just... this one's going as high as a kite.'

*

Whoa, up I go!

*

'Hey, McTavish, can you see a strange shape against the Northern Lights? Get a fix on that beauty. Wait, what is that? It looks like... could it be–'

  'Sir, please turn and look at the lighthouse. Most important, sir.'

  'Why? Wow, it's blinding me!'

  'Sorry, sir.'

  'I can't see it anymore. Did you see a... well, a spaceship, McTavish?'

  'Can't see anything from up here, sir.'

*

'Look, Buffalo, here he comes!'
 'Have you got him?'
 'Safely on board.'
 'Thanks, Dad, I knew you'd come. I've had an amazing time.'
*

Over a third whisky in the lighthouse, the staff reviewed their day.
 'I still don't understand why you asked me to look at the lighthouse. You nearly blinded me.'
 'I'm sure I didn't do that, sir. But it's been a confusing day.'
 'What happened about your extra-terrestiral?'
 'Extra-terrestrial, sir? But you don't believe in them.'
 'Of course I don't.'

Grandmother knows best

by Oliver Bussell

Owinye first heard the voice of his dead grandmother at work. He had been punching numbers into a spreadsheet and fantasising about lunch when the words appeared, unprompted, inside his head. He knew nothing had been said out loud because there was never a break in the rhythmic tapping of plastic keys and the tireless whirr of the photocopy machines, but there had been his own voice, mentally choosing sandwiches, and now there was another voice, unmistakably that of his long-dead grandmother. *That man is not long for this world*, she said.

Owinye knew he must be overtired – exhausted from another long week at the office – his girlfriend Esi had been telling him for weeks that he needed to slow down, to take his foot off the gas. It was an argument they'd had countless times before, and he would bite his tongue to avoid the spiralling anger, the shouts, the smashed plates, not repeating the words that enraged her so: that it was only with this job that they could maintain their lifestyle, that without those extra hours he put in, she would have to go back to secretarial work and they could kiss goodbye to that fancy car she loved to parade around town. So Owinye didn't tell anyone about the voice inside his head, and had almost forgotten about it, and its message, when his boss, the following week, died in a car accident.

Owinye was not a superstitious man, and for him to draw connections between these two events – a voice in his head and a tragic death – would have been illogical. Hearing a voice was one thing, but believing what it said was something entirely different. Besides, from memory it had only been a vague prediction, the same as if the voice had said *the rains will soon come*, when of course the rains would come eventually – it is easy to predict the future in sweeping gestures. An oracle vagaries do not make.

But it was while he was having these thoughts, pushing, once again, the memory of that voice out of his mind, to pretend he had never heard his dead grandmother say anything at all – as he watched a suited man show one of his colleagues the new office that this sudden death had granted her – that the voice returned and said, *I told you so.* It seemed that either madness was already upon him, or his dead grandmother really was inside his head, shining a light into his future from beyond the grave.

Owinye had few memories of his grandmother: sweet pastries on a high table, wet kisses on foreheads, and the fabric entrance to the Fortune Room. It was here that she would toss the shells for him and tell him things like *you must marry a nice local girl*, and *you should not live abroad*, and *grandmother knows best*. But these were things that grandmothers said, and although young Owinye would watch with fascination as she cast a question into the universe, scattered the white shells across the woven mat and recited his fortune in her gravelly voice, this was the magic of youth. It was a time when he still believed in gods and ghosts and fairies, each of which would shrivel in the harsh light of reality, as death, sex and anxiety rushed to fill the void they had left. He would grow up and move abroad and date an American and ignore his grandmother's wishes.

And yet here she was, his long-dead grandmother, never to be ignored, tossing her shells inside his head.

With this, there will be new beginnings. And as Owinye rolled his eyes at yet more ambiguity, he felt an instant surge of guilt flood his torso, as if his grandmother were standing before him, for he never would have been so discourteous to her face. He wondered if perhaps it was her that was goading him from within and so he apologised, saying he would try to believe it was truly her; he would try to rekindle that wonder of youth, the suspension of disbelief.

And so it was that Owinye came to believe this death would lead to new beginnings, and it was the following day, as had been foretold, that his new boss – not twenty-four hours earlier a colleague that had shared his complaints about the weather – fired him. And for the first time in seven years, Owinye was without a job.

You have the sight, said his grandmother, *use it.* And so, when he got home that night, he crept past the television room where Esi was watching one of her shows and climbed the ladder to the attic where he kept the old shoebox that held his grandmother's worldly possessions. He dusted off her wooden necklace, slotting it over his head, discarded a broken burner that would have once filled the room with sweet-smelling smoke, and found, on top of her expired driving licence the small black velvet bag that held sixteen white cowrie-shells. He could not find her woven mat but remembered with horror (although he realised the horror was not his own), that they had been using it as a table centrepiece for years.

He tiptoed back downstairs and stood over the mat, pouring the shells from the bag into his open palm and watching their hungry mouths gape up at him. *Ask them a question,* said his long-dead grandmother.

What should I do now? Owinye thought and his hand released the shells as if he had intended it himself, and they tumbled out, landing surely at random, some up, some down. But he could not begin to fathom what they meant, if anything. He suddenly felt foolish for ever going this far with any of this, for truly believing, even if only momentarily, that the voice in his head was actually that of his grandmother and not the early rumblings of mental illness. But then his grandmother said, *Read the shells.*

And so Owinye leaned over the shells, and suddenly saw the patterns – he saw that they made a picture, that they made words, that each shell told a story and through his eyes his grandmother read this story to him and said, *Now, use your gift.*

Owinye was elated, for he now had a way to talk with her directly, to manage these sporadic prophecies.

He first asked a question that had been keeping him awake at night for months: Should I marry Esi? He released the shells and immediately the response came: *I never liked her. She will seek pleasure elsewhere.* And Owinye suddenly felt his grandmother's scorn, believed her disgust, understood what was to happen if he did not act, and although the feelings were not his own, it became hard to distinguish where his grandmother's distaste ended and his own apathy began.

From that moment, it was impossible to shake the feeling whenever he saw Esi, it was a dark stain that he could not rub out. He was jealous of her wayward glances at other men, suspicious if he returned home to her already made up and smelling of floral perfume, and he grew tired of their arguments because he no longer had the energy or resolve to weather them.

And so, after another day spent sitting in a cafe to avoid telling Esi he had been fired, he summoned his grandmother's anger and walked into the television room – switching off the series she was watching, to shocked protestation – to tell her that the two of them were through and that she needed to leave immediately. A fight ensued and she beat at his chest and wept, but he already knew the future and so he understood that pain now would prevent what might otherwise have come.

There was silence in the wake of her departure. Sadness too, but also relief. He sat in his chair in the empty kitchen and pushed the shells with his finger, the image of Esi already beginning to fade in the shadow of the unimaginable power he now wielded. Because it was with this gift that he would make his fortune, and with that he would travel the world; he would be adviser to presidents, to kings, he would steer the world in righteous directions, averting disaster, spreading joy.

'What does my future hold?' he said out loud, for now there was no one around who might cause him shame.

Death, said the shells. *It is not safe here. You must return home.*
But Owinye was already home, for this had been his home for many years, one of the few things he owned in this country. And then he remembered that it was his grandmother who spoke through his eyes and so he understood that *home* could only mean her home – the country he had been born in.

So, because he knew the future, he sold his things, sold his house, sold Esi's dresses and the shoes and the car, for he knew she would never return, and he bought a ticket to the village where he had grown up, and there he bought a plot of land. He paid local labourers to build him a great house that sat atop the faded footprint of his grandmother's house, long-since demolished and cleared for farmland. He knew when he saw the spot that this was what his grandmother had meant by *home*.

Sitting in the darkness of this new house – for the power was out across the village and he was yet to install a back-up generator – he tossed the shells again and by the light of the candle he heard the voice that read the signs and it said, *You must find a nice local girl to father your children.* Although Owinye protested, asking if the time was not now to use his gift to see the world – to change the course of history – he was reminded by the voice inside his head that thanks to her he had escaped death already and that because of this he should trust her. *Listen to your grandmother.*

And so he went out into the village and asked the elders if they knew of any unmarried women and to his surprise, despite being far beyond the age of desirability in the city he had left, the prospect of this man from over-the-water attracted a wealth of families who laid out a buffet of brides for him to choose from. Although he had not cast the shells, the voice in his head said, *that one*, and so he picked a shy-looking girl with wide hips whom he came to wed.

They had little to say to each other and she was meek and frightened where Esi had been empowered and spontaneous. On their wedding night he bedded her with his eyes clamped shut, saving himself the shame of his grandmother witnessing the act, and afterwards, as he lay beside this woman, he knew that his new wife would bear him a child. She bore him two more children after the first, in quick succession – a single night spent together between pregnancies and he would close his eyes, knowing before he had even left the bed to shower that an infant would flower in this woman's womb. At intervals, when the children were asleep upstairs, he would ask the shells whether now was the time – whether now was the moment for him to share his gift with the world – but the answer would always be the same: *Build your life here.*

And so Owinye came to have a job in a local shop, the same shop in fact that his grandmother had worked in, and he tossed his shells for a fee at night as she had done before him, in a small tent in the yard, but he received little in the way of money and the fortunes he offered were vague. It was after the birth of his fourth child, a little boy, that the voice of his grandmother finally stopped.

He was sitting at the kitchen table, his exhausted wife upstairs, the new baby swaddled beside her, the other children asleep in their rooms, when he thought the words – I am not happy – and although it was not a question he tossed the shells nonetheless and for the last time the patterns aligned themselves and his dead grandmother, from deep inside his skull said, *Stop this complaining at once, you have everything I ever wished for you.*

And with that, she left.

Unexpected Turns

by Abigail B Vint

Lena pressed her fingernails deep into her palms. It was the smallest movement of force she could make without Marshall seeing. He was humming along to whatever the local radio station had on, his face calm and hopeful, like a small child's. She couldn't bring herself to pass along her own unease.

The air smelled stale, recycled from within the car and, after the four-hour ride, it was beginning to make her feel sick.

Flat fields as far as she could see stretched out ahead of her. The light yellow and brown tones of an arid July landscape. Dried grass swayed in the heavy breeze and the flatness of the journey was laid out in front of them, going on for miles and miles.

She rolled down her window.

'Sweetie, can we turn the A/C off? Just need a bit of fresh air in here.'

Marshall turned the dial to OFF and gave her a wink. She admired his cheeky grin, a smile appearing on her face. He always knew just how to calm her. She waited for the inevitable joke.

'Sure, babe, got a craving for a whiff of dry cow shit?' Marshall wrinkled his nose as he rolled his window down a bit and took a jovial deep breath in. 'Ahh, that's better,' he said, coughing.

She shook her head and turned to take in a blast of the warm air now floating into the front seat. Her stomach was none the better, but she felt less contained in a tin can, hurtling along the highway.

Marshall turned the radio up, the sound getting drowned out by the wind flapping against the edge of the open windows. A scratchy version of 'Song Sung Blue' by Neil Diamond came on.

They exchanged rolled eyes and Lena snorted.

'What?' Marshall jested. 'You're not a fan of the soothing static-y sounds of the-middle-of-nowhere radio?'

Lena let out a half-hearted laugh, her hand pulled up to her mouth, released from the pinch of her nails.

'We're going to lose reception so may as well enjoy it while we can. After that, it will be us and the sounds of tumbleweed along the highway,' he said.

Lena lifted her bare feet and gently placed them down on the car dashboard.

'Whatever you say, DJ,' she said. Then her face turned more serious and she dragged her hand through her long, knotted hair. 'Anything to pass the time.'

She turned to Marshall, revealing her anxiety. He reached over and rubbed the top of her forearm, giving it a squeeze before he spoke again.

'Not long now, sweet pea,' he said.

She gave a soft smile but pulled her arm away, caving into herself and nodding furiously to prevent the tears before looking back out at the dry farmland.

*

She hadn't been sure what to pack that morning, what to bring.

They were told they would need to stay a night or two before they could leave. It seemed odd. Lena wondered if they were still being assessed.

Marshall had called from the kitchen for her to hurry, shouting something about getting on the road. She flung the three dresses and four tops she had dragged out of her closet into a duffel bag. The final outfit choice would have to wait until the next morning.

First contact, the woman had called it on the phone. It sounded so clinical, so business-like. For months they had been on their best behaviour, putting their best selves forward to get to this point. This hardly felt like a first anything.

She grabbed the bag and took one last look at their room. Bed made, Marshall's doing of course. He could never start his day properly, he said, without the bed looking tidy.

He had even made the bed on the worst day of their lives.

That morning, when she woke in pain, an uncomfortable urge to use the toilet. The sea of red that followed, the intense panic that set in, her calling for him.

They had left in a rush; the emergency operator had told them to hurry. But Marshall had still managed to pull the duvet up over the pillows.

She had been angry then, mad at him for putting in so much effort during a critical time. She told him later that day, when they were both sitting, numb, on the living room sofa.

He winced when she mentioned it and then he spoke. 'My mother used to say, it's the small things that make a difference when your world is falling apart.' Lena remembered him biting his nails and looking down at the floor before he spoke again. 'She made the bed every day when we were in the shelter. Temporary or not, it was our home.'

Lena had never questioned him about it again.

Heading down the corridor towards the front door this morning, she had glanced at the spare bedroom, the bed also made, a few small plush toys sat at the top. This room would feel so very different when they returned.

*

Lena had been the one to bring up starting a family a few years ago, probably one year into their marriage. They had fallen in love quickly, two forty-year-olds ready to take the domestic leap. Lena had spent her youth on a cruise ship as a server. It was the best and the worst kind of life. Deep relationships with people that lived the same nomadic lifestyle but not many interactions with people on dry land.

Marshall spent most of his time teaching English in South Korea, raising enough money to pay off the student debt from his illustrious master's degree in history. He too, spent time with roving wanderers, maintaining tight knit friendships with a handful of other teachers or *foreigners* as they were known.

These paths less travelled bonded them in their respective love of exploration.

They were married in a small ceremony in a park near her parents' house, surrounded by friends and family and blazing hot sunshine. Lena had insisted, after years on a cruise ship, that she wanted no beach side or seaside wedding, nothing water-related for their special day. Even the pond was off limits for the photographs. Marshall surprised her at the reception by putting on a lei and dancing around to the *Love Boat* theme. It was received with great laughter and admiration, most of all from a blushing but giggling bride. She, in return, had him served his least favourite Korean dish, the red paste and rice cake dish of *ddukbokki*.

'Wow, my love, you shouldn't have,' he said, playing along.

He tried a few bites, wincing with each chew, much to the entertainment of their guests. She finally put him out of his misery and had the staff serve him what everyone else was eating: grilled steak. Even at the wedding, people began to talk about what great parents they'd be, what a great team.

After the honeymoon, Lena had brought it up in earnest.

Marshall hesitated. She could never quite place his uncertainty. Gentle but persistent, she urged him to think about it. Her patience and confidence eventually brought him round to the idea. He even got into googling baby names.

'What's wrong with Bob?' he called to Lena one day from the home office. 'Bob's a solid name. Everybody loves Bob.' Through laughter, Lena had continued reshelving her books in the living room and simply shouted no. 'You can name the dog Bob,' she said. 'But I draw the line at humans.'

They hadn't counted on the losses. The many, many losses. Marshall was checked. Lena was checked. There were no obvious anomalies, the doctors said. Her advanced years in her mid-forties may have had something to do with it but she was healthy, they said. Sometimes it's not one big thing, just a whole bunch of small things.

Lena wondered if they were being punished, being made to pay penance for getting down to this domestic life so late.

*

Lena looked at her watch. The old digital clock in the car had stopped working years ago. Parts of the numbers had died out, so the time was always a secret.

On long car rides, Marshall and Lena used to play a game, each taking turns to guess what the actual time was. Lena usually won. She was intuitive about most things: directions, restaurant menu selection, seat choices on a plane, people.

There was that one time she was wrong about a person. She had been so certain that teenage girl was not ready to become a parent.

'You're going to give her a great life, aren't you?' Lena remembers the girl, Tilly, asking during their final meeting, as she rubbed at her large belly bump.

'Yes, Tilly, yes, we absolutely will,' Lena replied, desperate.

Marshall was biting at his nails, Lena gently pulled down his arm to stop him. Sitting on his hands, he had leaned closer to Tilly.

'She will be very loved, Tilly. I can promise you that.'

They had both shed a tear and Tilly fell into Lena's arms, collapsing under all the weight she was carrying. When she finally pulled back, Tilly dragged the back of her hand across her cheek. 'I believe you,' she said.

Lena and Marshall had bought a crib, some baby clothes essentials and even a few toys. It took all Lena's persuasive efforts to stop Marshall from buying the video monitor.

But in the end, Tilly changed her mind. Marshall didn't blame Lena, even though Tilly had been her choice. Lena blamed herself for putting them through it.

'We've got to stop this,' she announced one night after dinner a few weeks after Tilly's decision. 'We need to focus on us, stop trying to get someone else's child.'

Marshall started to gnaw at his raw fingertips, and turned his back on Lena to start washing the dishes.

'If that's what you think,' he muttered, his voice soft and broken.

Lena crossed her arms, unsure whether she was angry at him for being so flippant or sad that he sounded so hurt.

'Well, it is,' she snarked and stormed out of the room. It had taken months before they spoke about it again.

*

Lena rolled the window up a bit, taming the wild wind that was now whipping around in the front seat.

'Well, we've been going for about five hours, we must be

close?' she asked.

'We've made good time, actually,' Marshall said, digging one hand into the bag of wine gums that sat between them. His mouth full, he spoke again, the sweetness of his breath filling the front seats. 'I'd say we're about ten minutes away.'

Ten minutes. Lena rubbed at the top of her legs, wiping her clammy, wet palms. She took a big breath and let it out.

Marshall ignored her this time, Lena catching him lost in his own thoughts. She decided not to ask him what was on his mind, instead turning to look back towards the passing fields.

*

They pulled up to the hotel right around the time Marshall had guessed and Lena clapped her hands with glee. She would still have to wait another twenty hours before this was all over, or all begun, but at least they were out of the damn car.

'I'll grab the bags; can you check us in?' Marshall said. She watched his face disappear behind the boot door as it opened, and she headed inside to the front desk.

'Room seventy-seven, ma'am,' the clerk said. 'You should buy yourself a lottery ticket because that's the luckiest room we've got.'

She thanked him and took the key, awkwardly holding the large plastic keychain. If all goes well tomorrow, she thought, her lottery would be won.

They settled into their shabby but clean ground floor unit, two queen size beds with scratchy thin floral covers and worn grey carpets.

'I'm not that hungry,' Lena announced after the pizza arrived.

'Aw, but, babe, you've gotta eat. Here, why not just have some crusts,' Marshall began to rip off the top bits of a few slices.

So parental already, she thought. She took a small bite and a sip of water.

They passed the time with some old re-runs of eighties sitcoms. Marshall finally broke the TV coma.

'Big day tomorrow. Gotta get some shut eye.' He stood to turn off the TV, the remote not working.

'Marsh?'

He paused before getting back into bed. 'Yeah?' he said, not moving.

'I'm scared. I don't know if I'm going to… I'm just not sure if I'm…'

He came up to her side of the bed and grasped her hands, squeezed hard. She stared into his bright green eyes.

'I'm nervous too. This is… this is big. But you know what, we can do this. We *are* doing this.'

She took a deep breath and pulled him in for a bear hug.

'Let's just get some sleep,' she said, before squeezing him tightly one more time and falling into her side of the bed.

*

Lena wasn't sure if it was the uncomfortable mattress or the nerves that ruined her sleep. Marshall was already up and showered. She kept her eyes pressed closed, hoping not to have to start the day yet. Maybe Marshall would just let her sleep, she thought. Maybe – but then he was there, sat on her side of the bed, rubbing her back.

'You're keen,' she muttered, using all her strength to get out of bed.

'Just awake, I guess,' he said, biting at what was left of his nails.

'Stop that!' Lena scolded and he scowled at her, shoving his hand into his pocket.

'Caught me again,' he said, heading towards the kettle to pour freshly boiled water over some coffee grounds. He turned to her, cup in hand. The liquid inside had a tan colouring, with a greasy film floating on the top. 'This stuff looks as good as it tastes. But it will sure wake you up.'

She laughed, took a tentative sip of the steaming brew. The styrofoam cup was hot but the smell drew her in. She took a few more slurps before setting it on the bedside table.

'OK, time for a fashion show.' Lena dragged her bag up onto the bed and pulled out the dresses and tops.

'God, Lena, how many days did you think we were staying?' he laughed, stepping towards the bed. 'And why are your clothes still in your bag?'

Certainly not something he would have done, she thought. Marshall couldn't help unpacking the moment he arrived in a hotel room. Lena did not share his desire to spread out.

'You only just noticed?' she teased.

Hands on hips, Marshall attempted to defend himself. 'I'll have you know, it took a lot of time to order that pizza and find that TV channel,' he said, unsuccessfully holding back a smile. 'I can't keep track of your shoddy organising all the time.'

Lena moved closer, threading her arms through his bent elbows.

'You're right, I'm a bit of a mess,' she joked, placing a light kiss on his chin. She turned back towards the outfits. 'I just wasn't sure what would be best.' She laid them out. 'And I was too flustered yesterday to decide, so, here we are. Which one do you think?'

Marshall looked and decided quickly. 'That one,' he said, pointing at the yellow sun-dress with white gerbera daisy print. 'My mother had a dress just like that,' he said, his voice cracked and he turned away towards the chair in the corner of the room.

Lena put her hand on Marshall's back and thanked him. He nodded, sniffing slightly and wiped his nose. Lena started her morning routine, giving Marshall some time alone.

*

They were sitting in the car park fifteen minutes early.

'It shows we're responsible.' Marshall straightened the shirt collar under his blue cashmere jumper.

'It shows we're desperate.' Lena patted her lips with gloss, pouting towards the mirrored sun visor.

'We're just trying to make a good impression,' he said. 'Let's go in, it's way too hot to be sitting in the car without the air on.' He didn't wait for her to reply, and Lena was startled by the sound of the driver's side door opening. By the time she had turned he was out of the car, standing, waiting.

She pressed her nails into her hands again. They were damp, puffy with sweat. She used the seat to dry them off.

Stepping out, she rubbed her feet against the asphalt to make sure she was really here.

A swift warm wind buoyed them towards the steps up to the building. Lena looked up and read the chipped black lettering on the door, *Sanderson Home for Children*.

'I can't.' Lena spat out the words and then froze.

Marshall was already at the top of the steps and turned back towards Lena. He did not move and said nothing, just stared at her.

'We can't do this. We aren't meant to do this,' Lena said, shaking her head, backing away from the steps. Big droplet tears streamed down her cheek, landing on the cracked pavement.

'We tried, Marsh. We really did. But there's something – God, the universe, I don't know – there's something that does not want us to be parents.'

Her face fell into her hands and now she was sobbing hard. Marshall rushed to her, skipping steps on his way down, and threw his arms around her.

'Yes, Leen, yes we are. This is meant to happen for us. We are meant to be happy.'

Lena kept shaking her head, her hands still over her face, her body now leaning into Marshall's chest. Her sounds were muffled, inaudible, and Marshall kept squeezing her tightly. After a few seconds, she pulled away from him; her hands slunk back by her sides.

He lifted her chin up so that she made eye contact. 'Look, I need to tell you something.'

Lena wiped her face, the mascara dripping down. She looked at Marshall, puzzled, and did not reply.

He laced his hands behind his neck, as if pushing the words out from the back of his throat.

'God, why did I wait so long to say…' he said, almost to himself. He began to pace now in front of the steps. 'I really wanted you to know but….' He paced a few more times before turning to face Lena.

'You know my mother and I ended up in the shelter? Well, there's a bit more to it.'

The couple stood on the pavement, still as statues. Lena could see Marshall's eyes searching for a reaction. She didn't want him to stop speaking. She kept her expression neutral.

'We did go to the shelter, to get away from my dad.' Marshall began to bite his nails. This time, Lena let him. 'But what you don't know....' He paused, eyes fixed on Lena.

'What I haven't told you... or anyone, for so long... we were only there for a week. And then we moved again.'

Marshall cleared his throat before speaking again. 'I was five years old. She took me to a....' He pointed at the front door. 'She brought me in, and she left me there, in a place just like this. I spent the next three years of my life waiting, just like all those kids inside....'

His voice began to crack but Lena didn't move and could say nothing.

'All that time, all I wanted, all I hoped for, is that someone, anyone, would come and take me away, take me home.'

'I don't understand,' Lena finally spoke.

Marshall went to sit on the steps. She shuffled towards him.

'Marshall, I don't understand. You said your parents were dead.'

Marshall nodded slowly, his elbows resting on his knees, his eyes fixed on the weeds growing in between the pavement blocks.

'They are dead, died right after I finished uni, that part is true.' He looked up, pleading, his eyes desperate. Then, his expression changed, his eyes became more solemn. 'Dad to cancer and Mum to a heart attack.'

A lone robin began to chirp loudly in the trees.

'But then... it doesn't make any sense.' Lena stood still in front of Marshall.

'I had a mother. And then, I had a mum and dad.'

Lena shook her head, speechless.

'After my mum's funeral, I was sick of the pity, sick of everyone feeling sorry for me.' Marshall pulled at some long grass beside the steps. 'The next week, I took off to South Korea. And when I came back, moved from all that was familiar and just... I dunno, I just wanted a fresh start.'

Lena had become abnormally calm. Something inside her relaxed, an intuition.

'I just don't... I just don't understand,' she said.

They sat in silence, the sound of robins singing to each other between the trees grew louder.

'Look, I can't believe I never told you this. I never meant to keep it from you.'

Lena felt his gaze and turned to find him facing her.

'I almost told you, that time in the kitchen, after Tilly....' He trailed off.

Lena's mind drifted back to what she said, the words she used. *Someone else's child.* Her stomach dropped at the thought of how deeply that must have hurt him.

'I was in a bad place, Marsh. I probably wasn't ready to hear it.'

'You were in an honest place, Leen. That's what scared me the most.'

Lena looked down, ashamed.

'When you finally came around to the idea of adopting, I didn't want to say anything that might change your mind. That might prevent some little boy or little girl....' His voice cracked again, and Lena leaned her head on his shoulder. They sat for a few moments, before Lena finally spoke.

'I'm sorry it took me longer to get to where you are.'

Marshall turned his whole body now and took Lena's hand.

'All this time when we were trying to have a baby, when we went through the ups and downs with Tilly.... There was part of me that knew, deep down, our family wasn't going to be built like that.'

Lena rubbed at his hand, twisting his wedding band round. 'Did you feel loved?'

Marshall frowned. 'Loved?'

'By your adoptive parents.'

'By my mum and dad,' Marshall corrected. 'Yes. Every one of those days for the twenty years they were with me.'

Lena took a breath and stood. 'Well, then, I guess that's all I needed to hear.' She grabbed his hand, started up the steps towards the door. Straightening her back, they both crossed the threshold onto the tiled shiny floor.

*

'We ask prospective parents to wait here in the blue room until we have your little one all ready to meet you,' the cheerful receptionist said in whispered tones. Her long arm motioned them towards a front sitting area, where a few other couples were waiting. They exchanged looks and nods, a rainbow of similar emotions firing around – excitement, shyness, pensiveness.

'Now, just a few more papers to sign and then you're all set,' she chirped.

'Thank you.' Marshall's calm voice soothed Lena. They took a seat in two plush wing-back chairs in the corner of the room to sign and wait.

*

Lena checked her watch. It had only been five minutes but, finally, an older, gentle-looking woman appeared, clipboard in hand.

'Mr and Mrs Perkins?' she said to the room and Marshall stood up.

Lena rose just as quickly, keeping her focus on the woman, trying to block out the eyes of the rest of the anxious people.

'My name's Rachel,' she said, her voice loud but soothing. 'Please, follow me.'

The door opened to a surprisingly big area. The building itself was originally a large family home; the rotunda above made for an airy entrance through to the wide, inviting staircase. The children must sleep up there, Lena thought. A flash of excitement burst through her as she followed Marshall and Rachel.

So many conversations and interactions must have happened in this space, she thought. A young Marshall appeared in her mind. She was halfway through her imagining when they arrived at the end of a long hallway, by a glass window that looked into a playroom. Rachel stopped them before they could approach.

'So, we're here. I assume you're ready to meet your….' Rachel trailed off. 'That is, if you're certain he's going to become part of your family.' She paused for effect, then smiled brightly. 'Just let us know when you're sure you're ready to meet him.'

Rachel placed a soft hand on Lena's shoulder and squeezed gently, looking towards Marshall and giving him a wink.

'I'll be right here, whenever you're ready.'

Lena held back a surge of emotion, raising her hand towards her mouth to stifle any sounds. They had seen his photos and read all about him, but now, here he was, playing.

'Thank you.' Lena's voice shook. She turned to Marshall, his eyes filled with tears, and grabbed his hand, running her fingers across his calloused knuckles.

'Let's just go in,' Lena said. 'I'm not changing my mind. Let's just go meet our son.'

Marshall rubbed his eyes, nodding, and Lena turned to Rachel.

'We're ready to meet him. We're ready to meet our son,' she said.

'Yes, of course.' Rachel put her hand on the door handle, then turned back towards Lena and Marshall. 'He's been waiting for this moment for a long time.'

Lena breathed in. 'So have we,' she said, pulling Marshall behind her and into the room.

'Teddy,' Rachel said, her voice sounding softer now. She stood at the door, presenting Marshall and Lena. 'There's some people here to meet you. This is Lena, and this is Marshall.'

The blonde-haired child looked up, jumped to his feet, and adjusted his clip-on tie. He was smaller than most five year-olds, but his face seemed older than his young age, a little life that had seen too much already. His fingers pulled at each other, his eyes content but nervous, a smile starting to emerge. He said nothing, but looked at the three adults; the book he had been reading lay open on the floor.

Lena raised her hands to her heart involuntarily and took a step forward. Marshall and Rachel seemed to disappear from the room. A few more steps forward, she stopped herself from sweeping him up in a hug. She crouched down to meet him eye-to-eye.

'Hi Teddy,' she said finally, the words breaking the tense silence in the room.

Teddy replied a soft 'Hi', his eyes drawn to the ground.

Lena looked down too, noticing his tattered but well-tied blue running shoes. His feet were tinier than she expected. She also noticed his book.

'I used to love that book when I was your age.'

Teddy looked up, surprised and happy.

'Maybe I could read a bit of it to you?' Lena offered. Teddy nodded, bursting into a small run towards the couch that was against the wall.

As Lena rose, she turned to see Marshall, eyes red, wiping his face.

'I'll leave you to your story, Teddy,' Rachel said, her eyes glistening as she gave Lena a nod and closed the door.

'Do you like stories?' Teddy asked Marshall.

'I do, Teddy, especially ones with a bit of adventure,' he said.

'Oh, you will like this one,' Teddy said, his small hand waving Marshall towards the sofa, which he then climbed onto himself.

'Will I? Well, OK then,' said Marshall, making his way towards Teddy, stroking Lena's back as he passed her. They exchanged a glance as Lena picked up the book and followed Marshall to the sofa.

'I don't think I've heard this story before,' Marshall said.

'Well, I won't spoil the ending,' Lena said, taking a seat on the other side of Teddy. 'But I can say Teddy's right about the adventure.'

She opened the book to the first page, and as she did so their lives played out before her eyes – bedtime stories, middle of the night bad dreams, dinners, family holidays, petty arguments, the sing-alongs on car journeys, tumultuous teenage years, sports tournaments, Friday movie nights, graduation, all the highs and a few of the lows, the years they would spend together, she and her boys.

She took a deep breath before starting the story. After a few pages a small head lay gently on her shoulder.

The New Term

by Rachel Waters

It had been a long and nauseous journey back to school, as ever, feeling slightly sick in the front of the car. Billie watched the various towns and countryside sights fly past in a pattern of barely glimpsed light flashes. She was lost in a haze of already missing home, while anticipating what was to come: a new year, another dormitory – hopefully with some friends from last year, though there had not been many.

Billie's stomach clenched with dread as she remembered some of last year's difficulties. For starters, there had been her name, as cries of, 'That's a boy's name!' echoed through the dormitory, an explanation that it was short for Wilhelmina had only made matters worse. Then there were her efforts to avoid eating meat, to which she had an aversion – especially to the meat they gave you at school, where the bacon was likely to come with bristles still attached to the rind. Smuggling out these greasy offerings preoccupied Billie and made her withdrawn at mealtimes.

She also tended to stick up for other girls who were being bullied, with the result that, on a Sunday walk, she and a younger girl had been pelted with cow dung by all the other girls. She could still hear the shrieks and feel the humiliation, and though she had tried to fight back, they had been outnumbered.

Billie's mother had come to the gate at home to wave her off, clutching her handkerchief. The dog whined slightly as she stroked his ears and whispered her goodbyes. She would miss them both so much that she could scarcely bear it. Now, as she approached the old building with its crumbling façade, her house for the next year, she felt dread descending, along with a measure of hope that this year things might be better.

An older girl met her and showed her and her father to the dormitory. She looked around and counted the beds, there were seven in all. Her father went to get the rest of her belongings: the violin she had not practised enough in the holidays; the cake her mother had made, which would have to be handed in to Matron; and the patchwork blanket knitted by her granny, which she now laid out on her bed, ready to spread out all her clothes and requirements for inspection.

She hugged her father close and said goodbye, fighting back her tears, and then she watched him walk out of the dormitory, turning back at the door to give a cheery wave. No more walks together along the Unsuitable for Motors track near their village with long, good humoured talks – at least, not until the holidays, and it was far too soon to think of going home. There was another girl already unpacking in the dormitory, and Billie remembered her vaguely from last year, so she now said hello and exchanged a few comments about the holidays. She took out all the bits and pieces that would live on top of her chest of drawers: the picture of home, with all the family and Treacle the dog standing outside, her little clock, and her hairbrush.

Billie unpacked her trunk, using the list her mother had packed at the top to lay out all the items in order. She was naturally untidy, so this was quite a feat for her. Eventually she had them all arranged ready for when Matron came to tick them off her own list: two pairs of shoes, a shoe cleaning kit, toiletries, three school blouses, three pinafores, three nightdresses, three vests, five sets of underwear, cape, gym kit, three towels (most things seemed to have been requested in threes), and a letter writing kit. As she held this leather zip-up case, which contained Basildon Bond writing paper and a special pen, Billie felt a pang of pain, realising that letters would be all that connected her to home. It was quite a challenge to write a weekly letter that would get past the teacher who presided over their letter writing sessions. Last year Billie's letters had been getting progressively sadder and, on several occasions, she had been asked to rewrite them.

Billie took out her teddy bear, which was a small otter, and placed it out of the way on her pillow. She remembered her mother's request that they think of each other every night at nine o'clock. This had also proved problematic as it was at this time that the other girls were usually deep in chats and stories and so Billie's attempts to connect telepathically with her mother tended to be perfunctory, and were often interrupted.

She wondered if her mother had already looked under her own pillow and found the note and pencil drawing Billie had left for her, and the brooch she always placed there, which her mother would wear while she was away. The brooch was silver, it had been given to Billie by Auntie Norah, a friend in the village, who brought it back from India where she had helped the sick and poor people there. Billie would, one day, over twenty years in the future, wear it to keep her velvet wrap in place on her wedding day. Now, at ten years old on this September evening, standing on the linoleum in the chilly dormitory, it was taking all her effort not to give in to tears, which gripped her stomach in a tight, aching knot.

Matron then came into the dormitory, greeted the two girls, and began to take her inventory of Billie's belongings. This cheered her up, since Matron was a kind woman. More than once, last year, she had found Billie wandering around the house late at night, consumed with home sickness and with a tear-stained face, and had taken her in to her small apartment for hot chocolate and a chat. Billie did her best to put on a brave face, and, thanks to her mother's care, she had all the requisite items, neatly named. Matron ticked off the other girl's belongings, told them that there would be a house meeting that evening at 8:30, and left with a cheerful smile, and Billie's chocolate cake, which would be given back to her in pieces at suitable intervals.

A few moments later, there was a commotion outside the door, which was then flung open to admit a tall man with grey hair and a handsome face. 'Come on, darling!' he called behind him, and into the dormitory came a tiny girl, about a head shorter than Billie, with tousled reddish-brown ringlets and greenish-blue eyes, opened very wide. Billie recognised that she was nervous and went over, saying as brightly as she could, 'Hello, I'm Billie, come in, this is the blue dormitory!'

For a short while, the girl looked at Billie's feet, she was wearing her red sandals, and then she looked up at her and, smiling, said, 'Hello, I'm Lara. I'm new, are you?'

Billie told her that she had been there a year, and they chose a bed for her, the bed next to Billie's. The gentleman stood there, beaming at them as they unpacked all Lara's belongings and laid them out on the bed. Lara didn't have a shoe cleaning kit so Billie lent her own to her for the inspection and said she could borrow it whenever she wanted. Lara did not seem to have many extra belongings but had a beautiful looking violin case and a guitar.

Years later, Lara told Billie's sons that she had taken one look at their mum's red sandals and had known that she would be OK. Billie was not to know it at that moment, but she soon realised that she need never feel lonely at school again, even when they moved up together to the next house, where the Matron was a legend for being as strict as she could be.

That evening, at the house meeting, all the girls listened as Matron gave them a beginning-of-the-year talk. Billie glanced to her left at Lara, who was listening intently. Then all the new girls were welcomed, and Matron told them about bedtime, and what they should do in the morning.

Thinking about the next day and the start of term, Billie felt a rush of excitement, and actually began to look forward to writing her letter home at the weekend to tell her parents all about Lara. As the weeks flew by, these letters would be filled with accounts of all the adventures the girls were having: trips into town for apple pie and cream in a tea shop, fits of the giggles in prep. Soon, Billie was writing home to ask if Lara could come to stay with them, so that, on the journey home at half term, sharing the back seat of her father's car with Lara, she was far too excited to even feel car sick. Lara would say hello to Billie's dog, Treacle, and then two of her favourite creatures in the whole world would be in the same room with her, and at home!

Billie quickly learned that a good friend at school could make all the difference, and that was the most important, life-saving lesson that she ever paid attention to.

The Right Choice

by Emma Crees

Scanning through the search results on Google, Susan clicked on a likely one. The website was clear and it seemed they would be able to do exactly what she wanted with the extension to her house. But she had questions, so she wrote a long query in the 'contact us' box and clicked send. To be sure she'd made the right choice, she went back to the search results and also contacted two other companies.

She spent the following twenty-four hours in a state of nervous anticipation before the answers started landing in her inbox. The first company to reply began their response with 'Hi Susan', so was rejected. They clearly didn't know how to correctly answer a business enquiry. The second response had a spelling mistake in the first word so she rejected that one too – if their staff were that careless when replying to emails then she could only assume they were also careless in the services they provided. She wouldn't be able to trust them. Next!

The third response took a little longer to come. Susan only saw it on her mobile phone when she was getting ready for bed that evening. It seemed a little strange that a response would come so late and that unsettled her slightly. But at first glance the actual content of the reply seemed very promising. Smiling to herself, she put her phone down and finished getting ready for bed. She would look at it properly and make her decision in the morning.

In the cold light of day the email looked even better than she'd first thought. This might be the right company to use. However, first thing in the morning wasn't the time to reply to an email – it was better not to appear too keen, as that was when companies took advantage of you. She didn't want to leave it too long but equally if she did make them wait a bit they might be more willing to negotiate on price.

*

Gathering up her car keys and shopping bags, Susan headed out to do battle with the supermarket. She wasn't a fan of supermarkets: too many people and not necessarily ones she wished to spend time among.

That opinion was reinforced when she entered the store and had to wait for a man in a wheelchair to move away from the potatoes before she could select the ones she wanted. Worse still, he appeared to be alone. Really, people like that shouldn't be allowed out, especially not by themselves. It wasn't fair to everyone else who had to deal with them. With a look of disgust on her face, Susan placed her potatoes in her basket and swept away.

After lunch, she returned to her emails and the matter of who could do the work she needed. This company, Didcot Building Design, did seem to be the best. And the email, signed by an A Longcross, the most professional. Clicking 'compose', Susan wrote:

Dear Mr Longcross
Thank you for your email. After some consideration, I feel your company may be best suited to undertake the commission I have. However, I would prefer to discuss the details via telephone. Please contact me at your earliest convenience...

Adding her phone number she quickly proofread it, and finding it to her satisfaction, pressed send.

*

Just after nine the next morning, Susan was washing the breakfast dishes when the phone rang. Gingerly removing her wet marigolds and placing them to dry, she hurried to answer it.

'Good morning, Susan Cornish speaking.' Her grandson had told her that it wasn't the done thing to give your name when answering your personal phone anymore. Something about scammers and identity theft. Susan, however, was of the generation who still considered it the height of good manners to introduce yourself.

'Good morning, Mrs Cornish, I'm calling from Didcot Building Design. Is now a good time to talk?' The voice was somewhat younger than she had expected but smooth and confident-sounding.

'Yes, I did say at your earliest convenience. Is this Mr Longcross?'

'Yes, it is. Sorry, I should have introduced myself. I've been looking at the project you enquired about and I have a few suggestions for you. Do you want me to take you through them now or did you want to explain how you see this happening first? I'm easy either way.'

The phrase 'easy either way' wasn't one Susan liked, as it implied a certain something about the speaker that made her uncomfortable. However, she knew it was important not to be judgemental so she let it go.

'I should like to hear your ideas first, Mr Longcross.'

The phone call that followed was very satisfactory and full of productive discussion. Mr Longcross and his company had clearly spent a number of hours considering her proposal since receiving her email the day before, and he was obviously very knowledgeable and experienced.

Susan thought he was likely older than he sounded on the phone, perhaps in his early fifties, and, from his enthusiasm, she suspected he would be into sports. She wasn't the most active person herself, preferring the more gentile pursuits that befitted a lady of a certain age, but she had a lot of respect for the skill and dedication it took to excel at a sport. Mr Longcross would be the sort of man who excelled at sport, she knew. Probably marathon running as he clearly had staying power. Or tennis, he might have played at boarding school, she thought.

Susan reluctantly drew the phone call to an end after forty-five minutes. All of her questions had been answered as well as some she hadn't thought to ask. And as much as she would have liked to continue to talk with this man, she had an appointment to get to.

*

Rushing out the door in a most unladylike manner, Susan was glad to see that none of her neighbours were in the street to witness her behaviour. One had to keep up appearances, after all. Luck continued to be on her side and, when she arrived at the dentist, she was able to find a parking space right outside. Despite leaving late she had managed to arrive just in time for her 3:10 scale and polish.

Once booked in, Susan turned to take a seat in the waiting area. Spotting the same man in the wheelchair she had seen at the supermarket the day before, she took a seat as far from him as possible and tried to avoid catching his eye.

'Hello,' the man greeted her. 'Have you got enough room to get past?'

If she hadn't been so surprised to see someone in a wheelchair alone – again – Susan might have noticed that his voice was somewhat familiar. But she was trying to avoid getting drawn into what she was sure would be an awkward conversation so she just said, 'Yes,' then took her seat.

Digging through her handbag, she pretended she was looking for something for the two long minutes before the dentist called her in. She was surprised the man in the wheelchair wasn't called in first, but she supposed he was waiting for a carer. Or a taxi home or something. After all, no one was going to let someone like that drive, were they?

*

Watching the rain out the window Drew hoped it would stop before his mum was finished with her last patient. He had been disheartened to see the woman who had glared at him in the supermarket the day before come in, and even more so when she had been so obviously uncomfortable with him and his wheelchair. Luckily the woman had gone in to see the other dentist at the practice so at least he wouldn't have to deal with the fallout of her sharing her opinions with his mum. He had had a busy morning and hadn't really wanted to come out and collect her in the rain, but luckily his conference call had finished earlier than he expected and he'd made it before the rain started.

As he waited he thought about work. He was finally working

in his dream job and had just been given a big project which was very exciting. He had spent hours on it the day before, much longer than he should have done, but he couldn't help himself. It might not make good business sense but he knew this project had the possibility to really establish him in the industry, so he wanted to give it his all. It would hopefully mean he'd no longer be known as 'that new guy, Drew – you know, in the wheelchair', but instead as an established player in his field, recognised for his work, something Drew had been fighting for since he finished his training two years ago.

*

Two weeks after first making contact with Didcot Building Design about the proposed extension to her house, Mr Longcross was due to visit to inspect the site and finalise the designs. It had been a long two weeks for Susan as she tried to contain her excitement about her extension.

It had also been a frustrating couple of weeks on a personal level. It seemed everywhere she went she saw someone who made her uncomfortable. It wasn't always the man in the wheelchair she had seen in the supermarket and at the dentist (although she had also passed him at the theatre one night), but it was always someone who wasn't what she considered *normal* and seemed to flaunt their difference to make others see it. Susan hated that. She supposed people who weren't like everyone else had the right to live their lives and do things – but she didn't think they should do it where she was trying to get on with her own life. It wasn't fair to make people like her see them walking around tapping their white canes or riding in wheelchairs.

Susan was up early and having a quick tidy round before Mr Longcross arrived. The house was as spotless as it always was, but she liked to be sure. Although she knew Mr Longcross would have formed an opinion of her from their phone calls and emails, this would be the first time they met in person and first impressions were really important. After all, you couldn't really know someone from the sound of their voice and their words on a screen, could you?

After an hour of unnecessary fuss – during which she fluffed the cushions on the sofa four times – Susan settled in an armchair to read for the thirty minutes until Mr Longcross was due.

But instead of reading, her thoughts turned to Mr Longcross. He would be an older, sporty man, she had decided, with vast experience in architecture. He would be well-travelled, and she pictured him as a family man. In their conversations she had discovered that Didcot Building Design was his own company. She believed it must be a good-sized company and that he would have built it up from nothing over several years. He would be planning to pass it on to his sons.

Susan had a good feeling about the meeting to come and knew she had made the right choice, contracting with Didcot Building Design for the extension. The doorbell rang, drawing her from her thoughts. Glancing at the clock she saw that he was right on time.

For a moment she thought no one was there. Then she saw that the person who had rung the doorbell was sat in a bulky eyesore of a wheelchair. It was the young man she kept seeing everywhere she went.

Trying unsuccessfully to keep the look of disgust from her face she asked, 'Yes?'

Holding out a hand he smiled and said 'Mrs Cornish? I'm Andrew Longcross from Didcot Building Design.'

Susan didn't know what to say. She just looked at him, pretending she hadn't noticed the hand he held out to her.

'I've come to discuss the plans for your extension?'

Susan was horrified. 'No, it would appear there has been some mistake. I won't be using your company. Didcot Building Design has completely misrepresented themselves to me.' Shutting the door before he had a chance to respond, she went away and made a coffee. Shaken, she realised that she had, in fact, made the wrong choice.

*

Drew blinked as he found the meeting abruptly ended, the door shut in his face before he'd even finished greeting Mrs Cornish.

He was hurt by her reaction to his disability but he wasn't exactly surprised. Reactions like that were getting much less common but they still happened fairly frequently, particularly from older or more sheltered people. And he was pretty sure she was the same woman who had blanked him in the dentist the other week.

What mattered more to Drew was the loss to his business: he had spent hours over the last two weeks working on her commission. And running a new business, it was a commission he sorely needed. Good business sense would suggest he try to reason with Mrs Cornish and make another attempt at getting the work.

But he knew her type. He would walk away rather than waste any more time. His painful past experiences with similar people meant it was the right choice.

Making Contact

by David Rudd

'Die, you Selenite dogs,' exclaimed Thomas, as his X-wing fighter ploughed into a phalanx of soldiers gathered on a ridge. 'Agh!' He echoed the cries of the troops as their bodies crashed to the ground.

There followed a squawk from another voice. I looked up to see the X-wing fighter laying waste to a peaceful tea party of Playmobil characters, which Elizabeth had been carefully setting up on the rug below where Thomas's space figures had their base on the hearth. As the destruction continued, eight-year-old Elizabeth squealed again and began physically assaulting her seven-year-old brother.

'It was an accident!' protested Thomas.

'Children!' Mum paused in her knitting. 'Be quiet, please. You'll wake Gran and Granddad.'

'But–' sobbed Elizabeth.

'Shh!' Mum put a finger to her lips. Thomas, however, was not to be silenced that easily.

'If she'd agreed to play with me in the first place,' he maintained, 'this would never have happened.'

'If the aliens had been friendly,' retorted Elizabeth, suddenly sob-free, 'I would've played.'

'They're *aliens*!' Thomas's tone was derisive. 'You expect them to sit down to tea?'

At this point, Father lowered his newspaper. Thomas and Elizabeth's noisy altercation immediately became a dumb-show of grimaces and cold stares. The paper was hoisted once again. Father was doubly put out, not only at this noise disturbing his evening reading, but also because he and Mum had been displaced from their favourite armchairs – one either side of the fire – by our grandparents: Mum's dad, Willie

McAllister, and his wife, Meg. They had come over to England to visit family, having emigrated to Canada with Mum's brother, Angus, many years earlier. Father and Mum, therefore, shared the settee, sitting at opposite ends, with our cat, Mandy, stretched out between.

*

I distinctly remember that evening, all those years ago, gazing round the living room at my family. It was as though I'd never really paid them much attention before. Looking back, we must have seemed an odd bunch: a family of loners rattling around the house. We got on well enough, that was no problem, but we were generally content to leave each to their own devices and do our own thing. It was only when someone overstepped the mark, as had Thomas, that any trouble began.

I, as usual, had my head in a book. HG Wells' *First Men in the Moon*, which I'd been given by Granddad and Gran for my tenth birthday. I'd thought the title was wrong at first, until I reached the part where the hero, Cavor, and his sidekick encounter the underground civilization of aliens, the Selenites. I had told Thomas about them, which might have inspired his game.

Before Elizabeth and Thomas had kicked off, the room had been relatively quiet. Gran and Granddad managed to sleep through the whole commotion.

They were quite a sight. Gran's mouth was wide open, and I could see that her upper dentures had left their gummy moorings and were resting on the lower set. Thomas and I exchanged meaningful glances, half wishing, I think, that we, too, possessed such versatile choppers. Granddad had his mouth wide open as well. He was really away, his head stretched back, Adam's apple prominent, his bulbous red nose pointing at the ceiling and his breathing stertorous. I remember carefully studying them both, for at the time they were the only old people I'd encountered at close quarters.

I was gazing at Granddad, his tongue worming its way across his dry lips, as if to moisten them, when, with a couple of little gloppy noises from the back of his throat, his jerky breathing suddenly stopped. One by one, other members of the family became aware of this hiatus and turned their eyes on him. Only Gran continued sleeping. 'Do you think he's alright?' Mum asked finally, nudging Father, who lowered his paper once again.

By now we were all holding our breath. Then, with a loud snort, Granddad's eyes popped open and he slowly adjusted himself to his surroundings, taking in the various members of the family staring back at him.

'Are you alright, Granddad?' Mum asked. 'For a minute, we thought we'd lost you there.'

'Well, now,' he said after a considered pause. 'That was… weird!' He did look quite pale.

Granddad's voice brought Gran back to consciousness, though she would always dispute that she'd ever been asleep. Merely 'resting her eyes' she would claim.

Granddad still looked quite confused. 'Well, that was weird,' he said again.

Gran was clearly unsure what was going on, but didn't want to admit it. She was preoccupied with ushering her dentures back into place.

'Were you dreaming, Granddad?' asked Mum.

'No,' he said emphatically. Then, after a pause, 'Well, mebbe.'

'Would you like to tell us about it?'

'I'm no' sure I can.'

'Please tell us, Granddad,' I pleaded.

'It was a bit… disturbing, Jamie.'

'Was it a nightmare?' asked Thomas, hopefully.

'No' exactly. But there were some aliens.'

'Aliens!' Thomas pounced on the word, unsettling Mandy, who had already moved from her place on the cushion between my parents and was pacing the back of the settee.

Father gave up trying to read his paper, folding it decisively. 'Come on, Willie, let's have this story. We'll get no peace till you share it with us.'

Granddad looked towards Gran, as though for guidance, and she returned an encouraging nod.

When Mum added, 'Perhaps you'd like a wee dram to calm you?' Granddad finally seemed to relent, ignoring Father's mutterings about it not being Christmas.

Some ten minutes later, after a round of drinks had been distributed – with pop for us children – Granddad began to tell us about his strange experience.

'I was sitting in this very chair, looking up at yon cracks in your ceilin', when I heard a voice calling to me: "Come away wi' us, Willie McAllister," it said.'

'Scottish aliens!' declared Father. Mum poked him with her knitting needle. She actually seemed relieved at his light-hearted tone, for the condition of the paintwork around the chimney breast was a long-standing bone of contention.

'...and the cracks in the ceiling seemed to peel away like the shell off a hard-boiled egg, and I could see right through to yon bedroom, above. I thought I must be going soft, and I rubbed my eyes,' – he demonstrated the action – 'but that only made me see more. I was now staring at the rafters in your roof. And then they too seemed to dissolve, and I'm looking directly up at the stars.'

'Cor!' exclaimed Thomas. 'X-ray vision. Just like Superman!' We found we were all staring up at the filigree of cracks in the alcove, no doubt caused by heat from the chimney. I think each of us was striving to replicate Granddad's experience.

'And one of these stars was slowly getting larger.' Granddad fingered the air as he spoke. 'It was travelling down towards me, and I could see it wasnae just a light, but a wee figure, all radiant and glowing.' His hands tried to conjure the vision. 'And I looked back, to where I'd come from, and I could still see mysel' sitting in my chair here.' He thumped the arms as though to confirm the solidity of his surroundings.

'In, er, *my* chair,' muttered Father, but everyone ignored him.

'And there y'all were, too, sitting round the room, busy wi' y'sel's and no paying me on'y attention – apart, mebbe, from young Jamie here.' He tilted his whiskey glass in my direction, and smiled at me out of his deep blue eyes. 'I thought my time had come, and I was being ta'en from y'all, and I was saying goodbye.' His accent was thickening as his eyes teared up. Gran, too, was reaching for a tissue.

Granddad was silent for a minute, bringing his whiskey glass to his mouth and pulling thoughtfully on the amber liquid, his thin tongue mopping up the stray drops round his lips. Elizabeth sidled across and clambered on his knee. 'What then, Granddad?'

'Well, bonny lass, this wee figure then pointed to a cloud that was suddenly hovering over us. And the cloud descended and surrounded us. Next thing ye know, I'm in what looks like an operating theatre, wi' cylinders and instruments all aboot the place, and there's more of these alien figures peering and poking at me.'

'Like the dentist's?' asked Elizabeth.

'Ay, but not so painful, wee lassie.'

'What then, Granddad?' Thomas abandoned his soldiers and sat himself on the settee between our parents, dragging a reluctant Mandy onto his lap.

'We… communed, Tommy,' he ran the word slowly round his mouth, in the same way that he savoured his whiskey. 'Aye, communed.'

'What's "co-mooned"?' asked Elizabeth.

'We talked, wee Lizzie, but no wi' voices. These alien beings seemed to be as much at home inside my head as I was, just looking round and seeing what it was like inside here.' He tapped his temple. 'It didna hurt. Very pleasant, in fact. Like having a warm towel wrapped round your head after a shave.'

'And didn't you ask them anything? Where they were from? Why they'd come?' Father's forensic tone drew disapproving looks from everyone, but Granddad wasn't fazed.

'I didna ask them on'ything, because it was as though I already understood. Ye ken? Everything seemed to make sense and fit together.'

I was suddenly chilly, sitting over by the window, so moved across to Granddad's chair, squashing onto the arm, where Elizabeth reluctantly made space for me. 'Didn't you ask to see round their spaceship?'

'No, I never did, young Jamie,' he said patting my leg. 'You'll have to try and draw me something.'

'Me! Me!' said Thomas, pushing Mandy away as he, too, bounced up onto Father's armchair. Father's complaints about his 'poor chair springs' went unheeded.

Elizabeth was tugging rhythmically at Granddad's arm and repeating, 'Then what happened?'

'Nothing really. We all just....' He paused at this point, his voice suddenly choked with emotion.

But Elizabeth and I were prepared, and finished his sentence for him: 'Communed,' we chorused. Granddad raised his glass to us in acknowledgement, trying to smile, but you could tell he was struggling to come to terms with something.

After he'd taken a long, slow pull at his whiskey, he continued. 'They just told me that everything would be alright and no' to worry.' And with that, Granddad passed me his empty whiskey glass, which I deposited on the table. 'They said I might experience a wee jolt,' and here he gave Elizabeth a gentle tweak either side of her waist, making her squirm, 'and that's when I found myself back among all of yous. All staring at me like *I* was an alien!'

In the firelight, his rheumy eyes twinkled with moisture. He caught Gran's eye, and they smiled across at one another. Mum put down her knitting and snuffled into her hankie. She came across to Granddad, who was almost buried beneath the bodies of us three children. 'We're so pleased to have you back, Granddad,' she said. 'You had us worried there for a minute.' Managing to find a bare patch of skin on his forehead, she bent down and kissed him.

We all felt good, our faces glowing in the firelight, although I thought Father was going to spoil it. 'Oi, you lot! That's not a spaceship you're on. It's an expensive armchair that's had only one careful owner… till recently!'

Mum looked daggers at him.

'Only joking,' said Father, as, to our communal surprise, he leapt to his feet, once again displacing Mandy, who thought she'd found sanctuary on Father's lap. 'In fact, I think there's room for *wan mair wee wan* on top here.' Whiskey bottle in hand, Father half-jokingly tried to lower himself onto what was now a squirming, fidgeting mass of bodies. We all yelled and shrieked in mock protest. Mum, struggling to drag him off, also played her part, while Gran hooted in the background, and

Mandy, not to be forgotten, was yowling at the living room door.

'I don't think you need any more of *this*,' said Mum, as she took control of the whiskey bottle, hauling Father away from his chair. Mum and Father stood, awkwardly clutching each other, before he was off again.

'Nonsense, lassie! It's wee tots all roond! Beam me up, Scotchy!' he concluded, throwing his arms in the direction of the alcove.

And with that, he launched himself out the door, pulling our giggling Mum after him. As their voices receded, I could hear Mandy's yowling once again. 'Always under my blinking feet!' Father complained. We all found ourselves helpless with laughter, the tears sparkling in our eyes.

*

Factually, I suppose, very little had happened, but that rare feeling of wellbeing has lived with me ever since. Unfortunately, it was Granddad and Gran's one and only return to England. After their stay with us, they cut short their tour of long lost relatives to go back to Toronto, where Granddad underwent treatment for a brain tumour. He pulled through, but was never well enough to travel again and, I'm sorry to say, we never made it over there.

But, as I look back down the years at our family gathered round Granddad in that armchair, like stray particles suddenly pulled into purposeful orbit, I realise how special the night was – for all of us. From then on, Father's chair was referred to as Granddad's, to the former's chagrin. And, for what seemed like years, one of our favourite games was to sit in that chair, head back, mouth wide open, tongue hanging out like a beacon, imagining ourselves being whisked away by aliens (I always pictured myself as Wells' hero, drifting up into space thanks to his anti-gravity invention, Cavorite). It seemed to be the one game that we could all play together, harmoniously, and we continued playing it until the chair was finally discarded, its springs worn out.

Even after the chair went, the tale of 'Granddad's alien encounter' continued to haunt us, and would, to the annoyance of our respective families and relations, often be revisited at social gatherings.

And it was I who turned out to be Granddad's staunchest defender, for I could never accept Thomas's view that Granddad had simply made the whole thing up after subconsciously hearing the alien-related squabble he'd had with Elizabeth.

'That doesn't explain why they suddenly returned to Canada,' I would contend. Someone, or something, I'd suggest, had alerted Granddad to the fact that he was not well, even if he didn't know explicitly that it was a brain tumour.

Elizabeth would then interject: 'Stopping breathing is a pretty good reason to get yourself checked out.'

'Except that,' I would respond, 'Mum insisted that Granddad never got *anything* checked out before they left England.'

And so the argument would run. But, as I have come to realise, my defence was based less on logic than empathy: an affinity I felt for the old codger, which, as I approach him in years, has deepened.

From Granddad's emotional state that night, I could never believe that he was simply spinning us one of his tall tales. To my mind, the only part that smacked of falsity occurred when he became so choked up that he couldn't go on. When, that is, he omitted to tell us what the aliens – or his subconscious, if you prefer (it really doesn't matter) – had communicated to him. For the sake of us kids, I think he decided to gloss over the details.

Now, as I gaze back down that long corridor of space and time, picturing us all in our living room, I realise what a seminal moment it was. Granddad had shown me how words could not only take you out of yourself as an individual but also bring you together as a family. All my own subsequent work as a writer has been an attempt to recreate encounters as meaningful as that one: seeking to make contact or, as Granddad more simply put it, to commune.

Reaping and Sowing

by Sarah Byrne

Decay

'Does she have any friends or family?'

I shake my head mutely. I don't want to be here, it feels wrong to be in this place so soon after such a tragedy. It's an almost spiritual transgression. I half expect a priest to emerge from the shadows and demand seven rosaries for crossing the threshold.

'We need to track down her next of kin,' the policeman says. He is patient and calm. I feel like he can see right through me, to all the vibrations in my brain; it's like my cerebellum is baking in my skull. There is a sour taste in my mouth. 'You come by here every day?'

'I do her shopping,' I explain. 'I come twice a week, Mondays and Thursdays. Mrs Rowe only eats fresh vegetables, no frozen. Then I do her garden every other Sunday. My husband used to do odd jobs sometimes too.'

'Has he been by recently?'

'No, he's gone.' I don't want to be here anymore. I want to go next door to my own home, crawl into bed, and never speak to anyone ever again.

'I'm sorry,' says the policeman. I suppress a shrug; it seems an inappropriate gesture for this moment, rude almost.

'I have a spare key,' I say. 'I don't know what to do with it. She didn't have any children. What will happen to the house?'

'The lawyers will sort it out, probably,' he says. 'You can give the key to them. There will have to be an inquest but the paramedic seems to think it was a fall. You last saw her on Thursday, correct? And yesterday was not one of the Sundays you do the garden?'

'No.' It comes out as a whisper. She fell. She fell a while ago.

Maybe as soon as I left on Thursday. I should have stayed longer, accepted her offer of a second cup of tea.

It's not good for a woman of your age – a young woman – to be on her own all the time. Loneliness can be deadly, worse than cancer.

'OK, thank you for your help,' the policeman says kindly. 'I have your details and we'll be in touch.'

I nod again. My head hurts, but my heart hurts even more. I want to go home but all I can do is go to my house; it doesn't feel like home today. Outside, everything is too bright and too loud. They are loading Mrs Rowe into the ambulance, she is shrouded in a white blanket. They have hidden her away, but I don't know if it's for her dignity or to protect the sensibilities of the neighbours who have swarmed into the street to gawp and gossip. As I study their bulging eyes and slack mouths I realise that I don't know any of their names and they probably don't know mine.

Inside my house the curtains have all been pulled closed. The radio is still on but it's turned down low so the songs are whispered to me. I want a drink but the cupboards are bare. No food in the fridge either, so I curl up on the settee and sleep.

It is dark when I wake up but it's winter so that doesn't mean anything. The clock reads six but I don't know whether it's am or pm and, since I haven't felt hungry in weeks and I'm tired all the time, my body clock is worse than useless.

The glow of the street light outside casts a hazy beam across the floor, the curtains swaying slightly. I didn't close the window properly before I left this morning. Or yesterday morning. I can't be sure and to be perfectly honest I don't care. Outside, the street is deserted, the spectacle is over and no one cares anymore.

Almost no one. From my window I can see Mrs Rowe's gate, and someone has left a small posy of white flowers there. They're Scabiosa, a type of honeysuckle known as pincushion flowers. What a strange choice. The pink or purple varieties are far prettier. There is even a dark variety, *Scabiosa atropurpurea* or mourning flower. Wouldn't that be more apt? People don't like black flowers though, even in funeral arrangements people prefer white. I don't really know why.

Part of me wants to bring them inside, to save them from the elements, but they aren't for me. I wouldn't be able to handle the guilt of taking Mrs Rowe's flowers. I used to bring her some from the nursery where I worked sometimes. She liked roses, everyone likes roses. Pink roses in particular, they matched her best crockery. We would drink chai tea out of delicate china cups with pinks roses on. Her late husband bought her the tea set from Paris when they were first married. She would take the pieces out of the dresser and show me; they were still perfect after all these years. It made her happy to think of him when she drank out of them, she would tell me pointedly.

Like I am not alone.

The next day, as if they have a will of their own, my feet take me to Mrs Rowe's house. I look up and down the street to check the coast is clear. I don't know why, but I feel like a thief. The Scabiosa are wilted, the petals dirty and trodden in on the path.

Inside, the house is dark and still, as if waiting for its former occupant. The phone is off the hook. I left it there when I let the paramedics in, and in the commotion I never replaced it. What if someone has been trying to phone? A cruel voice at the back of my mind says that no one has, and to silence the voice I replace the phone, a small triumph against something I cannot name. I sidestep around the floor in the centre of the room where I found her and head to the kitchen. I don't know why I'm here, only that I feel more at home here than my own house. For lack of anything else to do, I wash the dishes in the sink. I go through the fridge and throw out the spoiled food. Finally I wipe down the worktops and mop the floor.

I wish I knew why it makes me feel a little better. I still want to cry but it's like I've delayed my tears somehow. I look for something else to clean or tidy, anything to keep me here as long as possible. I dust her bookshelves, pack away her knitting, fold some laundry I find on the dining room table, and go to carry it upstairs.

Here I pause. It is odd enough I let myself in to a dead woman's house to clean, but going into her bedroom seems an invasion too far. I stand halfway up the stairs, pyjamas and bedding in my arms, unsure what to do.

A tidy house equals a tidy mind.

Mrs Rowe would forgive me, I decide, so I finish my ascent, heading straight to the bedroom to store the laundry away. The bed is unmade but I don't have the courage to change that. I avoid even looking at it as I work out which drawer and wardrobe is home to which items.

I feel slightly better when I am done but I don't want to investigate why that is. Nor do I want to return to my empty house next door. I hover, halfway between here and nowhere. Wondering what I should do next, I head back downstairs. The sensation of feeling slightly better has vanished already. I want to cry. It feels invasive to cry here. I head out to Mrs Rowe's garden. It's a much better spot for crying and I let it all go. To calm myself down I do laps around the garden and say the Latin names of all the plants out loud.

Planting

The tears have stopped. Everything is OK. I feel like I have been given silent permission to leave and so I lock the back door and double check all the windows. I am about to go when something catches my eye. Underneath the sofa something is sticking out, I didn't notice it as I was cleaning. When I tug it free I realise it's an address book, old and worn, with a pale pink fabric colour. Inside, the pages are thin and faded. I think back to the policeman whose name I cannot remember, and the book comes with me to my house. I don't even think about it, it just stays in my hand until I'm sitting at my own kitchen table in a house that feels colder and emptier than Mrs Rowe's. She is dead and her house still feels lived in. I am alive and I haunt mine.

A cup of tea and a biscuit that's far too soft later, and the address book lies on the table in front of me. I run my fingers over the cover. The stitching is delicate but done by hand rather than machine, and in the bottom right hand corner is a beautifully embroidered Dutch Hyacinth in pale purple cotton with DR stitched beneath in dark blue.

I don't know Mrs's Rowe's first name, I realise sadly. Daphne?

Deidre? Denise? Doris? Panic crests within me and then crashes just as suddenly, leaving a guilty residue. I don't know because I didn't ask.

At the top of the first page is the name Antony and a phone number with a London area code. Something else was written there before but has been erased with messily painted corrector fluid, so that Antony now has pride of place. The writing seems newer than the rest of the entries on the page.

David and Michelle have been crossed out separately and their address in Cornwall scored through. Nicolette's surname has been changed no less than four times and she too has been crossed out. On a later page, Martha has addresses ranging from Scotland to Canada to Singapore to Costa Rica, all diligently recorded in Mrs Rowe's tiny, precise writing. Sometimes a couple's names have been replaced by those of people I assume are their children. Sometimes there are notes that say a number is disconnected or an address doesn't exist anymore. Many of the names have dates by them and a small upright cross. There are postcards and In Memoriam cards slotted within the pages. I find photos and newspaper clippings and even the birth announcement for a little girl born in Australia ten years ago. There is a crowd within the pages of this book.

I turn back to Antony at the top of the first page, a half-formed idea swimming in my mind. Against my better judgement I grab my phone and begin dialling.

'Antony Rowe. Hello? Hello?'

'Hello. Can I help you?'

Yes? Maybe? I'm not sure what to say.

'Who is this?'

'I'm... I live next door to a Mrs Rowe. She passed away recently and I found this number in her address book.' That was the wrong way to start this conversation. 'I don't know if she had any friends or family so I'm looking for people who knew her.'

Why? This is none of my business. In my panic I almost miss the sharp intake of breath.

'Dahlia Rowe? Of 22 Hawthorne Street? That Mrs Rowe?'

'Yes!' I squeak. 'I'm so sorry for contacting you like this, I–'

The line goes dead. I sit stunned for a moment, backtracking over everything I have just said and identifying the myriad ways in which I went wrong. Everything clashes in my head and I can't pull it together and make sense of it.

Two days later I call the policeman and he pays me a visit. His name is PC Birch, according to the card which I had forgotten I had until doing some laundry. He has a kind face but looks mildly concerned as I tell him about finding the address book and calling Antony. I apologise profusely throughout the story. I only wanted to help. That's not true, I needed to help.

'I think I understand,' he says as he flicks through the pages. I squirm slightly at that. I expect a reprimand for interfering with police business, but nothing comes.

'You live here alone?'

I nod. PC Birch nods too.

'No friends or family? Other than Mrs Rowe, of course.'

'No.'

'Do you mind if I ask what you do for a living?'

'I'm a botanist,' I reply with a frown.

'At the university?'

'I'm currently on research leave. I have a greenhouse and a whole system back there.' I wave my hand towards the back of the house. 'They let me email in my work and consult over the phone.'

'So you're alone a lot.'

'I like that,' I lie. PC Birch nods again.

'We'll try and get in touch with Antony Rowe,' he says. He copied Antony's address into his little notepad. 'He's probably her next of kin, so her solicitor will want to speak to him and we can deliver her effects.'

'And? That's it?'

'What else is there?'

I don't know how to answer that.

A week passes and no one comes to Mrs Rowe's house. I return the address book, leaving it on the sideboard, and I clean, keeping the dust from settling, airing the rooms so it feels lived in. The air is heavier every time I enter, the weight of the house pressing down on me more and more until I feel like I should be crawling around on my belly like a snake.

One of my colleagues from the university calls to see how I'm doing.

I'm dying, I want to scream, *I was supposed to be getting better, but I'm getting worse. I can feel my body decay cell by cell as I stand here talking to you.*

'I'm feeling better,' I say gently. 'I've written a few things and done some work.'

'That's brilliant.' I can hear the smile in her voice. 'Do you think maybe you'll be back soon? We could use your teaching experience in the autumn.'

'Maybe,' I lie, before saying goodbye and hanging up. I do not leave the sofa for the rest of the day. I don't sleep. Instead I watch the shadows drift across the room as the sun climbs higher and then sets. The shadows are replaced by a dirty yellow beam from the street lamp, which is in turn replaced by the red haze of morning.

Harvest

I stay still, fused to the sofa like fungi on a log. My head thrums and my stomach rumbles, but still I lie there. Every so often my mind stills, forgetting I am there, and then must hurry to catch up with my body. Hour after hour slips by at a different pace until a banging at the door jolts me into alertness. I half roll off the sofa before pausing.

I should let it go.

As I settle back into position someone bangs on the door again and a muffled voice that I do not recognise calls my name. I don't have the right to be annoyed, I think as I pad to the door. It's not as if he's disturbed me from anything important.

The man banging on my door is not handsome, and I feel guilty that this is the first thing I think. His face is thin and pointed, the sharp lines accentuated by the grimace his features are twisted into. His hair is mousy and with his milky skin he looks washed out, like he has faded in the sun. He repeats my name as a question. It occurs to me that I could say he has the wrong house.

'Yes.' My voice is croaky from underuse. I almost do not recognise the sound.

'Antony Rowe.'

'Oh.'

We stare at each other for a moment. His eyes flick up and down as he takes me in; at least he tries to hide his disdain.

'You called me,' he says.

'You hung up on me,' I retort. He flushes at that, though whether from anger or embarrassment I can't tell. I am so tired. Too tired to defend myself, too tired to rise to whatever challenges this man is throwing down. 'What do you want?'

'I... I don't know.'

'I told the police your name. We reckoned you were her next of kin.'

'They called me. I don't want the house or any of her things.' He looks sad all of a sudden, like he has shrunk slightly in his cheap suit, his shoulders sagging, the grimace replaced by a look of anguish.

'Do you want to come in?' I ask against all better judgement. For a moment I hope he is going to decline but a flash of something like hope or relief lights up his eyes and I move aside to let him pass.

We sip tea and nibble some biscuits that are barely the right side of stale. He compliments the garden. I thank him. The air is thick and I want to lie down again. Mrs Rowe never made me feel like this. With her, all silences were comfortable, like exhaling.

'Who are you to her?' I ask. 'She didn't have any children.'

'Nephew.'

I take another biscuit, despite the fact they taste disgusting and I have no idea why I bought them in the first place. I don't need to know who this man is, and the entitlement I feel to know anything about him is misplaced. I know this but I can't stop feeling I have a right to know.

'Why are you here?'

'I still don't know.' Antony stares at his tea. 'Part of me just wanted people to stop calling me about her. I thought if I came they would.'

'And the other part of you?'

He pauses and finally looks at me. If a single look could break a heart it would be this one. Of all the emotions that can eat at a person, guilt is the most corrosive. It's acidic, burning everything and leaving an acrid aftertaste that never leaves.

'You don't have to tell me,' I say quickly. I am desperate to know, though, as if solving this mystery will satisfy me or give me a purpose that allows me to move on. Other people's demons are often easier to face than one's own.

'I lived with her for a little while when I was a teenager,' he says thickly. 'My parents… it wasn't nice at home. Then we had a falling out, and now she's dead.'

I know that asking 'What did you fall out about?' is not appropriate, despite my burning desire to ask it. Instead I shift a little in my seat and take a sip of tea. It's gone cold.

'I'm sorry,' I say, and I am, more than I can express. 'I know a little bit about regrets like that.'

He raises an eyebrow.

'My husband died last year and the last conversation we had was an argument,' I explain, and the lightness I feel after saying it out loud for the first time is a revelation.

'Oh, wow,' says Antony. 'I'm so sorry.'

'The funny thing is, I can't remember what the argument was about. I doubt it was important.' I have spent so long avoiding this. Since Mrs Rowe's death, however, it's like the spectre has picked up pace, it's chasing me down and I am struck by the fact I have a choice to make. Either I keep running and run myself to death or I stop and face it.

'Dahlia and I fought about my parents,' said Antony. 'I wanted to give them a second chance and she said I needed to let them go and move on, they were never going to change.' He paused. 'The thing was, I didn't stop speaking to her because she said that, I stopped speaking to her because she was right. I went home and things got worse. I couldn't face her after that.'

I don't know what to say. All of a sudden it feels very close to home. I wonder if he came here for an answer and he expects me to pass on some words of wisdom that will alleviate his guilt and rewrite his past. I should be sad. I should be weeping with despair because we are in exactly the same position, but I'm not.

'You were the first name in her address book,' I say. 'She kept meticulous records, updated names and addresses, and erased people when they passed away. But she kept your name and she kept you in her will.'

'She hoped I'd get back in touch.' Antony's voice cracked. 'I never tried.'

'Neither did she,' I point out.

He blinks.

'I only knew her as my neighbour. The nice old lady who kept me busy, stopping me wallowing in grief. I know she was tough, though, and I know she was stubborn.'

'I should have tried.'

'So should she,' I say. 'None of us, even the most isolated person, lives in a vacuum.'

Antony says nothing. We sit in silence for a little while, staring out into my garden. It is time to stop, I realise dully as I look at the thick grass that I have let run wild, and the weeds choking my beautiful flowers. I can still see them, flashes of pink and blue poking through the sea of green and yellow. If I go out now there is a chance to save them.

'Did you do hers too? I noticed there are a lot of the same flowers.'

'Yeah, it's kind of my thing. Mrs Rowe liked to know about the history of the plants, how they grow, where they come from.'

'It was all vegetables when I lived here. Every season there was a glut of fruit or veg and then weeks and weeks of soups and pies and whatever else she could make.'

'That sounds nice.'

'We once spent a weekend going round all these weird fairs looking for specific seeds.' Antony stares into the middle distance as he remembers. 'It was raining and cold and we were at it for hours and hours.'

'Did you find the seeds?'

'No,' he laughs. 'All that and we never found them. It was still one of the most fun days we had.'

The smile fades from his face as he returns to the here and now.

'A relationship is more than the last interaction you had,' I say slowly as the realisation comes to me.

The breeze outside shakes the apple tree in the corner of the garden. There is no fruit yet, it's far too early, but there are thick blossoms. Then the fruit, then winter and bare branches, and then eventually blossoms again.

'I have a spare key to her house,' I say quietly. 'I've been keeping the house clean.'

'Thank you. I'm glad she had people looking out for her. Still looking out.'

Something strange happens when I hand the key over. I feel released, like I have completed a quest or passed the baton in a relay. Except neither of those analogies is accurate. I have lost something, too. Perhaps it was meant to be lost.

I let Antony explore the house alone. He is there for hours and when I see him again to say goodbye his eyes are red.

'Thank you,' he says again before leaving. I nod, not really sure what to say, and, after I watch him drive away, I head back into my own house. It hasn't felt like home in a long time but now it no longer feels like a prison.

'Nothing happened,' I argue to thin air. 'Nothing's changed, not really.'

I phone up work to let them know I can come back soon, I email friends I haven't seen for a while and ask how they are. I don't make plans but I reach out to the world tentatively. For the rest of the evening I browse property websites and try and imagine myself in a new house. It all feels a little tender, like pink skin after a wound has healed.

The next day I walk to the shop at the end of the road to buy a few small items. The day after, I catch the bus into town. The next two days I stay indoors. I sit on the sofa feeling a mixture of frustration at myself and fear that this whole thing was a fluke, and I am not healing after all.

The fifth day I leave the house once more. I pause at the gate to wonder how summer crept up on me. The sun is overwhelming and the colours are more vibrant than I remember. A voice startles me.

'Hi.' Antony leans over the fence between our two gardens, one hand raised awkwardly in greeting.

'Good morning.' I try not to let my surprise show.

'I'm going through some things,' he said. 'Taking stock, donating some stuff, that sort of thing.'

'How's that going?'

'Very slowly. I'm getting upset over receipts and cracked mugs and loads of other rubbish,' he says, 'but little steps are better than no steps. What are you up to?'

'I'm going to the university,' I say, deciding there and then. 'I'll just drop in to get some books and papers. It will be good to say hello to some people I haven't seen for a while.'

'That sounds nice,' says Antony. 'Maybe when you get back you could come in for a cup of tea?'

'Yes.' I smile. 'I'd like that.'

People I Know

by David McVey

I had only been on the garden seat for a few minutes. It was approaching ten o' clock, the sun had just cleared the roof and the night-scented stock hadn't fully closed, so, as I relaxed, their pastel dream-fragrance drifted over me. I opened my book and began to read.

And then Declan appeared next door. His French windows opened and he strutted out, wearing a pair of three-quarter length cargoes and flip flops that clattered on the decking as he walked. He wore nothing on his top half. Declan was short, squat and puffy; with his strutting, cocky air, he was like a large man who had been squashed into a smaller package, perhaps by a kind of giant wine-press.

As he emerged, he bellowed into his mobile. 'Aye, Ricky, aye, nae bother, whit I'll do is I'll fix that job we done the other day – naw, the gazebo thing, no the extension – aye, an' then… aye, that's right, good, buddy, I'll see ye later oan, right?'

He ended the call and clattered about the decking for a bit. A frenzied scratching, demented yapping and his greeting of 'REILLY! Whitchy daein wee man?' told me his small, yappy terrier-thing was also on the decking. Declan then switched on his radio, filling the air for several gardens' width with the inane tunes and chatter of a commercial radio station.

'Howzitgaun, Andy, eh, y'awright?' he said, on seeing me.

I nodded, and tried to carry on reading but he started jabbering away about work and how he was doing really well and the younger girl was now doing dance classes and they'd gone out for a meal the other night and it had been really nice, steak, you know, and…

I was about to protest that I was trying to read, waiting for a break in the endless stream of gibberish, when there were noises behind me, indicating that Paul or Janey had emerged in the next garden.

Declan interrupted his splurge of talk and stood up straight and yelled, 'Yay, PAUL! Howzitgaun, big man?'

Declan never used one word when he could use ten, never spoke when he could shout and often broke into song, sounding like a drunk uncle doing karaoke at a family wedding. He was a builder and always communicated as if he were on the other side of a noisy site from the person with whom he was conversing. His wife, Frances, was a dopey, simple woman who always submitted to Declan's voluble suggestions and directions. The two girls, aged twelve and seventeen, were rarely seen and almost never heard. When they were, they were usually being told what to do and where to go by Declan's reverberating running commentary. The older one, Nickole, was now at college on some singing-and-performance course, the fruit of many years' careful study of *X Factor*.

And then something in the thundering Declan-Paul conversation being carried on between gardens, over my head, caught my attention.

'What was that?' I asked.

'It's the night,' said Declan. 'We've got Vinnie and Robbie and his wife and the weans coming along. We'll eat in the garden then hae a few jars and get the sound system out. Should be a good night.'

I groaned. There would be little sleep until the very small hours.

Declan disappeared soon after, though he left the radio on so that it could be heard only by people who didn't want to hear it. Above it, through the open kitchen door, I caught Declan's side of a typical Ross family conversation, with only his bellowed contributions audible. 'Where's that twenty-four-pack, Frances, is it in here? You gaun tae yer pal's hoose, Kaileagh? Ah'll gie ye a lift. Naw, no the bus, ah'll gie ye a lift… Frances, tell Kaileagh ah'll give her a lift. Get yer stuff Kaileagh.'

And then there was a brief burst of something like rifle fire – Declan and family getting into or out of a car always seemed to involve at least ten car doors being slammed noisily shut. The car scrunched away and then Frances appeared in the back garden, clattered onto the decking, lay on a sunlounger, and turned the radio up. As she lost what she had in terms of consciousness within the pages of *OK!* magazine, I retrieved my book and went into the house.

*

Vinnie and Robbie were also builders, or something in the construction industry anyway. Vinnie, Declan's best buddy, was between divorces again. Robbie and family arrived first. Robbie and Declan were talking just inside Declan's kitchen door when I opened my own. They were engaged in a typically loud, lager-fuelled exchange of bawling. I paused, laid down the recycling I'd been taking to the bin, and listened.

'Will the guy next door no' complain if we're bangin' the tunes aa night?' This was Robbie.

'You mean Andy?' bellowed Declan. 'Who gives a fuck? He's a fuckin' wanker anyway.'

'What does he do?'

'Och, he lectures in some college place. Fuck knows what he teaches. Some fancy, up-yer-arse thing.'

'Standin' up talkin' shite. It's no' a man's job, is it? Is it just him that stays there?'

'Aye.'

'He's no' a *poof*, is he?'

'Naw, his wife died a few year ago. Another car smashed intae hers. He disnae drive.'

'I noticed there was nae car in his drive. No drivin' is just like bein' a poof.'

Declan agreed and laughed explosively.

I spent most of that night in the living room. A small room, but one that had always seemed large and echoing and empty to me since I lost Sarah. I didn't go out a great deal these days. I had grown to value quiet, the space to think and remember and recreate, qualities Declan did not rate and which he made it hard to enjoy. As the clock inched towards 1.30am, and as Lady Gaga gave it large in the back garden (albeit still nearly drowned out by Declan's great animal roaring), I resolved to do something about the situation. Declan might well dislike me, detest what I was, and dismiss what I did for a living. But

I *knew* people. You see, Declan, that thing I lecture in is *Criminology*. And from projects and research old and new, I have contacts. And, Declan, you would not like some of the people I know. Perhaps I would go back to some of them and call in a favour or two.

*

'Yes,' I said on the phone. 'Next door, number 41. Anything, whatever you think. But it *has* to be within those dates, when I'm not around. And it has to be carried out at considerable arm's length.'

I was asked where Declan might be vulnerable.

'He's domineering, has to be the centre of everything and his two kids are like wee mice when he's around. Suggest something dodgy there? His best pal's another builder, Vinnie Johnston. He often comes over when Frances isn't there, because she doesn't like him much. Suggest they're an item, Declan and Vinnie?'

A few minutes later my first contact rang off. He would now call one of *his* contacts, who'd call someone else, who would issue instructions to people *he* knew in the mysterious Chinese Whispers of the city's dark side. The thought of the people in the chain, of the world they inhabited, made even me shudder.

*

'Gaun away, Andy?' roared Declan, over the radio-cacophony of one of those football phone-ins where the panel are audibly irritated if callers want to talk about something other than Rangers or Celtic.

He'd just come out of his car, a lengthy Merc convertible with a tasteless personalised number plate. He switched the radio off and began clattering car doors in a seemingly random fashion (like I said). I was standing, locking my front door, ready to hoist my rucksack onto my shoulders.

'Aye,' I replied. 'Hillwalking for the long weekend.'

'Hillwalking, eh? We've got some folks comin' ower the night. PART-AY!' he boomed and chuckled at his own imagined waggishness. I made to head off for the bus stop as Declan unlocked his front door, but after he'd swung the door open, he turned and asked me in his characteristic bellow, 'Whit is it you dae the lecturing in?'

'Criminology,' I said.

'Ooh!' said Declan. 'Fucksake, man, how fancy is that!' He disappeared into the house and the door banged behind him. Before I set off, I picked up a couple of small stones from the pavement and pinged them towards the badly-parked Merc. I was pleased to see one of them strike the rear windscreen and summon into being a faint star of cracks. He wouldn't know it was me, he was always pranging the thing.

I went off, whistling, down the road.

*

It rained most of the weekend and I saw little of the Cairngorms, yet I was in good spirits as I alighted from the bus and returned home along our dreary street of 1970s whitewashed semis. I was pleased to see that there was a lot of activity outside Declan's house. The exterior was being painted, and window panes were being replaced.

As I unlocked my front door, Paul, Declan's friend from the other side of my house, appeared and beckoned to me. I laid my rucksack on the front step and went over to him, a grey-faced, grey-haired, hefty lump of a man in a Celtic top and manky jogging bottoms.

'Look, Andy, jist so's ye know, there was trouble at Declan and Frances' on Saturday night. Broken windows and, like, stuff painted on the walls.'

'What kind of stuff?'

'It said, well… never mind what it said. But they were making out that he, y'know, *does* things tae Kaileagh and Nickole.'

'That's terrible.'

'Aye. They're aa really upset and that.'

Not so upset that, in the evening, they couldn't console themselves with music and TV and shouted conversations competing with each other as usual, reverberating through the shared wall as if it wasn't there. Next morning I saw Declan, still in the boxers and T-shirt he'd've worn in bed, driving Kaileagh down to the school bus (the stop's just three hundred yards away) and the girl's white, frightened face made me feel a little less good about myself.

A few weeks later I was away overnight at a conference in Edinburgh and it was then that I was expecting the second and final attack on the Ross household. As I fought back the dozy realms of sleep during a keynote address on the second day, I wondered if it would look suspicious that on the two nights the house was targeted, I was absent. This time there should have been explicit graffiti suggesting that Vinnie and Declan were an item. But it didn't happen.

I got a call from my contact. At first this fazed me. I had stressed that he should never approach me, and I feared that something had gone wrong and I was in trouble. In fact, something unexpected *had* happened, but nothing that would rebound on me. He told me the planned operation had had to be cancelled.

I returned home to learn that Frances and Nickole were in hospital recovering from overdoses, Kaileagh was in care and Declan was in police custody. There was, of course, no graffiti and no damage to the house. When my more distant contacts had arrived at the house sometime after midnight, they had found all the lights on, doors open, police cars everywhere and dozens of nosy neighbours in dressing gowns peering at the house over police incident tape. And they had, understandably, scarpered.

'Turns out it wis aa true,' Paul said to me later. 'He's been interfering wi' the girls for long enough. Nickole couldnae cope with it coming out intae the open, with everybody knowing.'

I felt sick, could taste the bile rising. What had I done?

'What about Frances? Did she know about this?'

'Oh, aye, it seems like it. But that's not *everythin'* that's behind her overdose.'

'Why? What else is there?'

'She's discovered that Declan, y'know, goes both ways. He and Vinnie have been at it.'

I gagged, fighting back the vomit. I had interpreted their closeness *correctly*?

'Nae wonder he's aye gettin' divorced, eh?' said Paul.

I excused myself, groped round to my back garden and retched into a flower bed. I had sought to impose and exploit an alternative interpretation of Declan, his family and his lifestyle, but I had inadvertently identified matters correctly. By bringing all of this into the open, how had I damaged those girls? Permanently? More, perhaps, than Declan had?

Paul saw me as I returned, green-faced, to the front garden.

'That guy that done the graffiti a few weeks back – he must've brought it all tae a head. It wis all for the good. Funny thing.'

'You think?' I said.

'Och, aye, surely. At least Declan cannae try anythin wi' them again, at least everybody *knows*.'

Paul thought a bit more, lit a fag, and said, 'Aye, I always thought there was something funny about that Declan.' He waddled, paunch wobbling like a half-set jelly, back to his house.

I dumped my bag in the living room. I had sought to disrupt Declan, but as soon as I intervened I set in train events which would ruin four lives, not inconvenience just one.

It was very quiet, though.

The sun emerged from the clouds with some force and brightness. I found insect repellent and sunblock in the bathroom and went out into the back garden and sat on the seat with my book. A blackbird piped in the trees and bumblebees hummed drowsily in the flowerbeds.

Harsh yaps interrupted the new calm. Reilly, the dog, was confined to the house next door. I felt myself wishing I'd asked my contact to arrange something for him as well.

Night Without End

by Stewart Greene

The Livu Square, Riga is alive. Music swirls like dancing ghosts set free from the bustling bars. A thousand neon coloured spotlights illuminate the enchanting Art Nouveau buildings that tell stories of times long past. The moon shines brightest of all, its silvery glow reflecting off rooftops, cobbled streets and smiling faces. There is that comforting evening smell that lingers after the blazing sun has descended.

A tribe of merry young Englishmen ramble over cobbled stones past a group of Latvian women strolling in the other direction. The groups come together, competing in good-natured banter.

For one of those men, at that moment, a story begins. In years to come he will be able to pinpoint the bookends. A city of hundreds of thousands in a country far away becomes a city of two people.

*

As she floated past, the world became quiet. He wouldn't ever forget that brief moment in time. They say we are made of the stars, that we were born when stars died. Well, maybe, just maybe, they were atoms that separated in the same star, one of a billion stars in a billion galaxies. They had been apart for billions of years while the universe sought to reunite them, if only for the briefest of moments.

The universe was plucking the strings, orchestrating the reunion; somewhere out there the energy was sparking the birth of a new star. For all of infinity, the light from that star will tell their story. But I'll tell it here now on earth. We don't have time to wait.

She smiled. It was graceful and effortless, like a movie star, a real movie star, a Hepburn or a Bardot. A tidal wave crashed through him, shaking his soul, working the atoms that make him dance in a frenzy. He stopped, stupefied. He couldn't tell you what he did or said at that moment, for he had ceased to exist. She, though, would tell you he smiled back.

While the world stood still, his tribe had secured an invitation to accompany the group of women to their next venue, an '80s bar fantastically named 'Oma's Briljants' (Grandma's Brilliant). As far as '80s bars go, this was a classy affair: rich red velvet seating, sultry lighting, pulsating with energy.

He wasn't nervous about asking if he could buy her a drink, as a young boy might be when speaking to a girl in school; he could only say that to speak to her for the first time caused him to tremble inside. Hard to describe, but whatever it was it wasn't nerves, perhaps just a precious first moment of discovery.

She drank tequila. Just a shot of tequila which she didn't drink all in one go, instead taking sips. He thought that was beautiful and magically cool.

Her English was good, though she said she was glad to have the chance to practise with an Englishman. She was a native of the city and, amusingly to him, named Santa. They sat while everything around them blurred into streaks of light – they were either moving very slowly or flashing by at supernatural speed. Only the two of them remained in focus as they talked together.

The shapes of each of their words perfectly fitted the gaps between those of the other. The words and passages from the pages of their lives rose up three-dimensionally, transitioning into an emotionally tangible object they could feel. The armour they wore as part of modern-day life was almost entirely discarded as they were magically set free.

She stood, and floated like an angel over to the DJ; his eyes never left her. Returning to him she held out her hand, requesting with her index finger that he stand.

They danced. The song was *Just like a Prayer* by Madonna. It was a fitting song. Had he not been with her, it's likely the lyrics would have flowed over and around him, but here they stuck, and at this midnight hour they felt powerful. The atoms swirled and their hearts raced. The universe had chosen the song and it became the musical score to their story.

The night played on. Only in the rarest moments will the universe use its strength to stop time, and even then it's only for a precious moment; the weight of time is impossible to resist. The event horizon was approaching. The universe began to shake, its resolve dissipating rapidly. It was valiant in buying time but eventually it gave out.

They were ushered from the closing bar into the city, now bathed in early sunlight. In the upper reaches of the northern hemisphere summer days are long, arriving early. In daylight the ethereal beauty of the city made him believe they had fallen into the pages of a fairy tale.

Linking arms, they grew quiet in contemplation, for at that moment they did not yet know how the story would end.

They stopped in a square. In the distance loomed the freedom tower. Her friends were shouting at her to join them, his had long since vanished into the night. Time was approaching light speed.

The one piece of armour neither had shaken was the fact that they were married. Married to other people. Atoms are atoms, and they danced, feeling a true and complete connection. A connection of chemistry and physics. Perfect mathematics, so rare in a world of seven billion people.

But despite this perfect match, the only place not made up of atoms is the soul. And the spaces in each of their souls was already taken. He looked into her eyes, he knew her answer, and she his.

They gazed at each other in a way that spoke as clear as the morning they had danced into. In the years that later passed he'd sometimes think of those rich hazel eyes and the atoms in his belly would dance.

The impatient beep of a taxi tore through their world, sending rivers of shattered glass throughout their cocoon. They kissed one another on the lips. It was the kiss of friends, not a full kiss. An unconscious exchange was made. They were now some small part of the other, and all that was left was for her to turn and go. In order to pull clear of his orbit, she turned aggressively and never looked back. He didn't looked away until she was gone, walking towards where the freedom tower stood.

The world around him reappeared in real time. He made his way to his hotel. His body felt rigid, and his old leg injury returned, stiffening to the point that he had to drag his foot. Some guy on a rickshaw took pity on him, offering him a free ride home. He declined: he didn't want the night to end just yet.

He meandered into a park through which a little stream ran, and smiled as he watched two blackbirds wash and playfully provoke one another, chirping happily. On he wandered, still feeling her silken lips on his.

As he neared his hotel he lay down on a grassy bank. The sunlight was massaging the swells of the River Daugava, a river of gold, the same colour as those eyes, he thought. He wondered about the power of the chemistry of their union, equations known only to the universe.

The city was just waking up, it was 6am. He found some cigarettes in his pocket, not that he smoked often, but he drew on one now. Two young men rode past on a bike and laughed at him. He laughed at himself as well. Everything but the soul is finite. His soul had been seized long ago by another heart and was a content and happy soul, the only antidote to the power of physics.

Gingerly he stumbled on, eventually arriving at his hotel. He felt warm and happy, for this had been a most unexpected episode, in which, ultimately, his soul held all the cards.

A short chapter was all it was. Sometimes, later in his life, he'd revisit this chapter and those hazel eyes, but that was all it could ever be, all he'd ever allow it to be. He hoped, though he wasn't to know, that she'd remember this chapter too.

He lay down on his bed and slept, and the final page was turned.

Handmade by Rosa

by Tony Lawrence

The Cotton Club, New York City, 25 July 1937
The young man peered nervously at the gloomy expanse beyond the stage curtain, hoping to catch a glimpse of her. A bead of sweat trickled down behind his right ear as his eyes became accustomed to the dim light of the nightclub. It was hot and the atmosphere was charged with animated chatter, the sounds of glasses and bottles chinking, and orders for more drinks being shouted out across the bustling bar. People jostled past each other to grab available seats at crowded tables and all around the room a bluish-grey haze of cheap tobacco smoke clung to the low ceiling like smog in winter.

As he looked out, he saw a sea of faces: hard-working men and women who wanted top value for their hard-earned dollars and woe betide those acts that didn't make the mark, for this was the Cotton Club, New York City. Recently relocated to a smarter neighbourhood in Midtown from its origins in Harlem, 'the Cotton' was famous for being the best jazz nightclub in town. The place was always packed and tonight was no exception. In these economically fragile, post-depression days, the Club owners sought to extract every cent they could by cramming in as many people as possible. Health and Safety had yet to be invented.

As the young man continued to survey the scene, a hand came to rest on his shoulder and he shuddered at the shock.

'Feeling nervous, boy?' asked a tall man, impeccably dressed in a tuxedo, his clarinet clasped firmly in his left hand and a knowing smile stretching across his friendly face. 'That's good,' he said, before his companion could answer. 'You need to be nervous so you can put on a great show.'

Leaning towards the boy's face he said, 'Breathe it in, GK, they're your people out there. Some of those men have worked double shifts for the past month just to get a ticket for tonight. They're hungry and weary and they need something to remember and brag about to their buddies.'

'But it's scary, Mr Hammond,' wimpered the boy. 'I don't think I'm up to it, sir.'

'You know, it's true what they say about the Cotton,' continued the man, ignoring the boy's plea. 'It can make or break you in one night. The reputations of up and coming performers are either made or ruined on this stage – I've seen it happen many times before. Tonight it's your turn to dazzle 'em and that's just what you're gonna do.'

'Yes, Mr Hammond,' said the boy. 'I'll try my best, sir.'

'It's not about trying, GK, it's all about the doing, remember that. And my name is Lennie, not "sir", remember that too,' he added.

'Yes, sir – I mean Mr Hammond, er, Lennie,' stuttered the boy. 'I'll do my best for you.'

Looking out again around the room, the young man wondered if she was here. Yes! Over in the far left corner, squashed into a booth with a group of older men, sat Rosa Jacobsen, her pale complexion radiating innocence and serenity among the boisterous crowd. He smiled at her, expecting that she would respond immediately, but even though Rosa was looking at the stage, it seemed she couldn't see him in the darkened club.

He was about to wave, but instead his hand came to rest on the handkerchief tucked into the breast pocket of his jacket. Rosa was still staring at the stage. 'Was it really only a few hours ago that we first met each other?' he asked himself. The day's events rolled about in his mind and he struggled to put them into chronological order.

First, rehearsals had started at nine o'clock sharp in the basement of St Patrick's Church Hall. It had been hard work and almost obsessive at times, the band leader relentless in his pursuit of perfection. He demanded top notch playing and every man knew it – under-performance meant someone else would be taking your place.

By noon the basement had become unbearable in the summer heat. 'Let's take a break,' announced Hammond. 'Grab a sandwich and a smoke and try on your stage jackets,' he said, pointing to a row of navy blue blazers hanging from a tailor's rack at the back of the hall.

The rack had been wheeled in by Brad Craddock, otherwise known as 'Fixer', so-called because his favourite response to any question asked of him was: 'Yeh, no worries, ayle fix 'er for yer.' Fixer was part-manager, part-medic, part-mechanic and full-time drinker when he got the chance. In short, he was responsible for everything non-musical in this band and had just been to collect the new outfits from Solly Jacobsen's store.

The boy walked over to the rail and found his jacket, the name 'Kennedy' scrawled in pencil on a scrap of paper pinned to the lapel. As he took the jacket off the wire hanger he instantly knew there was a problem.

'Fit yer OK?' enquired Fixer, as he watched the boy holding up the jacket with a worried look on his face.

'Er, yes,' he replied. 'I'm just gonna have to roll up the sleeves a little.'

'You'll do no such thing!' interjected Lennie Hammond, who had overheard the exchange. 'I'll have elegance in my band, no exceptions,' he said firmly. 'Fixer, get him over to Solly's and back here double quick time. We've still got a lot to get through today.'

'OK, Lennie, I'm on it, ayle fix 'er for yer,' came the reply, and Fixer took the boy's arm, leading him and his new jacket to the outside door.

Solly Jacobsen's was five blocks away from St Patrick's, and comprised a working men's outfitters and upstairs workshop. Solly was a personal friend of Lennie Hammond and they had grown up together as children in the same neighbourhood. Making outfits for musicians was something of a labour of love: getting paid was tricky at the best of times, and instead of dollars, concert tickets were often traded as currency in return for their stage-wear. Still, it meant Solly got to go to the gigs and enjoy the music for free, and he said that was better than collecting IOUs.

Solly was upstairs studying a clipboard of orders when Fixer arrived with the boy. The room was crowded with people, materials and machinery. Women hunched over sewing tables, while flat-capped delivery men threaded between them carrying bolts of cloth on their shoulders, jostling for space with busboys who were moving out finished garments on wheeled hanging rails. Rolls of cotton and woollens of all colours and weaves were stacked wherever there was space, and finished goods – shirts, suits, coats – were hanging from every available overhead cable, hook, nail and pipe.

It was a hot, dusty and oppressive workplace and the relentless pounding from the sewing machines assaulted the ears. Everyone seemed to be haranguing everyone else, and in a variety of languages. To the casual observer the scene was pure chaos, but the focused look on Solly's face said this was simply work in progress.

Over the din, Fixer shouted something into the ear of Solly, who yelled out the name 'Rosa' in response, and pointed to the far end of the room. 'She'll get you sorted,' he added.

The boy looked to where Solly had pointed and saw a young woman at her sewing machine. Rosa had shoulder-length auburn hair tied back under a pale blue headscarf, she wore a matching dress buttoned under her chin. Her face shone like sculptured porcelain in the murky workshop light and her dancing dark eyes had a magical, enchanting beauty. The boy was captivated and instinctively walked over to her, spellbound.

'Hello, how can I help?' asked Rosa, her smile reducing him to a bag of nerves.

'Er, it's my jacket,' mumbled the boy, feeling like a child, though he was nineteen years old, as he put the garment on. 'The sleeves are too long,' he said, his face reddening.

'They look fine to me,' replied Rosa.

'No, I mean, they're fine, but I need them to end here,' he said, pointing to a spot just above his wrist. 'I play the drums, you see, and my sticks get caught in the ends of the sleeves otherwise,' he explained. 'I can roll up them up, but Mr

Hammond will fire me if I do that.'

'OK, give it to me and I'll make the alterations.' Rosa smiled again. 'Sit down for a while, it's really hot today,' she said, pointing to a wooden stool at the side of her bench.

The boy did as he was told. His face reddened further when he saw Rosa noticing the damp patches under his arms and along the front of his crumpled shirt.

'Sorry about my shirt,' he said. 'It's just that I get hot when I'm playing and we've been practising all morning.'

'That's OK, shows you're working hard. So you're in a band then, are you?'

'Yes, I'm in the Lennie Hammond Orchestra and we're playing tonight at the Cotton. It's my first big show and I'm really nervous.'

'And what kind of music do you play?' Rosa asked.

'It's jazz, or what we now call big band swing,' replied the young man. 'Have you heard it on the radio? All the kids love it.' He felt his initial shyness ebbing away.

'What's your name?'

'Gerry. Gerry Kennedy, but people call me GK for short.'

'I'm Rosa Jacobsen,' she replied softly. The boy leaned towards her to make sure he caught every word. 'Solly is my uncle and I've been working here for three years now.' Rosa spoke as she worked, her fingers a blur as she handled scissors, pins, material and machine simultaneously. The boy watched in awe, fascinated with her speed and manual dexterity.

'How long have you played the drums?' she asked. 'You don't look very old to be playing in nightclubs.'

'I'm not,' replied the boy guiltily. 'In fact I'm not old enough to be allowed in but everyone's keeping quiet about that. I've got a chance to make a name for myself and one day soon I want to have my own band.'

'A boy trying to make it in a man's world,' declared Rosa, a note of teasing in her voice. 'Well, that's a good thing and I wish you luck with your ambitions.' Before he could answer, she handed the jacket back to him.

'Here,' she said. 'Now take this over to Bessie for steaming, then come back here for checking.' Rosa pointed to an elderly woman leaning over a table, surrounded by a cloud of steam coming from a clothing press.

The boy did as he was told and returned a few minutes later, his face beaming as he put on his jacket. 'Look, it's perfect,' he said, twisting his arms to show his bare wrists to Rosa. 'Thank you so much.'

Rosa smiled. 'Here, this is for you. I've made you a pocket square.' She handed him a crisp white handkerchief, neatly folded and with the initials 'GK' stitched onto one corner in blue thread. 'In case you get sweaty,' she added with a grin. 'Put it in your top pocket, for luck.'

The young man's face flushed. 'Why, thank you so much,' he stuttered. 'It's great – just the job.' He pushed the handkerchief into his breast pocket and patted it down. 'And it's been handmade by Rosa as well,' he added.

'I like that phrase,' she said. 'It's catchy, like your jazz music. I'll remember it.'

The boy was about to say something when he felt his arm being tugged by Fixer. 'Time to go, GK,' he said. 'Flirtin' time's after the show.' He led him away from the workbench.

The boy glanced back at Rosa. 'Come to the show,' he said hurriedly. 'It's tonight. Your uncle has some tickets,' he added, as Fixer weaved him across the crowded workshop floor. 'I'll see you there,' he shouted, all traces of shyness disappearing. 'I'll look out for you!'

His thoughts returned to the present as he looked again from behind the stage curtain and brought out the handkerchief to wipe his forehead. Turning the square over in his hand he smelled a sweet fragrance of perfume and saw the outline of a lipstick kiss on the corner. 'For luck,' he recalled Rosa saying, and he smiled at the memory and looked at her again.

'Two minutes to curtain up,' yelled a stage-hand behind him, interrupting his thoughts.

'OK, boys, tune up and line up. It's show-time,' announced Lennie.

The band members gathered up their instruments, the boy dropped the curtain edge and came over to join his colleagues.

'Time to show the world what you're made of, GK,' whispered

the band leader to the boy. 'Let's give 'em something to remember.'

*

The band had been playing for nearly two hours and Rosa had been transfixed from the outset. She was fascinated as people around the bar nodded their heads and clapped their hands or tapped their feet in time with the music, while the bolder couples jostled and jived on the crowded dancefloor below the stage. Everyone was happy, and at the end of each piece they cheered and whistled their appreciation. The place was jumping and so was Rosa's heart. She was mesmerised by the young drummer and everything else around her seemed unimportant. She thought about their first meeting earlier in the day and smiled to herself at the gift she had brought along for him tonight.

The young man pounded his drums at the opening of the band's finale piece, *Sing, Sing, Sing*, and, as it came to a triumphant climax, the crowd went wild and surged towards the stage, knocking over tables, chairs and glasses in their wake. GK was surrounded by people congratulating him, then he was lifted up high on their shoulders. He'd done it! The boy had conquered the Cotton.

'That young man's going places,' said Solly, as he stood and steered Rosa out of the booth towards the exit doors before the rush. 'You mark my words, we've seen history being made tonight.'

'Just let me say hello to him before we leave,' pleaded Rosa, turning back to join the crowd of people milling around the stage.

'What the...? Why, are you sweet on him or something?' asked Solly, puzzled by her eagerness. But Rosa didn't hear him as she edged forward.

The house lights had come on but Rosa's petite frame meant she couldn't see past the taller men in front of her. Grabbing an empty chair she stood on the seat yelling out, 'GK, it's me, Rosa, I'm over here.'

The boy heard Rosa's voice above the cheers and whistles and looked over. His dark hair was damp and tousled and it fell forward over his forehead. Beads of sweat were running down his cheeks and neck. As their eyes met he smiled at Rosa and took out the handkerchief and waved it at her. 'Rosa, meet me out back in ten, I have something to ask you...' – the rest was drowned out by the cheering all around him.

'We need to go, Rosa,' said Solly, lifting her off the chair and hustling her away from the crowd. 'Come on, before we get trampled.'

Rosa turned back towards the stage but the boy had disappeared among his adoring well-wishers. 'Did he just say meet me outside?' she asked her uncle. But Solly didn't reply and instead moved behind her, his hands on her shoulders, guiding her towards the exit.

'No, wait a minute,' Rosa insisted. 'I need to collect something from the cloakroom to give to him. He said I was to meet him, I'm sure that's what I heard him say.'

Solly shrugged in resignation. 'OK, be quick, I'll wait here for you,' he said.

*

As Rosa disappeared, Fixer ambled towards Solly from the bar.

'Great show tonight, Fixer,' said Solly. 'That young drummer's going to make a name for himself.'

'Aye,' replied Fixer. 'He's killed it, fer sure.'

'My young Rosa likes him,' mused Solly.

Fixer looked perturbed. 'The boy don't need no distractions at this time,' he said, simply.

'I'm not sure we'll get much say in it,' Solly said. 'After you both left the store this afternoon she stayed on late to make him a gift and – ha, here she is now.' Rosa returned, clutching a tailor's cloth bag in her hand.

Fixer eyed Rosa and her bag warily. Turning his head he said, 'Here, let's get out of the crowd this way,' and steered them through the tables to a set of double doors on the opposite side of the room where a neon 'fire exit' sign shone above the doorway.

Fixer pushed the metal bar so that the doors swung open to reveal a stone staircase leading down to the sidewalk on 52nd Street. A dim orange glow filtered down from an overhead light and a warm breeze blew up the stairwell from the street below.

'Exit this way, folks,' shouted Fixer signalling with his arms to the people around them as he allowed Solly and Rosa to step through the doorway in front of him.

As they reached the top of the stairs, Fixer looked around, half-turned his body, and shouted, 'Take it easy at the back, folks,' and at the same time put his foot across Rosa's left shoe and pushed her hard in her upper back with his right hand. There was nothing to grip hold of, and Rosa screamed as she flew forward down the stairwell past Solly, missing the steps beneath her feet and landing in a crumpled heap on the stone slab.

'Rosa,' cried Solly, hurrying down the steps after her, followed by Fixer. There were gasps from the crowd behind them as they realised someone had fallen. Rosa lay silent and unmoving on the grey stone and blood started to spill and pool around her head. People were gathering for a closer look at her prostrate figure.

'Quick, Solly,' said Fixer, 'get 'er to the hospital. St Vincent's is only one block away.' Taking off his waistcoat, he wrapped it around Solly's hand. 'Hold this against her head to catch the bleedin'. She'll be fine, you'll see, now git moving.'

Solly was in shock and did as he was instructed, picking up Rosa in his arms and reaching under her shoulders to cradle the back of her head. Rosa's blood dripped steadily onto the sidewalk beneath them. 'Go, Solly, I'll take this to the boy,' said Fixer, plucking the cloth bag from Rosa's hand. 'Now move back, folks, and give 'em some space.'

The small crowd parted and Solly headed towards St Vincent's carrying Rosa in his arms, moving as fast as he could. 'Stay with me, Rosa,' he pleaded, tears filling his eyes. Rosa didn't reply. She was unconscious and her blood continued to trickle through Solly's hand, gathering around her neck and shoulders. Ahead of them, the illuminated cross of St Vincent's Hospital shone in the night sky, a hundred yards away.

Fixer watched them for a few seconds then turned to walk in the opposite direction, round to the stage door on the other side. Reaching the corner, he opened the bag and pulled out a navy blue blazer. Pausing for a second he held the jacket up in front of him, grunted, then tried it on. The sleeves were a little short but otherwise it fitted his frame reasonably well.

Looking down at himself, Fixer pulled open the jacket front and stared at a white silk label that had been sewn into the lining against the inside breast pocket. It read, 'For GK. Handmade by Rosa.'

'Hmm,' he mused. 'Cute.' Pulling a penknife from his trouser pocket, he began to pick at the stitching around the label until he was able to tear it out, whereupon he crumpled it and tossed it into the gutter together with the cloth bag. He continued down the alley behind the building, to the stage door.

Fixer paused briefly as he saw the stage door open. A young man stepped out and looked expectantly into the gloomy expanse beyond.

*

The boy was hot, sweat still trickling down behind his ears as his eyes became accustomed to the darkness of the alley. Behind him he could hear the excited chatter and the sound of beer bottles and glasses chinking as the post-show party got underway.

'Here's the star,' said Fixer, coming towards him. He placed his arm around the boy's shoulders in a congratulatory gesture. 'You did us all proud tonight.'

The young man smiled and nodded. 'Thank you,' he replied, but his attention was elsewhere. For a moment he thought he caught a familiar scent of perfume in the air, but then it was tainted by the smell of rye and beer from Fixer's breath. He glanced over his shoulder into the alley, but nobody was there.

'C'mon, GK,' said Fixer, 'let's join the party, nuthin' to see back here.'

Fixer led him in through the door. Despite the night's heat, the boy felt that the arm around his shoulders was cold and heavy and it sent a shiver down his spine. 'Keep lookin' for'ards 'cause you's the king tonight,' said Fixer. 'Tomorrow we're off to Philly.'

Laughter and noise surrounded them, and the boy realised it

was true. Tonight he was the king and tomorrow the band was starting its east coast tour in Philadelphia. Everyone was jubilant and celebrating. Across the room Lennie Hammond raised a glass to him and smiled. It was his moment, yet the boy couldn't help feeling that some part of him, a part he couldn't quite understand or explain, was missing – perhaps forever.

*

While the boy struggled with his feelings, Solly and Rosa reached the emergency department at St Vincent's. 'Please, I need some help here, fetch a doctor now,' Solly shouted as he backed through the doors. A duty nurse came over from her desk to assist. Together they laid Rosa on an empty gurney in the corridor and the nurse hurried to find a doctor.

Rosa lay still. Her breathing was shallow and laboured and her face was marble-white from the loss of blood. Solly stood over her, whispering and fretting, his hand still supporting her head with the blood-soaked waistcoat.

A doctor appeared, took one look at Rosa and began shouting out urgent instructions to his nursing staff. Rosa stirred slightly at the raised voices, opening her eyes and blinking at the unfamiliar surroundings.

'Oh, Rosa,' said Solly. 'Lie still now, you've had an accident, you're in the hospital.'

Rosa looked at him and whispered, 'It was a great show, Uncle Solly, I won't forget it,' before her eyes closed again and she slipped into unconsciousness. As she was wheeled away to surgery, Solly watched, helpless and distraught, agonising over whether Rosa would ever open her eyes again.

Exoskeleton

by Grant Waters

The queue shuffles along in slow procession, Edwin waits patiently, his ticket ready in his hand. Ahead of him, a heavily tattooed doorman is tearing tickets and handing back the stubs to people before letting them pass. Edwin appreciates the crudity of the ritual, it befits the band that he is about to see. The Stranglers have been going since he was at school. Once, they portrayed a menacing presence, but nowadays it's a good-natured affair: punk nostalgia for the middle-aged rebel.

Now it's his turn, he stares at the doorman and tries to read his features, but they are disguised by the blackened ink patterns that adorn his face. What do they hide? Perhaps an earlier, more amateurish attempt? The doorman is oblivious to Edwin's musings, he is fixated on removing the correct portion of the ticket. Edwin looks at the doorman's hands, there are more patterns entwined around his fingers. He is about to look away, but then he sees it, in the fleshy wedge between the thumb and forefinger, a faded grey name: 'ARNOLD'. Could it really be him?

He finds himself inside the auditorium. Should he allow himself a drink tonight? Should he secure a place in front of the stage? He feels his heart beating faster. Is it him? After all these years, could it be Arnold? He distracts himself by looking at the crowd: it is mainly male, and mainly his age.

'Now, how do I tell which ones the ageing punks are when most of them are going bald?' he thinks. T-shirts and well-worn motorcycle jackets might be a clue. No matter, they are here for the same reason as him, whoever they are. They wish to feel the music go through them once more, to cheer in recognition at the opening chords of the hits, to lose themselves in the moment, to clap at the memory.

The lights dim and a recording of 'Waltz in Black' begins, to loud applause; the band will be on in a few moments. He sways with the crowd, but he is not there. He is back in the moment, *that* moment. Suddenly, he is afraid. Now the band have taken to the stage; JJ Burnel picks up his bass guitar and thunderous notes emanate.

*

He thinks back to that day, the day that he met Arnold. Back then, he was a delicate, gentle creature. He read books, he played the piano, and he studied insects. He always worked hard at school and would surely go to university.

On a cold November morning, as he walked across the park, an older youth approached him. Edwin looked at him, then quickly averted his gaze. In 1979 few people were tattooing themselves and, if they did, they were rarely drawing swastikas on their foreheads or writing 'Skin Head' on their cheeks.

'You frontin' me? You fuckin' are!'

Edwin felt the punch before he even saw it. He didn't know it yet, but his elfin nose had been broken. He was dragged forward by his hair and held in place while a brown boot thudded into his face. First there was the smell of damp leather and then came the tobacco stained fist with 'ARNOLD' emblazoned across it.

'P-P-Please,' was all he could offer in return. It worked for a moment: Arnold was amused by his stutter.

'G-G-Give me your m-m-money,' Arnold mocked. The few coins in Edwin's pocket were willingly handed over.

How long did it last? A minute? An hour? He had tried to block the memory. He would later refer to this as his 'ragdoll' moment. A helpless, useless ragdoll. *Ragdoll, ragdoll!* Finally, he was thrown into a ditch and left there, curled up into a ball. His satchel had spewed its contents across the ground, scholarly endeavours scattered about among the autumn leaves: biology, Latin and maths. He had always been so precise with the answers he wrote.

He could feel that rain-sodden ditch all around him once more. He could see again the sympathetic look of the lady who had discovered him still lying in a foetal position. He couldn't look her in the eye, he couldn't explain what had happened. How could he articulate the lack of control, the fear and the shame? He did not even know himself yet, but he would never be the same again. Arnold had changed him.

*

'Down in the Sewer' is next on the set list and there is pushing and pulling in the crowd. A moment later Edwin's hair is soaked in beer. He looks around and immediately spots the culprit. He reaches out, grips the man's shirt, twists it and pulls the drunk towards him. He leans in, he speaks into his ear. The band are playing too loud for anyone else to hear, but the culprit does; he has been warned. The man looks into Edwin's eyes and considers briefly the possibility of escalating the situation, but then thinks better of it. Edwin remains calm, his broken nose the only outward sign that might hint at his familiarity with aggression.

There are approving looks from some of the men around him, 'What an arse'ole.' One of them shouts. Edwin is used to this, he has long since learned that a sturdy torso gains respect.

*

It was never merely a case of pumping up his body, no, that was the easy part. His mind came first, he needed to reconstruct his mind.

He had retreated to his bedroom after the attack. Always something of a recluse, this did not cause immediate concern, but his lack of activity did. The piano playing that had brought his parents such joy was abandoned, and later his teachers could not hide their disappointment at his exam results. As the days turned into weeks, he was possessed by dark thoughts. He still ate a little, he still spoke if spoken to, but he was slipping helplessly, he was falling into the darkness.

There were outbursts of anger from time to time that his parents did not understand. For the most part, however, he would lie curled up on his bed for hours on end. He slept too little, or sometimes he slept too much. Then, one morning, he slowly stretched out his body, climbed from his bed and staggered to the bathroom. There, looking back at him in the mirror was an emaciated body.

'I need rebuilding,' he thought.

He decided that he should attain an acceptable standard before he entered a gym, so he screwed a pull-up bar into the bedroom doorframe and he began. He ate raw eggs; his mother was perplexed but pleased that at least he was eating again. He explained that he was building an exoskeleton, so that no harm could come to him.

*

The band are playing 'Tank'. Edwin used to listen obsessively to this song. The aggressive sound played through his Walkman over and over, and he would rewind the cassette to just the right place to hear it again. He knew that it was talking to him personally.

His mother asked if he was going to resit his exams, or perhaps get a job. 'Your father can't support you forever.' Soon he would, soon it would all be sorted out.

He attended the local karate club and would bow with great respect to his Sensei. He did precisely what he was told, he practised all the exercises the requisite number of times, he attempted to embrace the philosophy of true karate, to discover the unity of body, mind and spirit, as Zen teaches, but dark thoughts still possessed him. He picked things up very quickly and was gratified to learn that he had good reflexes. Back at home, he would wash his karate suit and, much to his mother's amusement, he even ironed it. He took a boy scout-like pride in every belt he obtained. Soon he would be ready.

A year later he resat his exams and did well enough to go on with his studies. He would nod an acknowledgement to other students and discuss work with them, but he did not have friends – he never really had, even before his encounter with Arnold. His Sensei was all he needed, but he could not even confide in him the way he felt.

He was ready now, he was more than ready, but the day never came. He would sit in the park, he would wander around the estates on the edge of town, all to no avail. How could you not find someone with a swastika on their forehead?

Eventually he moved away to university. He studied entomology and he studied Shidokan Karate. He gained an upper second class degree and in time he gained a black belt.

Encore

It's time to speak to Arnold. The encores have started, and Edwin walks away from the stage and out of the auditorium. He finds Arnold standing on his own along the corridor. He holds out his hand and smiles. 'Arnold! You've lost the swastika, I see.'

Arnold is confused but takes the hand offered to him. 'So, who are you?' he enquires.

'Oh, I knew you briefly, but then I went away.'

'Yeah, I been away a bit too!' Arnold gives a knowing look and chuckles.

Edwin tries to examine the chronology of the inkwork. He is surprised by how at ease Arnold appears. 'I'm back now though, to see my parents. They're the only family I have.'

'Lucky you, mate! I've got four grandchildren, don't get no peace!' Arnold laughs, it sounds a little disturbed. Edwin recalls it: there was a lot of laughter that day in the park.

'I've cured my stutter,' Edwin says. 'I've rectified a lot of things, but not quite everything. I came looking for you when I was ready, but perhaps you were "away" by then.'

He recalls a detail of the attack. 'You're left-footed, Arnold, I know that because I had more bruises on the right-hand side of my body – so many you couldn't put a pin between them. Do you know what an exoskeleton is?' He detects confusion on Arnold's part. 'Bugs, Arnold, I study bugs. I have developed my own exoskeleton. I could have done with one when we first met. You have a very simple and, if I may say so, predictable technique. Nonetheless, it was effective enough at the time. Tell me, do you still urinate on your victims?'

Arnold has long since learned to strike first and he lets loose a punch. His arm is caught, locked, and he is turned to the ground. Edwin concentrates, and feels the arm cracking. Now his forearm is pressed against Arnold's neck and he chokes the breath out of his prey. Should he continue the pressure? Blood swells in Arnold's face, revealing itself behind the mesh of ink. Edwin looks into the bulging eyes of an aging man: a thug, a grandfather and now his victim.

In the auditorium, JJ is teasing the crowd with the introduction to 'No More Heroes'. The show will soon be over. Edwin steps away, he lifts Arnold up and sits him against the wall. He politely calls for help from the doormen at the entrance. They do not suspect for a moment that Edwin could possibly be the cause of such an assault. He steps back and allows them to take over.

*

He walks towards his parents' house, then he breaks into a run. All the while he feels achingly hollow inside.

He thinks about that gentle boy who existed all those years ago, he thinks about him studying for his Grade 8 Piano exam: Schubert, Allegro ma non Troppo (Sonata in A Minor, D537), to be practised nightly. He always worked at it so diligently. Edwin wishes that he could protect that boy. He wants to cry, he wants to scream, but he cannot.

Serving Tea to God

by Marina Favila

Martha knew early on that she'd never get to heaven, not a dead man's chance in hell. So she began inviting God to tea on Tuesdays, a standing invitation on a low-trespass day: after the terrible angst of Monday, with its quick fall from Sabbath grace, but before the rousing intent of Thursday or Friday, when weekend plans for sin and riot begin to rise in earnest.

Martha timed her invitation to the minute. Too early, and God might think her presumptuous, though He probably didn't sleep much, being God and all. Too late, and she might look insincere. After all, she would want his full attention, and who could compete with vesper prayers at the local St Mike's, not to mention the fervid anxiety rising like smoke at the Baptist Singles Barbecue? Martha settled on 2pm.

But let's be clear: Martha did not expect God to show up. Her careful planning was a gesture of respect, a way to pay homage to the god who made her but would not invite her into His heaven. No hard feelings, really. Martha believed in the substance of style, and being, now, not one of the elect, why, style was all she had. A way, she thought, to stand on her own as she trod the many bridges she'd built away from the Almighty. A comfort she neither understood nor questioned.

Style is inherited. Martha knew that, for she had been carefully taught by her mother, her grandmother, her great aunt Sis, how to set a table, craft a menu, design a place card, arrange flowers and fruit bowls and favours, and create that general sense of ease and comfort found in the best of homes. Nothing to do with money, just the proper care taken by a good hostess happy to wed function and beauty. Look at her table:

First published in *Wraparound South*, summer/fall 2015.

Indian teak, polished to a fault and pulled up close to the window seat. The afternoon light set the gold of the grain on fire, and the open window let in pleasing hints of mint and sage from Martha's garden. A lit fire in the parlour banished the chill from the lingering winter, and the warmth added cheer to the room.

But the aesthetic of a high tea was also important, and Martha took pains there as well: a sheer white scarf draped over pearl-grey lace on the table, and a vase of bluebells to decorate the centre. Her china was plain, exceedingly so, but blinding white in the light of the sun, and edged with a thin line of silver. If you leaned in close, you could see a minuscule star poised on the lip of each delicate cup, and three tiny stars on the platter. Antique pewter spoons and forks were wrapped in linen napkins and tied with a single twist of silk. And in the background, barely discernible, Cole Porter ballads played so low the melodies seemed to hang in the air like a whiff of perfume or some vivid, happy memory its listeners couldn't place.

And the tea? Lest God doubt her earnestness, Martha set out a spread for a king. In the first year, she favoured China Black, piped up hot in a copper kettle, humming on the stove and ready to pour, always, it seemed, on the verge of whistling, but never quite reaching that piercing wail. By the second year, she was more adventurous: raspberry-honey or passion fruit chai, with little dishes of lemon and peach slices on the table, and extra placed on the sideboard for scent. Regardless of her chosen tea, served hot or cold, with milk or sugar, Martha always added a platter of homemade baked goods, their quality and variety such to make any baker blush with envy. Cookies, muffins, Bundt cakes, teacakes, cinnamon rolls, chocolate croissants and iced macaroons came out of her kitchen at record speed; no season passed without at least one serving of her great aunt Teenie's Scottish shortbread, slathered with caramel and dark chocolate bits. She even toyed with offering sandwiches, diagonally cut with the crusts removed – cucumber and cream cheese on white, chicken salad with pickle on rye – but she feared God would think she presumed too much. Tea was one thing, brunch quite another. Martha wouldn't get to heaven, but she was anything but rude.

Besides, Martha liked God, appreciated the many gifts He shared on a regular basis: the quiet dignities and second chances offered on holidays, birthdays, and funerals. She thanked him for her health, for a good head on her shoulders, and even for the cups of tea she offered, if ever He decided to come. But most of all, she praised his morning, the pale yellow of it, with the sun stealing up over the mountain, lighting the meadows in her backyard, and her neighbour's backyard, and his neighbour's backyard, all the way to the riverbed, dry now, yes, but in spring the Shenandoah would roar down the mountain and overwhelm that sandy pit with a rush of icy-cold importance. And Martha loved that too, for she could hear the waters ushering in April from her back porch swing.

So, you see, she really did want God to think He might enjoy His time with her, even if He wasn't coming and even if He didn't want her in His heaven. An invitation to tea was all there was between them. She would make the most of it.

After 2,184 high tea preparations, at the age of eighty-two, grey-streaked and wrinkled, though beautifully coiffed and dressed in a new linen jumper, with a white collar and a simple pearl brooch, Martha answered the front door of her little white bungalow on the last Tuesday in March, in the Year of Our Lord, 2015, at 2pm exactly.

'Welcome, uh, welcome…' Martha wasn't sure what to call God, but she recognised him immediately, in the way you recognise the natural leader in a group of boys on the playground, or the president, out and about shaking hands, kissing babies, or the prince of some Mediterranean principality, greeting his subjects in a long-line parade. Not by how they look, no, never by how they look, not their height or their hair or even how they dress: that's not how you know who's in charge, not how she knew who stood before her. It's how they move through their world, how He moved, now, right through her open door: a marked fluidity; quiet, light-lit assurance; grace. But Martha, in all her many daydreams of having tea with God, had not expected the large German shepherd that quietly padded into her kitchen that afternoon.

*

'Would you... would you like to sit down?' Martha gestured feebly towards her dining room chairs, delicate and straight-back, with embroidered green satin seats and cut-out violin backs. They weren't real antiques, but Louis XIV copies from Pier One, beautiful all the same, and Martha had saved the good part of two months' salary for them.

The German shepherd looked around, taking in the room with a knowing glance: the beautifully set table, the low, flickering fire, the soft Persian rug in gold and rose set before an ivory-white couch, overstuffed and inviting, a cashmere pashmina with plum-coloured tassels draped over one arm. He circled the room once, carefully, slowly, then circled it again, then circled the rug in the middle of the room once, twice, three times, as if to catch his own glorious upraised tail before settling down on the carpet's plush centre of yellow roses.

'Tea?'

The shepherd's head lifted, just a bit, then gave an almost imperceptible bob. His eyes were chocolate brown, gold and green-flecked, and there was an intelligence there, shining, and perhaps a touch of melancholy too. Martha, usually afraid of dogs, felt a calmness and awe sweep over her. God was here. Her hostess mode clicked in.

'Of course, of course, you want tea; what am I thinking? Or perhaps something more refreshing?' She scurried to the refrigerator, where she had prepared a pitcher of water with slices of lime and cherry. Reaching for a teacup she realised how ridiculous that seemed. Her eyes lighted on a deep-red, cut-glass punch bowl, a retirement present from colleagues at the Tarryville Library – happy to be rid of her, she knew, all of them, even her boss. Her fastidiousness, her insistence on detail and procedure, had irritated them no end. But she had not hated them, had even admitted she no longer fitted into their generation of eBooks and Nooks and Kindles and shared computer files. But she hated that bowl: its gilt edge and eighteen matching goblets mocked the fact that she never had occasion to use it. And they had known that, they knew when they chose it, for it was well known at work she was a fabulous hostess without any guests.

But now, how perfect, a proper chalice for a lord! It was heavy too, and would not easily overturn. She happily rushed to fill it with the citrus-touched water and a handful of shaved ice. Martha carefully placed the bowl at the dog's feet. She was still a bit afraid of him, but his eyes were kind and, she thought, grateful, as he thirstily lapped up what she had to offer.

When he was finished, the shepherd stretched out on the rug, his body massive, muscular, his coat thick and well cared for, and more velvety than the carpet he lay on. When he yawned, Martha could see the triangular snap of his powerful jaws, with teeth as sharp as a saw, Martha thought – as sharp as his tongue was soft and wet. He drooled a bit, stretched again, then settled into a half-sitting, half-lying position. God looked tired, but he stared back at his hostess with alert attention. He seemed to be waiting for her to begin.

*

'My name is Martha… oh, I guess you know that already.

'I've invited you here – I've been inviting you here for a long time now. I'm not complaining. I know you have many things to tend to. I didn't really think you'd come. But I'm glad you did. I'm honoured that you're here.

'I guess I just thought it would be nice to meet and talk, you know, given our situation?'

Martha waited to see if God had anything to add. He did not.

'I wanted to say that I've appreciated everything you've given me. My parents were supportive; my sister was kind, she shared all of her dolls and her books. My education was certainly good enough, and the master's degree too, really, more than enough. I've always been able to support myself, and to buy, with a bit of saving, everything I wanted.' She gestured proudly around her living room and kitchen, which sparkled with care and colour. 'But, as you well know, I'm missing something, some… gene of empathy, some ability to care for other people.'

Again, she waited. The dog was silent, like a sphinx.

'I do all the right things. Believe me, I do. I follow all the rules, obey laws, fulfil society's expectations, my family's expectations, like a champ. I chose a profession where order is imperative. In that sense I'm like you: I brought order to the chaos of hundreds of mindless people, just sauntering into the library as if they had nowhere to go. Browsing, they called it, picking up books they had no intention of reading, putting them down, here, there. I twice found a book in a toilet cubicle! Or worse: they put them back on the shelf in the wrong order, or on the wrong shelf, or in the wrong room. But I dutifully picked them up, all of them, every single one of them, and put them away, and I never said a mean word to anyone.

'And when I wasn't doing that, I was cataloguing new books, or repairing old books – books torn by thoughtless patrons, ear-marked and spine-bent, or erasing silly comments made in pencil and pen, or cleaning the grime of sweat and years of dust that settled on their covers and smeared their pages, the imprint of dirty hands and sticky fingers – children's sticky fingers! – their pudgy little digits smudging up gorgeous picture books with sticky toffees and Cadbury stains. Of course, homeless people were the worst: they stank, for one, and the lounge chairs always needed vacuuming after they left. And when a blind person came in, oh my god, with their service dogs panting and slobbering, brushing up against chair legs and pushing their wet noses into magazine racks, well, I might as well have left the vacuum running all day.'

Martha paused, recognising her faux pas. She cleared her throat. *Do I try to explain, apologise, cover up, or rush on? What would Dear Abby do, what would Martha Stewart advise?*

'Sorry, I didn't mean to imply you've made imperfect creatures.' *Good, Martha, good, generalise the mistake, that'll cover it up.* 'Cleanliness is next to godliness?' Martha sighed. 'I only meant that I did try to care for the world you gave me. I just don't seem to care for the people in it.

'Yes, I recognise that *that* is the problem, the unforgivable sin. I'm not a stupid woman. I understand that people are worth more than the things around them. But I can't seem to change. I don't desire it.' Martha shifted her glance. 'Isn't there some part of heaven where a person can live quietly alone, say, on the edge of Elysium, one street over, in a little condo with a private bath and a view of the mountains or meadows in the distance?'

The German shepherd rose up on the balls of his feet, stretched and yawned, then padded through her door with more grace and dignity than one might imagine from a large-bodied dog. Martha took that as an unqualified 'No.' The screen door swung quietly shut behind him and Martha got up, went to her closet, and pulled out her Hoover WindTunnel self-propelled upright vacuum cleaner. But there were no hairs to remove from the expensive plush Persian, not even from the raised patch of roses in the middle. God, apparently, did not shed.

*

Martha's second visit from God was even stranger, perhaps because she wasn't expecting his return. They had left things unsettled. She had made a request, surprising even herself, for she hadn't a clue such a query would rush from her mouth – and as soon as she met him, for god's sake. Nor did she expect his quick and obvious rebuff. But oh, how embarrassing and such an un-hostess-like thing to do. And it didn't make sense. She had come to terms with the idea of not going to heaven years ago.

So when God returned the following day, she wasn't sure whether to let him in or not. What more was there to say?

The soft repeated thud on the front door from the German shepherd's tail did not seem to herald a godlike entrance. Surely a choir of angels was in order, or a trumpet or harp or at least some bell-ringing? Martha opened the door halfway and was awed again by his majestic stance. His ears were up and pointed, his black and gold muzzle reaching well above her waist. The shepherd's eyes held hers with serious intent.

'I'm afraid I haven't prepared anything, God. It's Wednesday.'

The shepherd nosed past her – not a bullying move, though he *was* a big dog, just pushing past in a way that made it clear he wanted to come in. He was panting a bit, too, perhaps due to the heat of the day, for the end of March in this part of the country could be terribly humid, and spring was well on its way.

Circling the living room, the shepherd stopped once to sniff the oven, where Martha had blueberry tarts crisping, three quarters of the way done. Then he returned to his favourite spot on the Persian roses, as if he had lived there all his life.

'I suppose I could get you some water,' Martha said with a sigh, though she knew, she just knew, by his longing glance, he was hoping for a tart, maybe two. And she'd only put three in the oven.

The two stared at one another, a long stare. God could stare down anyone, Martha thought.

*

'Two, no more!' Martha pulled out the hot steaming tarts with a quilted mitt, fat blueberries bulging through the interlaced crust, crunchy with cooking oil and liberally brushed with melted butter. 'No one ever cooks with both,' Martha murmured to herself.

The smell was overwhelming and filled the room with a vanilla sweetness as powerful as the Eucharist. Martha blushed at the thought, hoping God wasn't listening to such blasphemy. She looked furtively behind her, where the shepherd paced back and forth, crowding her as she placed the tarts, one by one, on the cooling rack. No, no, his mind was only on the tarts, she was sure of it. Martha searched the cupboards for an appropriate dish.

Five minutes later, both were seated in Martha's living room: she on her white sofa, with a blueberry tart on a Wedgwood plate, the two startling colours, berry and thistle, deepened by mounds of glistening whipped cream; and he on his roses, lapping up chunks of blueberry mush in a make-do aluminium mixing bowl. Sugar crystals dusted his handsome black beard. Martha felt, rather than heard, the companionable hum of his heavy breathing as the dog slurped up the afternoon treat. Seconds later he looked up, and Martha felt that too. The German shepherd seemed startled to have finished before his hostess.

'Forgive me for saying this, God, but I believe you were hungry!'

Without thinking, Martha broke off a chunk of her tart and offered it to her guest. The dog rose, and with a great bounding hop came to gobble the tart from her hand. Martha laughed as he licked her fingers to get every last drizzle of berry juice and cream, and Martha patted his head, and then pushed him down to the floor. Really, it wouldn't do to have even God slobber on her ivory couch. So she was doubly pleased when he made no protest but contentedly settled in a heap on the floor, his large black head resting on both of her feet.

Martha finished her tart without talking or thinking. Nat King Cole's 'From This Moment On' played softly on her antique turntable, or was that a memory? Her head fell backwards on the embroidered pillows of her overstuffed couch, and she slipped into a peaceful nap. When she awoke, God was gone.

*

Martha marvelled at the thought of these heavenly visits each and every day. The pattern had been set, and the shepherd never deviated. At some point – morning, noon, or night – he would arrive, his wagging tail or friendly nose knocking at her door. And Martha would open it wide for God to bound in.

And it didn't take long before she started to plan different types of 'teas'. Teas that required a whole new slew of ingredients. Even her shopping patterns changed. Baking tins and rolling pins were pushed back in the cupboard. Frying pans, soup pots, and large casserole dishes were purchased, along with a new set of knives. Martha negotiated special cuts of meat at the gourmet butcher shop on Edgerly and Vine. She read cookbooks, watched cooking shows, and cut out recipes from women's magazines. She even did research on the dreaded internet to find out what German shepherds liked or needed or required, for surely God could not live by blueberry tarts alone. And she bought hamburger meat and holiday hams and whole chickens (which she deboned herself), and fresh sausages, locally stuffed, and now and again a huge T-bone steak to give God a bone to gnaw on. And at TJ Maxx she found an enormous porcelain platter with hand-painted angels swirling around the edges – made in Italy, too, home of the Pope! – on which she served old-fashioned meatloaf and chicken Française and pork roast with plum sauce and steak tartare. And now, always, the beloved cut-glass punch bowl was set by the fireplace, filled to the brim with lime- or lemon-laced water, ice cubes added for a last minute chill. And God devoured it all, everything she cooked, licking the plates, lapping up the citrus water and never spilling a drop, or not a drop that Martha noticed. God, it turned out, was the consummate guest, and if he ever did let a morsel dribble from his sharp-toothed mouth, why, he must have licked it up in a flash, or swept it up with his powerful tail. Martha's house was always as clean after God's visits as it was before.

Soon the two were not just sharing meals, but taking long walks too. In the morning, they would stay close to home, wandering the streets of the neighbourhood as the sun came up over the mountain and lit her valley with a warm yellow glow. Martha would gather ideas on how to redo her patio or plant her spring garden or shingle her roof, and God would follow the scents of various squirrels and rabbits, splash in and out of rain puddles and lawn sprinklers, and chomp, then spit out, dandelion weeds and rose thorns, which always made Martha laugh.

On late afternoons, God would hurry Martha down to the park, through the playground, around the dog trails, and over the old wooden bridge. And the two would carefully cross those haphazard logs over the rushing Shenandoah, always stopping midway, where God would jump into the river with a swan-like dive and chase fishes and frogs, while Martha sunned herself or read until dusk. Once they went walking at night, up a rarely used trail on the Blue Ridge Line, where a meadow of unsurpassed beauty was hidden in a circle of pines. 'It's a cloister!' Martha gasped. 'A cloister of giant raggedy spears!' Only the light of the stars could penetrate such darkness. Their brilliance was almost painful on that moonless night, and Martha's eyes watered considerably.

It wasn't long before Martha began to long for these visits, to depend on them, plan for them, and she liked to think God did too. Why wouldn't he? It must be so tiring to be God, she thought, people always making a mess of the world and expecting Him to clean it up, to tidy up the chaos of their mindless wanderings and bring some meaning or order, or illusion of order, to their curiously vapid lives, and demanding things, always praying and pleading for them, bargaining, begging for them. Knock and the door will be opened, ask and you shall receive – that's the verse they hold onto. Asking, asking, all of the time, for things to make their lives better or brighter or easier, as if God didn't have things of his own to attend to. 'Even I,' Martha stammered, 'even I had to ask for a place on the edge of heaven, with a private bath and a view of the mountains, where I didn't have to care for anyone but myself.' Maybe God wanted that too.

Then one day the visits stopped. God no longer came to her little white bungalow, to eat in her kitchen or rest on her Persian roses. Martha grieved for years.

*

Before Martha died she dreamed that God came to her one evening. As always, his coat was thick and shiny, his ears pointed and alert, and he motioned with his head for her to get up and follow him. In her dream, Martha tried to tell him, patiently, but clearly, that she could not go because she was much older now, and dying. Martha knew then, too, even in her dream, that she would not enter heaven, and she refused to ask, after all these years, from her dear, dear friend, this boon of a place on the side of his home, with a private bath and a view of the world, where she could live by herself alone.

But the shepherd refused to take no for an answer, and he pulled at the sash of her robe with his teeth, and Martha found, in her dream, that she *could* get up, and she *could* walk, and her arthritis was gone, and the cramps in her legs were gone, even her breathing was easier, in and out, in and out, as even as the wind stealing in through her bedroom blinds. Martha dreamed that she followed God outside, down her neighbourhood streets and into the park, up and over the old log bridge, with sure steps now, not even a stumble, skipping over the Shenandoah River that rushed and thrashed beneath them, the sound of its furious water a great whoosh in her ears.

And then Martha dreamed they were back in the meadow, fir-scented and freshened by rain. The night was so black in that circle of pines, and the stars so bright, pulsing on high, that the contrast between night and light, and the distance between them, seemed to blind her. Martha stumbled to her knees, and to steady herself reached out for God, and buried her face in his soft thick fur.

Pandemonium

by Kathryn Wills

Commander

Our craft landed on the new planet, our new home. The holy man, our priest, clambered down first, and raced to plant his lips on the red-brown soil. This wasn't the plan, as well he knew, to 'consecrate' the homeland with his old religion. At least, and we were grateful for it, he wasn't wearing a spacesuit, as we had all been surgically adapted for low gravity and zero oxygen. Can you imagine the fool, the priest, Axel, bouncing off the soil in an oxygen mask like a gigantic turd?

The Shanghai Protocols said all colonisers had to be careful and respectful of their new environment, despite the fact that all prospective planets had been checked to death by the nerds who worked for NASA. There was always a chance of something having been missed. Ignoring my stupid paranoia and bearing in mind my unblemished mental health rating, I followed the regulated procedure and made a short welcoming speech inside our living biome. We drank fermented honey and ate banana peel confits from our own blue planet, now blackened by the appetites of capitalism.

Life-force

We drift, unknown, below the red-brown crust of our home. Once we had voices, muted ones, before this galaxy murmured into life, and now we silently hum, like the immeasurable stars. You cannot hear us, for we are eternal solitude, though we are legion. When there was water, we surged, innumerable, and devoured the mud, multiplying and dividing, ready to become more. And then there was no water, but hotness and dying, silently, with plant matter decaying, strangling. We failed to respire, drowning in the sea. Yet some of us have a half-life, a collection of dried up spores, waiting, dreaming of life, of a drop of moisture to bring us new life, a tremulous hope in the acrid plains.

Commander

And then, a few weeks in, let's face it, annoyingly, our resident holy man and a few others, agricultural workers, started to complain about the effect the planet was having on their bodies.

'It's weird,' the priest moaned at me, during our weekly 'chat'. 'My skin is, like, well, like a baby's. All my scars, marks, stubble, it's all gone! I mean, I feel stupid for complaining – people at home would give their eye-teeth for such youthfulness, but I can't help thinking, what does it all mean? What's going to happen next?'

I looked at him. He was right, at fifty-four he shouldn't look like this. Even in the harsh glare of the morning sun, he looked like a movie-star version of himself, creases and lines ironed out. It was shocking, but he had identified the problem as well: who could complain about such an upgrade in our self-obsessed culture? Yet why were the farm workers also affected? They spent a lot of time in the sun – wouldn't that be more likely to damage than enhance their skin? Anyway, what on earth can I do? I'm afraid I gave him short shrift – wasn't he supposed to be part of the solution to others' miseries?

Priest

When I spoke to the commander, he seemed unconcerned about my skin's youth, and I wanted to scream at him: something's going on! Today, however, I feel much better – my skin feels almost radiant, my mind powerful. Even though my dreams are disturbed by vivid images, almost incandescent, of my past life, I am reassured that I dream of my friends from earth, my family, all together in some ethereal domain – heaven, perhaps. I seem to have been given power, to emanate spiritual energy, just as my body is also newly dynamic. I shine. I am like some divine mediation from above.

But, I digress. There are people to see, people to console, some of whom are in a terrible state missing home, plagued by apocalyptic nightmares. It's not as though they can just jump on a plane and ease the pain.

Life-force

Suddenly pulsing with life, we hear the sounds of others' thoughts, the jolts of desires, and it is as though we are alive for all eternity. The muted humming of ours, the lowly ones, is now a susurration, like a cosmic exhalation. We were dead and are alive, lost and now found.

How do we become larger, more, shake off our lowliness? No matter, there are aeons to work it out; we do not need yet to burst through the rocks and soil, pulverising, and enhancing ourselves. There will be time. We will spray ourselves somehow, like myriads of seeds, and flow through the impoverished atmosphere, searching for minds – minds that press on us, that have thoughts and desires.

Commander

Being the commander is getting harder by the day: people are complaining of bad dreams (what?) and feeling strange – well, you would, wouldn't you? It's a strange planet!

Axel is behaving bizarrely as well: he comes in like some kind of royal, like he's got a halo suddenly – serene, and almost other-worldly (interesting phrase), and you almost expect him to say he's here to save us. Actually, maybe he could save those who spend their time moaning! That would put a hole in his wings.

Priest

And now something else has just happened to me. I was counselling someone distraught, with a beautifully young face, who has reported himself plagued by 'hideous nightmares', when I moved to touch his hand. A moment later, I became aware of a sudden terrible thrumming in my ears and a jolt like static, as though something was waking up within me. There was a sudden raging of something almost evil growing. I ran to the commander but he was uninterested, always so rational, almost insulting, as though my grandiosity, imagining that I have special powers, has triggered some delirium – a nemesis.

I went to my room and lay down to recover, as he advised, praying for calm. Baffled by the anomalies of my soul, I fell into what seemed a soothing sleep. Yet the infection thrust through the healing power of rest hideously.

I am now assailed by appalling hallucinations, monstrous apparitions, amalgams of all those whom I've loved, now dead, and chopped into messes, then reassembled by some clumsy Dr Frankenstein!

I know from mental health training days that this isn't real, its's the mind reacting to a bug, but part of me has decided that this is the devil's work, the work of some cosmic force of evil I have sworn I don't believe in, or have sworn has no power over me. Only God has such power and yet, in the heat of an alien sun, I find myself wondering if God has reneged on us, abandoned his favourite child – man. Is he perhaps a God who has lost his power in the vast wastes of interstellar space?

I start to howl in my extreme mental pain. I hear my door lock.

Life-force

Minds murmur around us, thoughts and live bodies thrum with energy, with moisture. We touch the life, we are growing, moving, our powers returning, our hope renewed like prayers in the wind.

Commander

I've had to confine him to his quarters. He came to see me yesterday, almost raving. The Devil was taking over, he was no longer Axel but Satan, creeping over the planet, destroying.

I've followed the protocols exactly, and protecting everyone else on the new planet is vital – what would happen if we all became hysterical or demented? We couldn't survive. There are no mental hospitals here and we can't section people.

Priest

I am lying on my bed, perfectly sessile. He has locked me in, despite my bitter tears and pleas, terrified that I am mad.

  I am not mad, I am just satanic; something Other is shifting in my blood stream, like noxious fats, moving and coating my organs with malice. I am no longer myself.

Life-force

We are new, we are pulsing, we are Legion.

Swarmer

by James Debenham

Chantelle was walking hurriedly up the street. It was already 8:15pm, the time she would normally be home, and she knew her Mum would be starting to worry. She had tried calling when she left the gym but realised her phone was out of battery, so had been walking at a quick pace for the last fifteen minutes. She pulled her phone out of her pocket and tried one more time to switch it on – nothing. And she was still ten minutes away.

She had put loose-fitting black jogging bottoms over her tight lycra shorts in the changing room at the gym, and then zipped up her purple Nike training hoodie and strapped on her watch. Then this sixteen-year-old black girl, with short cropped hair (that her mother hated), said goodnight to anyone who was left, picked up a rectangular Reebok kit bag that was almost as big as her, and walked out. That was two miles ago, near City Road in East London, and now she was halfway up Pitfield Street and starting to feel the weight of the enormous bag, due to having to walk so quickly straight after such an intense training session.

She passed the off-licence on the corner and crossed the street towards Royal Oak Court: a collection of six-story council blocks that were set back two hundred yards from the main road and had plenty of green grass all around to separate them. Time check: 8:25pm.

Chantelle had seen them when she'd crossed the road by the off-licence: five young boys, no older than her, dressed in dark hoodies and grey tracksuit bottoms, all standing around smoking, with a few of them straddling push-bikes. And now she was approaching them because they were hanging out right in the middle of the small road that led into her estate, a hundred yards past the large green entrance arch that had Royal Oak Court written in large white letters through its middle.

This wasn't the first time she noticed them. They'd been hanging around for a while – not every night, but a few times over the last couple of weeks when she returned from the gym. They were usually on the main street, or off to the right, a little further up. But now they were right in the middle, blocking her way, and there was no way around them without looking stupid and climbing over the low fence that ran either side of the entrance road, and she didn't have time for that.

She had passed under the green arch with its faded lettering and hadn't even got close enough to ask them to move before one of the boys stepped out from the group and blocked her way. He was a fresh-faced mixed-race kid wearing a hoodie that was zipped up to his chin. She didn't speak, but watched as he tried to give her what she thought was probably his best effort at looking serious, trying to 'give it' in front of his friends, who were all following the action from behind him.

'Wanna hang?' Zip-Up said, standing only a foot away from Chantelle, but not exactly towering over her: he was only an inch taller, putting him at around five-seven.

'No thanks,' Chantelle said.

'Why not, man?'

Chantelle moved her eyes from Zip-Up over to his four pasty-white, skinny friends and then back again.

'I don't like crowds.' Chantelle knew she had to get home and was surprised, when she stepped to her right, that Zip-Up didn't block her way.

'Well how about you just hang with me? No one else around?'

Chantelle stopped and turned to see that Zip-Up had followed her a few feet and was staring at her with piercing blue eyes.

'And what would we do?'

'Anything you want.'

Chantelle looked at this guy, thinking he suddenly looked normal, cute even, once separated from his troop of gormless monkeys.

'And what do you think you're gonna get out of it?'

This set the monkeys off, who all whooped and jeered as Zip-Up smiled and glanced back at them, Chantelle feeling that he'd have to come back with a disgusting answer just to keep them entertained.

He turned back to her. 'How about a kiss?'

Whoa, she wasn't expecting that. She waited, then, suddenly feeling in control. 'Well, you'd have to earn that.'

'Give me long enough and I will.'

'I'll give you two minutes.'

'That's no time.'

'That's the deal. Take it or leave it.'

Zip-Up turned back to his skinny white troop. Chantelle wanted to say, 'Don't bother, they don't have any answers,' but Zip-Up was looking back to her already.

'OK. Did you wanna start now?' he said.

'No. Tomorrow morning.'

Zip-Up tutted. 'Whaat?'

Chantelle remembered he was still just a boy, putting-it-on in front of his friends. 'At seven,' she said.

Zip-Up erupted into laughter now, along with all his monkey friends, giving time for Chantelle to check her watch: 8:35pm. She really had to go.

'You for real?' Zip-Up said, still laughing.

'For real. Meet me at the top of Shoreditch park, near the tennis courts.'

'Outside? I thought we'd be at your place or something?'

'Not on the first date. If you want your two minutes, it has to be outside. In a public place.'

Zip-Up didn't answer, but didn't look back to his friends either, making Chantelle wonder if he was actually considering this?

'OK.' He said.

Chantelle was already backing away. 'And by the way, I lied.'

'How's that?'

Chantelle waited a moment, having fun with him now.

'I do like crowds, so bring your friends.' She didn't hang around because she knew what was coming, so walked quickly towards her building, listening as all the skinny white monkeys erupted into whoops and jeers behind her. *Damn,* she thought, *Mum is going to be so mad.*

*

Chantelle dropped her spare training vest onto the grass. She was at the top of Shoreditch Park: a large open green space that was usually reserved for football matches and dog walking. But this morning it was quiet, and about to be used for something different. She walked a straight twenty paces south, away from the three tennis courts that marked the end of the green space with their tall wire fences.

Dressed in tight black tracksuit bottoms and a green running top, she reached into the large kit bag over her shoulder and pulled out another spare training vest, which she dropped on the ground.

She looked out across the empty park, the low October sun barely up but casting a warm orange light across the open space. Looking west, towards the very bottom of the large park, her right hand clutched the strap of the bag. The cars appeared as mere blips as they sped up and down the main road behind the treeline that cut off the end of the park. She always felt good at this time of morning, alone, one of the first people to greet the day.

She wondered if Zip-Up would show? Standing there, in the cold light of the morning, she felt the whole thing had been stupid the day before, and was unsure why she had taken things as far as she did, and hadn't just gone straight home. Then she smiled, remembering how the blue-eyed boy had agreed to all her demands, despite being in front of his friends. The idiot.

She checked her watch: 7:58am. It was doubtful he'd appear, but still she turned ninety degrees to the right, paced another twenty steps and dropped a third spare vest from her bag. Turning again, she headed another twenty paces back up towards the tennis courts and this time dropped her bag, creating a four-point square that was twenty foot by twenty foot. Looking west towards the sun and feeling its warmth on her face one more time, she was about to check her watch again.

Which is when she heard something.

*

Rubin walked across the park from the south. He remembered where she'd told him she'd be but was still surprised to see her standing there, pacing away from him and then reaching into her large black bag and dropping something on the ground. What was she doing? He was also surprised that his four friends had bothered to get up so early to join him. Maybe they hadn't slept? Rubin sure as shit hadn't. He was too curious as to what this girl had in mind for these two minutes.

Chantelle. He'd found out her name long ago because he asked around after seeing her that first time, with an old woman he guessed to be her mum, as they were heading into Royal Oak Court – across the street from Rubin's block of flats, and a lot nicer (still a council building, but way better than his).

After he found out her name, he stopped asking questions about her, because all he wanted to do was meet her, which is when he'd started hanging around outside her building most nights, or at least the nights he could convince his friends to hang with him, so he didn't look like such a freak.

She had passed by a few times, but Rubin had never had the balls to get her attention, or even known what he would say if he did. He hadn't actually intended to step out in front of her the previous night, and still wasn't sure how or why he'd done it. Just instinct taking over, he figured, meaning he was totally unprepared when he did, and just made things up as he spoke. And now he was totally confused as to how things had developed the way they had. But he was glad they had, in a nervous kind of way.

When he saw Chantelle in the mornings she was always with her mum, and in the evenings, heading home, she was always alone. She never came home with a guy, as far as he could tell, which filled him with hope. He liked the way she was always wearing training gear, not the sort of baggy stuff you wore just to hang out, but the more serious stuff used for things like the gym. It was always colourful and looked great against her beautiful black skin.

Getting closer to her he could see she wasn't wearing too much colour today, she looked more serious than usual. He kept walking while his four friends circled around him on push bikes. He fixed his eyes on Chantelle as she dropped her bag to the floor and looked out across the park. He was so close now he wanted to say something cool to get her attention, but all he could come up with was a 'Whoop-whoop!' He immediately regretted it, seeing her look at him with a face that said she thought he was an idiot. She didn't respond, but waited for him to get closer, forcing him to speak first.

'What is this?' Rubin asked, stopping several feet away and looking around at the four markers she'd laid down.

'It's a twenty by twenty square.'

'What are we gonna do? Wrestle?' he said, smiling, but genuinely confused, and feeling butterflies in his stomach.

'Close.'

This was immediately followed by whoops and jeers from his cycling monkey friends. And even Rubin was half smiling still.

Chantelle was edging slowly backward, not taking her eyes from him. 'It's the exact size of a regulation boxing ring.'

Rubin paused. 'You wanna go at it?'

Chantelle was over at her kit bag now and Rubin watched as she pulled out two pairs of boxing gloves, one blue set, and one red set. 'You said you'd give me two minutes.' She was walking back towards him, to the centre of the ring, and holding up the gloves. 'You go two minutes and knock me down inside this ring, and I'll give you what you want.'

There were guttural jeers from the monkeys, who had all stopped cycling and stood straddling their bikes behind Rubin, a few feet clear of the ring.

Rubin stood still, putting it all together in his mind, waiting for the punchline.

'You wanna box? For real?'

'For real,' she said.

Shit, Rubin thought – there was no punchline.

'But, if you don't knock me down or get me out of the ring, and I knock you down, I get something from you.'

'You actually wanna fight?'

'No, I wanna box. I want your best for two minutes. If you think you've got what it takes?'

'I can you give you my best, but that might be more than you can handle.' Finally he'd said something clever, he thought, something he knew would get jeers from his friends, which it did. The only problem was that he didn't believe his own bluster.

'That's a yes.' Chantelle said. She threw the blue set of gloves at Rubin's chest, which he barely caught.

Had this girl really planned all this? If she had, it meant that she wasn't fucking around, Rubin thought. Although, at this point, he wished she was 'cause he was past the point of backing out and knew his friends were hooked. But what was he supposed to do? Back out and look scared? Or say yes and try and throw punches at a girl? So what he did next surprised even himself: he stepped forward, unzipped and removed his hoodie and, dressed in tracksuit bottoms and a loose T-shirt now, started putting on the gloves.

Chantelle did likewise, a serious look on her face.

'You are about to spend two minutes trying to punch a girl in the face – how do you feel about that?' she said with no expression.

'Come at me,' he said, his nerves showing in his voice. 'Only...' he hesitated. 'What about gum shields?'

'You're a big boy,' she said. 'And don't worry, I'll be gentle.'

'I was more thinking about you.'

'No you weren't,' she said, still not smiling.

Fuck, he thought. She was right.

Chantelle stepped to the centre of the ring and beckoned him over.

'No punching below the waist. If you step outside the ring you immediately lose. If one of us goes down, the other has to wait until they're back on their feet. And when I say break, we break. And one more thing.'

'Yeah?'

There was a moment.

'What's your name?'

He struggled to remember. 'Rubin,' he said.

Chantelle looked surprised. 'OK, Rubin. Now touch gloves.'
And they did.

*

Chantelle didn't expect him to go past a minute. Which is why she didn't bother setting the timer on her phone to count down from two minutes like she usually did when she sparred with someone. She figured she would be able to apply enough pressure – never letting up, bobbing and buzzing like a bee – that she would be able to wear him down quite quickly. With her slender size and weight, her trainer had always told her she was a natural swarmer: someone who, despite not having a long reach or a large physical frame, could overwhelm their opponent with relentless punching and good footwork. And that was exactly what she was going to do today: shower Rubin with hits, force him to move, eventually tire him out.

But for any of that to work, she'd have to get him fully engaged, to treat it seriously and throw actual punches at her. If he was anything like the other boys she boxed with, he'd hang back and try to let the clock run down because he was fighting a girl. Which is why, as soon as they'd touched gloves, she stepped forward and gave him two quick solid jabs to his face. Which certainly sent him the right message, based on the surprised look in his eyes.

*

What the fuck was happening? He'd only wanted a date with the girl and now he was getting his face smashed in. He hadn't wanted to hit her, and still didn't want to, but then, suddenly, there was a stinging pain in his nose, and he wanted it to stop. So he had to retaliate. But the more he tried to focus the more she moved, and the more he felt the pain of her punches. Then, every time his vision cleared enough to throw a punch in the direction of her head, she was gone, and he just felt tired, and struggled to breathe. And she just kept coming!

So when he tried to back away, and she wouldn't stop, he was forced to bring his arms up to cover his face, blinded now as he felt blows to his ribs and one to his stomach that sucked all the air out of his body and, without him realising it, put him down on his knees, which was when she finally backed off.

Above his desperate, gasping breathing he could hear her counting up slowly from one, over which were loud shouts from his friends telling him to 'Get up!' and calling him a 'Pussy 'ole'.

He could taste acid, his lungs burnt fire, and his arms felt like lead. How many punches had he thrown? A lot. How many had he landed? None that he could remember. How many seconds were left? And what were his friends thinking, watching him get a proper beating like this without intervening? He wanted the ground to swallow him up. He wanted to forget this whole thing and be put out of his misery. And fuck his friends. They should try it.

'Six... seven...' he heard Chantelle say. Already? He used everything he had to get up, to try to make it to the end of the two minutes.

*

Chantelle was impressed by the way he took it. Especially as she didn't let up, throwing flurry after flurry of jabs and crosses while constantly dancing around him, so he never knew where she was coming from. She wasn't putting a lot into the punches, but still, the guy had some real staying power. And he was careful not to step one foot outside the ring and put himself out. But, truth be told, Chantelle never pushed for that, having too much fun with him inside. When she knocked him down and backed away, she took a lung full of air, impressed with her own footwork and timing this morning. She didn't relax, though, as she walked away, counting slowly to ten, figuring he would get up on about seven or eight, thinking about the name Rubin and how she liked it.

'Eight...' she said, and watched him struggle to his feet, listless and breathless. And then, in that moment – barely halfway through their two minutes, she reckoned – she decided she'd tormented him long enough.

Once the word 'Ten' left her lips, she didn't hesitate and, leading with her left foot, stepped forward and quickly brought herself within a few feet of Rubin who was too tired to move but had already brought his hands up to his face to protect himself. Chantelle paused, choosing her moment before feinting: moving her left glove low to punch him in his midsection, but pulling it short, causing Rubin to flinch and instinctively bring his gloves downstairs to protect himself, leaving his head totally exposed – meaning that, when she threw her right cross and it connected with his jaw perfectly, the punch could have floored an eleven-stone middleweight, let alone a skinny hoodie kid who was just looking for a kiss.

*

When Rubin opened his eyes he didn't know where he was, but then saw Chantelle looking down at him and it all came back. She had already removed her gloves and was clutching the strap of her bag.

'I said,' – she heaved the kit bag onto her shoulder – 'if you lose, I get something from you.'

Rubin pushed himself up on his elbows, feeling his jaw on fire. He looked across the park for his four monkey friends, and spotted their retreating backs across the grass.

He said, 'Was that you giving it to me gentle?'

'It was.'

'I remember.' Rubin said, bringing his glove up to feel his face.

'East City gym. Next Wednesday at six. Be there.'

'What for?'

'Sparring practice. I need a new partner. And you never know,' she said, looking in the direction his mates had gone, 'you might find some better friends there.' She looked down at Rubin now. 'Keep the gloves. Bring them with you on Wednesday.' And then she got up and walked away.

That's when Rubin let his elbows give and collapsed onto his back on the grass. He stared up at the morning sky, wondering if his jaw was actually broken and, more importantly, how the fuck he was gonna get the boxing gloves off.

But then he smiled, realising he'd just got a second date.

The Dressmaker

by Deborah Freeman

'Do come in,' says Madame Colette Safran, beckoning. I may be sixty-nine, but this is my first ever visit to a dressmaker. A narrow corridor with a rich dark carpet leads to her workroom. The walls are lined with photographs in diamond-studded frames: women look radiant in fashionable settings; celebrities, ball gowns, sequins, men in bow ties. This could be a dream, except it isn't.

'So. Tell me how I can help you.'

'I have this dress. I bought it for a friend's wedding. Then I found the front was too low. For me, that is, personally. Embarrassingly low.'

'Really?' She raises an eyebrow. 'Let us regard the offending garment!' Her accent is French, or perhaps Belgian. She eases the dress out of its cover, rests it over the back of a crimson chaise longue. It lies there, limp, innocuous. Her posture is erect, soothing. There is something in her dark, watchful eyes, her gently regal smile: a veritable *curriculum vitae* pours out of me.

Myself. My mother (*late* mother). My husband. Our sons. Our daughter. I relate how Julia strayed for a while. Goth, anarchist, born-again, she is now a college librarian with an interest in refugees.

'And tell me,' purrs this dressmaker I selected from Yellow Pages Online, 'more about the dress. You say that your dear mother *instructed* you to find a dressmaker?'

Have I already told her that? I have been babbling.

'She did. Almost the last thing she told me, not long before she died.'

She died months ago. I'm supposed to have passed *the first stages of mourning*, as they refer to it in books. I'm supposed to be remembering the good things.

Tears threaten.

This is the moment when I turn my head and spy six pale anxious-looking women gathered around me. I frown at the first one, who frowns back. I look again and see the same woman to my right. The same to the left. And one over there in the corner. I notice the shabby tunic-top. *Mine.* Colette Safran's workroom is not simply hung with a mirror or two, as you would expect. Three walls are made of two mirrors each, nothing but mirrors. In the last mirror this woman, late sixties, coarse hair that needs a trim, turns towards me. Accusingly.

'*Et alors.*' Colette gathers our green dresses softly over her outstretched arms. I fix my gaze on her so I won't have to stare at these six illuminated versions of me. They stand in tight pantie-girdles and too-tight bras, stomachs bulging between the two garments. And their legs: not that fat, actually, but far too white. Venous estuaries above the knees gleam blue and purple. Our almost black support socks look dense, obsidian, vulgar.

'*Voila.*' Colette seems relaxed, unlike the six women, whose faces now freeze in one tight, puzzled, determined expression. Like my mother at the moment of death: she sat up straight, her mouth set stiff, not going gentle into any dark night, thank you, wide eyes glaring.

Mirrors surround me. The women in the mirrors share one expression. Nice to meet myself, at long last. I'm slipping into a cage of cold light. Self-awareness. At my age.

The mirror on the left flickers to get my attention. I turn round, my face close to Colette's. She is manicured, poised, made up. Me, I never wear make-up, I look my age; people stand up for me on the tube. Colette positions herself behind me. I feel the pressure of her hands as she pulls the dress half an inch higher. 'I will,' she explains, 'simply stitch it up on the shoulders, and then the low V will no longer be low!' When I wear it in future no one will get that view again, the sweaty creek between my two big breasts.

'So.' I take off the green floral dress, fling it on the chaise longue, put my trousers and shirt on quickly, whip my brush out of my shabby handbag and run it through my hair.

'We need to arrange a time for a fitting. When is convenient?'

I am standing with my back to the mirrors, my eyes on the front door, but I sense movement reflected in them nevertheless. My six doppelgängers frown in their reverse universe, their mouths open and close. I feel cold. I don't want this. But I don't intend to panic, just because I am in a room full of mirrors. I take out my diary and we plan the next fitting.

'That will be delightful,' she says.

We're saying goodbye. I wish Colette would close the workroom door but she doesn't, so I am still at the mercy of the mirrors as I cross the hall. The women seem wary, watchful. As I withdraw and they distance themselves I think they are whispering. To my relief they retreat, turning back into their mirror world, but, next thing, someone comes skipping past them towards me. A small figure. Yes, a small figure that runs, leaping towards me.

That is me! I'm five. My hair is dazzling auburn. I'm in the park. My young body, my one and only own little body is perfect. It can do anything. I can jump, skip and hop. My mother is peeling a banana for me, my first one!

I walk shakily out past the thyme and mint, real scents mingling with those coming back to life in Colette Safran's workroom. As the front door closes, I hear her phone ringing – the old-fashioned filigree silver version. I may be shaking but I'll have to return.

*

Tuesday, Colette welcomes me like a friend. She slips the dress on me casually, and the mirrors light up. I stand stiffly, view myself in all the mirrors at once. Six identical images. Or not, not exactly. Out of one corner, out of the grey glassy background, some movement. It's here, in the second mirror. A figure is slowly coming into view.

Is this a spirit, or a dream? No, not at all. It's me again, growing up now. What am I doing? I'm hurtling towards myself. Here I come. From fifteen to sixty-nine, teenage me races towards the present.

Or not. Not that either. Not out of the mirror. Teenage me is running just the way I did then. I run in and out of my childhood home. I am sprinting, breathless. From front door to kitchen, to biscuit tin, then back to front door. Yes, running, panting. Oh no, God, no. Before my eyes – this is the day I couldn't stop eating ginger biscuits.

Madame's hands smooth the dress to subdue a wrinkle, no, a wave, no, the tidal wave of chiffon which has appeared since my last visit here. There might be a fault, she says frowning. The alteration isn't working yet.

Can't she smell the ginger biscuits? They are in the cubbyhole in the kitchen dresser of my childhood. I'm at the front door, it's half past one, time to catch the bus back to school. Summertime. My emerald uniform skirt tightens week by week. This might be what teenage pregnancy feels like, but I'm not pregnant. Only pregnant with frustrations, hatred for my sister, resentment of my mother who tells me to eat when I'm not hungry and to stop eating when I am. All the while, I'm getting fatter.

The house stands between bus stops. Till now it was a game. You hear the bus stopping at Woodland Road, which means you have two minutes to run, in advance of it, to the St Michael's stop, and get there gasping for breath. An obsession I share with my sister, who today is not here. She's at school, skipping lunch, losing weight. The family pattern. We go like this: fat, thin, fat, thin; mother, daughter, sister, cousin. See us at weddings and Christmases.

I nip back inside to get a third ginger biscuit, then stand at the front door, sun on face, and crunch. My great monster of a greedy soul tumbles in the sky, swooping down to capture me in a tornado of need so strong that it lifts me a foot in the air. *Keep eating biscuits until the bus comes.*

I do. I do. And incredibly that same scene replays itself whole, all these years later, in Colette Safran's mirrors. There I go. Crunch, munch, watch for bus. Run inside, flip cubbyhole, get biscuit, reach porch, gobble, glance up the road, then run back for another one. Like a panting puppy, I play the game over and over again.

'*Et voila!* I see how to solve our problem.' With Colette's voice the taste of ginger leaves my mouth. 'I'm sorry, you will need to come back for another fitting.'

'Thank you for your hard work,' I smile falsely. She clasps my hands as I leave but I pull away. I could hate this innocent dressmaker, whom I hardly know.

*

Julia called earlier. For some reason (she's never cared before) she asked me about the dress, the dressmaker, and we got onto wedding dresses. She asked me what mine was like. Plain, I said, and on we chatted. I mentioned that my mother had motioned me not to speed towards the wedding canopy.

'Don't run,' she'd whispered, a twinkle in her eye. 'You'll knock the Rabbi over!'

It's Wednesday afternoon, two minutes to three. I've had time since the last fitting to reflect carefully on what is happening. I have a theory, so I skip past the thyme and mint. I know that today there will be a different scene in the mirror. A sweet one, and it will make me happy. Because my body did not remain unlovable, did it? Oh no, definitely no. How could I have forgotten! Size eighteen or not, I found love. I found love, and *it* found love too.

So today I will seek out *that* body in the mirror, and ignore the irritation of Colette's fingers, tugging gently at flaps of cloth that are still not behaving. I won't mind if the dress is not yet satisfactory. In fact I hope it isn't.

Because today I'm here willingly. Today I peer eagerly, my eyes avoiding hers. My past plays brightly in her mirrors, and it is my good fortune to have been alerted to this. Yes, there I am. I'm there in a white wedding dress, my husband beside me looking nervous. There is my mother, radiant in her fifties. Years younger than I am now! She puts out a hand. 'Don't run, darling.'

'We will need yet another fitting,' Colette's voice comes from very far away.

I'm immersed, now, in this game. I'm learning. The mirrors want to play with my past? Let them. I'll play too. And I'll choose my own moments.

Such as this one now, for example. Yes, this one. Here I am, moving purposefully through the glass walls of dressmaker time towards one night I *want* to remember. Through the shadows I see that night. A moment, walking across a shabby landing. It is that landing, the only reality now is on this landing. *That night.* What happens that night?

We've been together two or three years. We are building what people call a marriage, although I don't see it myself, this thing with that name, I see us.

We have a small furnished house on the outskirts of the city. The floors are fitted with lino which has an uneven relationship with the walls. Lino, never quite fitting snugly. Dark stains where moisture gets in. Damp from the windows, spilt coffee, spilt wine. I'm on the landing, my feet are cold on the threadbare carpet. Floral patterns, rhododendrons and roses. Bare patches are dull-brown puddles.

I'm walking across this landing, musing. Only men believe thinking and bodies belong in different spheres. What happened in there? That room? I turn round, and see the end of the bed, the Portuguese bedspread I bought for five pounds. Malcolm's feet are splayed in the half-light. In between three sensational orgasms, best ever, I'd been asking questions: who are we? Who is he? Who am I? Who was I? Who will I become?

Will I ever feel this again, this particular sensation of damp, richly scented Being Alive in the middle of a night? (What are the smells? Walking on a forest floor, perhaps. Bitter, dark, mossy perfumes.)

I stand at the cracked sink and turn on the tap. I see the flannel and soap. Imperial Leather. The flannel is brand new, the water hot, and I wash myself slowly, luxuriously. Two hooks wobble on faded tiles with blackened grouting. Whoever hammered them in, whoever those people were, they lived in a very grubby house. Me, I live in a palace.

By now I am half asleep, ready to go back to bed and cover my husband's sleeping body. That's what he does: falls asleep after sex, wakes up an hour later saying he's cold. An answer inscribes itself across my inner eye, even though I'm so drowsy I no longer know what the question was. But the answer is a shout, a revelation, a resolution. 'We are at peace, my body and

I. There is peace between us.'

'I'm happy with it as it is,' I tell Colette today, who keeps passing her thin fingers over the material, instructing it to behave.

'You may be happy my dear, but me, I am a perfectionist.'

At the next fitting I am in labour. By the time Madame Safran is inspecting her handiwork, checking whether she has it right this time, I am ready to give birth, one more time, to Julia! The miracle of the mirrors, I'll call it. I stare. My selves stare back. Then the pictures come.

Midwives, nurses, everyone dancing, and I'm singing. The slow movement of Beethoven's Choral Symphony. The rise and fall of the melody matches my contractions.

People in white wipe faces and hand me Julia. My girl, after two boys. Slippery but snug, carried by my body and ushered by it out into the world, Malcolm beside us looking pale. The smells of fresh blood, disinfectant, sweat, dissipate as Colette's voice closes a curtain over the mirrors. She's sweet, actually. I'm having a great time. Next week, another fitting.

*

I've absolutely got it. I understand what's happening. I've been entertaining myself in Colette's massive mirrors as a protection against *anxiety*. I would otherwise be far too fraught, forced to gaze upon my half-naked self. SIX MAGNIFICATIONS OF MY BODY IN MERCILESS LIGHT. This week I come with a jewel of a scenario in mind. I thought of it in the shower last night.

I am forty-three. My mother is sixty-nine, the age I am now. Julia is eleven. We are having a day out at Hampton Court, and my mother has provided the picnic. Her face is flushed by the sun, her arms harsh red in places, because when it's hot – we don't know if it's insects or not – she scratches obsessively. White skin, capillaries staining it at the slightest irritation.

'I've brought the same for each of us!' She puts three melamine plates on the grass. Two sandwiches, crisps, three pickled cucumbers, two tomatoes, three rounded fish balls on each plate.

'No fish balls thank you,' says Julia critically.

'But we're all having the same! Don't you see? Why not have

three like the rest of us!' My mother thinks Julia is too thin and it's my fault. At the end, her plate still holds a mountain of uncrunched crisps. My mother looks troubled.

'Your crisps, Julia. *Do finish them.* Look – our plates are empty!'

*

Colette seems to think she has solved the problem. One more fitting and the dress will be perfect. All she needs to do is unpick it again. She gathered too much material on this side, here. A whole centimetre or two.

'It would help,' she says, 'if you could stand up straight. And do me one favour. Don't keep tugging at your bra strap.' But I can't do what she asks. And why should I? I'm too uncomfortable.

'Please,' she repeats, 'your strap.'

But, like that day years ago when my will gave way to the ginger biscuits, it now gives way again. My reflections and I are unable to refrain from pulling at our bra straps, which slide inexorably over our shoulder bones – which are not like other people's. They are crushed. Our hands tug, stretching the dress a little. We eye Colette defiantly.

'This is getting out of hand,' she observes coolly. 'For some reason, you will not relax. Please. Do me the favour of becoming calm. *Ma pauvre*, you are tired of these fittings.'

I assure her benignly that I'm having a great time.

My six reflections catch me in the lie, and we all smile knowingly.

Their faces. All six of them, with that same self-knowing smug smile. Are they with me, these reflections, or against me? This time I drive away with a sense of having been caught out. Back home I can't stop thinking about them: their persistence, their ability to focus. Presumably I deserve their displeasure.

*

Warily, I have come for the last fitting. Colette busies herself with a new problem, her back to me, leaving me alone, half dressed, surrounded by my several selves. This time I look at them with real coolness, and they look back at me coldly.

It's as if they want something. They glare, all of them, with the same searching glint. Six pairs of eyes.

I put up a hand, in a gesture, and they all raise their hands at me. But then, suddenly, we split, we separate, yolks from whites, or whites from yolks, and they're free, or I am – or, actually, I'm not, because now they're beckoning, they're calling me, all of them, and it's in this moment of weakness that I become theirs. They reach out, pull me, out of the crimson room, and into the other place, their cold reflected world.

I am drawn back by the shameful betrayal of my very own reflections, to the room, the bed on which my mother lay an hour before she died.

*

I'm here first thing. I'm beside our mother on the day of her death. Again. From nine in the morning, I sit by her, in the small hospice ward that has opened its arms to us. My sister is due at one. My mother and I have until then. She is hooked up to oxygen, and morphine. She says quietly:

'I was going to ask you to put the post in a pile, and I'd sort it out when I get home. But then I thought: oh no, I won't be going home.'

A rattling behind me comes from a trolley, wheeled in by a bearded elder in a Stetson hat. I read Professor Edwards on his name tag.

'Morning tea, ma'am?' this volunteer asks.

'Do you have cold milk?' my mother asks.

'Ask the nurses,' he replies. 'What would you like for lunch?'

'What is there?'

'Soup. Fish. Potatoes. Green beans.'

'Is the soup *hot*?' my mother asks assertively.

He inclines his head. 'It will be so.'

'What were you a professor of?' my voice asks as if it means something, which surprisingly turns out to be the case.

'Geology,' he replies, scratching his beard.

I think of mountain ranges, valleys and rock faces, and that the universe is billions of years old.

'Find a nurse, darling. I'd like a glass of milk.'

Nurses are plentiful here, and I find one immediately. The

milk is full fat and cold, and my mother drinks it with appreciation.

'Was that alright?'

'Another, please.' I witness my mother drinking two glasses of milk at eleven o'clock, then hot soup at twelve – I steady the spoon. With my help she manages more than half the fried fish, mashed potatoes and green beans. And I read her thoughts. *I am calm because of the morphine, relaxed by the oxygen, but here's a discovery. My appetite is not bad, under the circumstances. I may be in a hospice, but I surely have a few good days left.*

No. Within an hour she will be dead, handled roughly by the ultrasound technician who will kill her by making her lie flat – the fluid in her lungs will burst like a dam and flood her heart.

That hasn't happened yet. At this moment, I'm experiencing an existentially illuminating revelation. I am counting the thousand connections between the threads of life, motherhood, food and bodies, so powerful they are death-defying. Metaphysical and feet-on-the ground at the same time. Descartes said, 'I think therefore I exist.' My mother teaches me, an hour before her death, 'I eat therefore I am alive.' Is it any wonder I have been a daughter on the plump side?

We set off for the ultrasound department. She is jolted from side to side by the geologist wheeling the iron bed, followed by me and now my sister who has, to my immense relief, come early.

The first time our mother dies my sister stays heroically beside her but can't stop shaking. Myself, I run away, too terrified. What kind of a mother is this, who has not taught us to accept her ending? 'Help us!' I shriek down the empty corridor.

I turn back into the moment, my heart thumping, and here is where the scene takes root, establishes itself, embeds. From now, it will simply keep happening. My mother dying her indelible death.

Her eyes roll back, right into her head. Her poor, poor head.

And me? I wish I had been able to show some real solidarity in the face of shock, instead of all that shrieking, leaping, escaping, shaking! But that's the way it truly was. That scene happened. So from now and for always it will roll like a box-office hit the minute it finds an opportunity. The truth. When I look at myself in any mirror, with honesty, it will be there.

I nod towards my reflections, and they nod back. It's a draw, I suppose, or stalemate or checkmate. Is it me or them, smiling in that grim and knowing way?

'Just for my satisfaction. Try this on one more time.' Colette's voice is crisp, but I refuse. So she sets about folding the dress, then swaddles it in tissue paper, placing it in a gold-fringed carrier-bag. Instead of handing me the bag, she sits down, folds her arms and nods, as if expecting me to sit down too and say something to her. Perhaps she wants me to explain my obsessive staring at her glass walls.

But I say my goodbyes standing, then turn to leave. I open the front door and see bees circling the herbs. She follows me to the path outside. I hold out my arm and wait for her to hand me the bag. I say, 'Thank you' politely, for her devoted work. Then I open the car, and toss the gold-fringed bag onto the back seat.

A Moment in Time

by Thomas Redjeb

His hand shook slightly as they sat together on the wooden park bench. They were spaced far enough apart as was socially acceptable for a first date, neither wanting to encroach upon the other's personal space, both second guessing if the other would even want this.

Looking down at his fingertips he could see them tapping lightly and, although he knew no one else would be able to see it, he felt as if the whole world was watching his slow anxious breakdown.

She was eyeing him now and he cursed inwardly as he met her glance, hoping she hadn't noticed his quirks. Something about her told him he needn't worry, but still, he wanted to be better for her, to achieve a level of cool-headed confidence he had never attained in his previous twenty-two years' experience. He was good at pretending, no one ever seemed to notice his anxiety, the way he clenched his fists, stared at his shaking hands or felt his heart pounding in his chest – slightly out of rhythm, which only worried him more. Still, people in his life would say that he was 'so chilled out' and 'so mellow', a sentiment which both reassured him that his anxiousness was not his defining feature, but also saddened him because it revealed that no one really understood him.

It occurred to him that neither of them had spoken for a long time now and so he turned to her, accidentally brushing his hand against her leg as he did so.

'Sorry,' he said.

She smiled and told him not to worry. Something about her attitude was calm, relaxed. As he admired her smooth legs, protruding from her loose-fitting black dress, he got the feeling she didn't mind his gaze. Still, he figured staring too long would be weird, perhaps not to her, but to anyone observing from afar. He often worried what people thought of him. Her attention had already drifted from him to the park and she seemed to see something there which pleased her.

'I love it when it's sunny like this,' she remarked. 'Don't you?'

This pleased him, because he did indeed enjoy sunny days, although he often felt a sunny disposition masked ugliness below the surface. Perhaps it was the fact that he knew it was fleeting, there was no way to keep hold of inspiring sights: soon they would fade away and be replaced by something bleak or broken.

But, not wanting to sound too crazy on their first date, he replied, 'Oh yeah, it's been great today.'

This probably came out more sarcastically than he had intended, but to his surprise he saw her mouth form a smile and she said, in a manner he could tell was heartfelt, 'It's perfect.'

The sentiment was so unexpected that he couldn't help but smile, and he felt her shift closer to him on the bench. She was mere inches away now, and he noticed her hand creeping towards his.

Earlier on in the date, they had walked by the river and he had longed to hold her hand. While she was speaking he had noticed her delicate fingers, which betrayed her own nervousness through bitten nails. But the moment for hand-holding never seemed to come – perhaps the other people walking by made him unsure, or maybe he simply didn't want to accept the fact that if he tried to take her hand she might reject him. He had settled for not holding her hand: that way he had not given her sufficient reason to leave, nor had he shown too much affection as to be off-putting. Sometimes he worried he thought too much.

He'd done this before, played the dating game. He'd got close to people, he'd even go as far as saying he'd experienced love. But, something about this was different. She was different. It was almost as if, if he touched her she might break, the perfect image of her might shatter like a mirror.

Something inside him yearned for her and, while he felt

anxious, the primal urge was stronger. He looked at her, their eyes meeting. It was not normal for him to look into a person's eyes, he found it unnatural to remain fixed upon someone and would often focus on something just behind them. With her though, it was different.

She was beautiful, he thought. She hadn't used much make-up, and she looked tired, a little pale, and had marks that were clearly the remnants of spots. But none of this mattered. The look in her eyes, earnest and honest; her chapped lips, rough but inviting; the curve of her smile, reassuring. Beauty was not the lack of imperfection, rather the fact that those imperfections told a story, the story of a person, of a life, of their emotions and their wants, desires, and dreams. He couldn't help but wonder if, looking back at him, she saw those same things.

'I want to do something...' he began awkwardly, 'but I don't know if you'll like it.'

She moved closer and laid a soft hand upon his. They lingered for a moment, both knowing what the other wanted. An unspoken bond shared between the two. Her lips moved towards his, his toward hers. His eyelids were dropping, ready to shut, a feeling of euphoria – alongside intense nervousness – gripping him. The hammering of his heart had begun and he knew that the next few moments would determine the path of his life. As a result of this moment, something would change.

Then, her lips touched his and it seemed as if they eclipsed his hesitation, his worries, his fears.

They were both lost, caught between physical action and mental reaction. His arms and hands seemed to move on their own, they moved higher, holding her back and pulling her closer. Then, just as quickly as the passionate outburst had begun, it ceased and the two moved apart, their hands still clasped together. He looked away, uncertain of whether the kiss had pleased her or not. He risked a glance her way and he could see her staring off into the distance again, smiling. Content, he relaxed slightly and leaned back against the hard wooden bench.

Looking ahead he couldn't help but feel different. There was something about that moment that was idyllic, so perfect. It was as if the world had frozen for a few seconds, a moment in time in which the sun hung at just the right point in the sky, so as to illuminate the lush grass, to highlight the branches of the trees, full of leaves, brimming with life.

Beside him, he could feel the heat radiating from her as she rested her head on his shoulder, still not removing her hand from his. The act was comforting and spoke to a new-found intimacy. He didn't want to speak, move or even breathe. If he remained still, he wouldn't ruin the moment. He wanted this to be theirs, this one perfect moment in time.

Yet, a moment cannot last forever, no matter how much one longs it to.

She removed her head and hand, and stood up. Looking back at him, sitting with a look of awe upon his face, she offered her hand again. Smiling, he took it, knowing that while one moment had passed, with her he had plenty more to look forward to.

Found and Lost

by Clare Marsh

It's so much harder to let Sam go this afternoon than when we left him at university last October. Today he gives me a hug, but it's obvious he's distracted.

'It'll be alright.'

'Will it?' I reach up to kiss his sandpaper cheek, inhale his aftershave. How I wish it was still his downy infant skin, smelling of baby lotion. I stroke his face with my hand, remembering.

'Come back in an hour, Mum, I'll introduce you then.'

'I understand. Whatever happens, your dad and I will always love you.'

'I know: *always and forever* as you say.'

With a grin he moves towards the hotel lounge and the plate glass doors swing shut behind him. It's as if the whole of Sam's childhood has vanished in a puff of insubstantial smoke and nothing will ever be the same.

When I sneak up to peer through the lounge door the receptionist raises an immaculate eyebrow contemptuously. I glare back. The agency advised us to arrange this meeting on neutral ground. Somewhere like this hotel. I watch Sam cross the room, then stop in front of a woman who struggles to her feet. Typical, she's both pretty and blond. I gasp as she stumbles into him, knocking her cup over. Sam reaches out his arms to steady her and they sit facing each other. A waiter dashes over to clear up the mess.

This is excruciating, like when I left Sam at nursery as a toddler then lurked outside to check he wasn't crying. As I make my retreat my bag jams in the hotel's revolving door, and then, blinking, I emerge into the sunshine, the heat so intense it's like another smack in the face.

The shops have lost their appeal, so I wander through the city to Riverside Walk and flop down on a bench in the dappled shade of a chestnut tree. A mother passes with her brood. There was a time when I couldn't watch other women with their children without breaking down, now I'm reminded of Sam's early years.

I smile at the gorgeous baby sitting with his mother on the next bench along, and am rewarded with a gummy grin, which reminds me of Sam at nine months. I only ever wanted to be a mum. Nothing else mattered.

I'd sell my soul to return to that time. Sam used to cling to me like a little koala bear, resisting being put down at all. He took hours to settle at night. Chris would say, 'Don't give in to him, Di, you'll spoil him.' But I knew Sam needed to be held close because the world was a black void when he was alone. In his mid-teens he became depressed, leading me to realise that some damaging experiences can't be put right by love alone. He refused to see a doctor or a counsellor, telling us not to make a fuss.

I hope today lays something to rest for him, but will one meeting be enough? What if it stirs up his old feelings of rejection? The agency has warned of the possible risks, but my headstrong lad wanted to plunge straight in.

The cathedral clock chimes. I wish the afternoon would evaporate in this heat haze so we could resume our lives as though this had never happened.

*

In the lounge I see my boy smiling, gesturing with his hands, looking animated. An unwelcome wave of jealousy washes over me.

'Mum,' Sam says.

'Yes?' Tanya and I reply together.

He laughs – it's the most light hearted he's been for years. 'That's right, I suppose you are both my mums.'

God, that hurts. I always knew he had a *birth mother*, but not another mum. Surely that was someone who was always there for you? Not a person who gave you away as a tiny baby, who didn't see you sit up, cut your first tooth or say your first word.

And I realise with a pang that I'd also missed those unique milestones. We were only introduced to our Sam when he was nine months old.

I'd fantasised she'd be slimmer and trendier than me, and she is, so now I worry that Sam will opt to stay with her during his university vacations. But genetics can be quirky as he looks nothing like her. I sense I've scored a point.

Sam tries again. 'Mum,' – he's looking at me this time – 'we've had a long talk, but Tanya wants to speak to you alone.'

This is a complete surprise. 'Mum, please.' He squeezes my hand and leaves us to call his girlfriend to tell her how his reunion has gone.

Tanya watches him leave. 'I hope you don't mind this? I wanted to say thank you for doing such a good job of bringing up my baby.'

'Your baby?' I spit the words out. 'You didn't want him.'

'That's not true. I'm adopted myself, and had the best childhood. I was only seventeen when I became pregnant – much too young to care for a baby – and I thought adoption would be better for him too.'

'Let's get this straight, Tanya, we didn't adopt Sam as a favour to you, we did it because we were desperate to have children. Fate dealt me a crap hand: I lost several babies early in pregnancy.' Tears are hovering. I dig my fingernails hard into my clenched palms to distract myself.

Now she's knocked over her empty cup again, and she's slurring her words. I can no longer contain myself. 'Besides, maybe Sam had a lucky escape.'

She looks stunned. 'What do you mean?'

'I noticed you stumbling about earlier and you sound pissed. Admit it, you're a drinker. My Sam deserves so much more from you than this.'

She crumples like a deflating balloon. God, the woman is crying. She doesn't win my sympathy, even when she concedes, 'I won't see him again if you think that's for the best.'

'Bloody wonderful, so now you're dumping him a second time.'

'No, it's not like that. I've done what I set out to do and

reassured myself that he's just fine, with a loving family and a great future ahead of him.'

She leans forward, losing her balance again and I sigh with frustration.

'What's the problem? Too much alcohol?' I'm on autopilot. This can't be me speaking. I sound bitter and vindictive after years of holding in my emotions.

She puts her head on one side, weighing me up before reaching under her chair and pulling out two walking sticks. 'I couldn't have got here today without a lift from my husband and these. I had no intention of telling you this today, but you mustn't get me wrong. Not now, not ever.'

'Go on.'

'Three years ago I had frequent falls. I became clumsy and forgetful. I went to my doctor and then for hospital tests. When they asked questions about my family I had little information about my birth parents. My genetic history was a virtual blank.' She pauses. 'Then they diagnosed me with a serious medical condition.'

My cheeks are burning. 'I'm so sorry I accused you of drinking.'

'Don't worry. Most people imagine that's the problem. I hope Sam didn't get that impression?'

'Probably not, they're so self-absorbed at his age.'

She continues. 'It's Huntington's disease.'

'But that's incurable isn't it?' I blurt out.

'There's no treatment, just medication to manage the symptoms and, yes, it is progressive. I didn't inform the adoption agency when they rang to say Sam had made contact. I wanted to meet him before it gets an even greater hold on me. It's reassuring that he's happy.' She paused. 'There's a fifty-fifty chance of him having the gene too. I'm a glass-half-full kind of person, so I hope and pray he will be alright. But now the burden has passed to you: you must choose whether to tell him and, if you do, help him decide about taking the test.'

'Perhaps ignorance is bliss?'

'Sometimes that's the best way to get through this dreadful disease. If he hasn't got the faulty gene there's no problem, and if he has, he can live life to the full before it hits without worrying. But… you should decide what's best. I was planning on writing to you via the adoption agency after today.'

I'm torn between overwhelming relief that she'll never take Sam away from me and fear that knowledge of this disease will have such devastating implications for us all.

In the new-found calm, we talk about Sam's early years and I show her the photos I'd grudgingly brought along at Sam's insistence, but never thought I'd share with her.

Sam returns and uses my phone to take selfies of the three of us together. Sam is in the middle, his arms round both his mothers. I promise to email the pictures to Tanya. We say our goodbyes and leave, as she has asked me to, before her husband collects her and without Sam detecting her mobility problems.

Later, in the car Sam breaks a long silence. 'I'm not sure I'll see Tanya again.'

'Much too early to say yet, Sam.'

'It's good you'll keep in touch with her by email though.'

'Sam, that's the least I can do.'

'Thanks for everything, Mum. I love you.'

*

Sam shoots out to meet his girlfriend as soon as we get home. I go through to the kitchen where Chris passes me a chilled white wine and gives me a cuddle.

'I've never needed a drink more in my life.' The tears are unstoppable as I give him a detailed account of the reunion.

Later, I research Huntington's disease on the internet. Strange, I always thought any potential hereditary risk would come from Sam's unknown father. Wrong. In the genetic shuffle at his conception the odds for poor Sam were three times worse than Russian roulette. I click on the Junior HD link and discover that only five to ten per cent of affected people show symptoms before they're twenty-one. So that's a relief.

Or at least it is until I read the article in more detail and the room spins. Last summer Sam had episodes of stiff muscles which he put down to too much sport. Sometimes in the past year he's been clumsy, forgetful and had mood swings. But isn't that true of any teenage boy? I'd attributed all his emotional problems to adoption and hoped today would resolve this.

The black shadow of grief descends again, taking me back to those desperate childless days.

'Chris, you need to come here now,' I shout.

Time's Corner

by John Ludlam

It all started with a task to research climate change for Geography. The old desktop PC was a birthday present to help with homework. Mole showed me how you could collect info using a web crawler, a special program he had set up. Everyone calls him Mole because he's always hiding somewhere in the dark, staring at a screen and connecting to the latest weirdsome thing he's interested in. He doesn't mind being called Mole and says there have been some very famous moles, and he will be famous in ten years' time but I'm not to tell anyone yet. Mole is a geek, he knows all about the internet, but still he couldn't help me get out of the mess I got into.

We have broadband at home so we're connected all the time. My parents say it's OK to look stuff up as long as I do everything I need for school. They come into my room to check sometimes, even though they don't understand what I'm doing. Anyway, I minimize the window when the landing creaks. That's the thing about our house. It's not like any ghosts roam about, but squeaks, clicks, and deep yawning sounds come from the walls as if there's a connection with other bits of the universe. My father says it's because our house is at the corner of Greenwich Road and Summer Close so we are living at time's corner, flipping between Greenwich Mean Time and British Summer Time. Whatever.

To nail our homework task – to research climate change – I used the web crawler. How was I to know the trouble it would cause? When I clicked the Go button, the message *WARNING!* flashed up. Well, Mole says that's normal. I stared at the screen. The machine hum became louder, turned into a throbbing, and the window showing the warning message got bigger, filling the whole screen, and then sort of overflowed, forming a bright flashing orange frame. As I looked away, shielding my eyes, I saw that the flashing lines were projecting scenes from old TV programmes onto my bedroom walls.

The room light went off and the room was dark except for these screens. One showed the first nuclear bomb explosion and then missiles being fired; the next showed forest trees being chopped down and a tsunami; on the curtains there were factory chimneys puffing out smoke, and then cars, buses and lorries all squeezed together in a traffic jam. Each screen repeated over and over in a loop. I looked behind me to see one showing starving children with round eyes staring at me.

I could see this was about how humans are destroying the planet. Well, I know this from TV and even from school. Looking back at the PC I saw two options, End or Next. I guessed End would stop the displays, so I clicked Next – well, wouldn't you? Then I stopped breathing when a window showed a fresh message:

'You can help save the world. First we train you. Then we give you a mission.'

There were two options, Accept or Reject. That's all, not a Don't Know or even Return Later. I decided to help save the world. Why not? I didn't think about being famous. I didn't think about how much trouble I'd get into. I didn't think about anything, except those staring eyes projected onto the wall behind me. I clicked Accept.

My room changed again. The walls became pale white and lines of small flashing lights strobed the ceiling, like in a shopping centre at Christmas. The PC monitor, now displaying a console, showed a new message: 'Welcome to Virtual Exotransporter 4D.'

I wanted to type, 'Who are you?' or something. Even to talk to someone like Mole, or Mum or Dad might have helped. I mean, where are your parents when you want one?

The Exotransporter started humming like a jet. Where were we going? I was off on a journey to who knows where, with who knows what in control, and I didn't have a clue what it meant by training and a mission. The more questions I had, the more the lights flashed. Looking at the screen I realised there were more windows showing different clocks and stuff. And now I understood the lights: they flashed when there was something on the console to look at. There were the answers to my questions: one window had a map which kept changing, and next to the clock I could see a line of numbers – at the end there was a year number which only changed slowly, until it stopped at fifteen-something.

*

'Hi. Call me Leo.'

I nearly jump out of my chair. At the sound of this voice, my room changes completely. It's like a room in some old painting, dark round the edges, but bright sunlight coming from a window. When my eyes get used to this, I can see there is someone else in the room.

He looks half like a wizard, the way he's dressed, but there are no stars or stuff on his cloak, and when he steps into the light the brightness is in his face. He is tall, standing next to a massive table covered with sheets of paper.

'So, you're wondering who I am. Good. The first thing is to question everything.'

I don't say anything, but he goes on anyway.

'Who we are is not important. Only what we do counts. Now, if you want to save the world, first try to understand the world.'

Understand the world! Does he mean everything?

'No, you don't have to know everything, but you will want to learn how to understand, and it's easy to start. We are given eyes to see with, but that's not the same as looking at something. If you want to understand why it is the shape or colour it is you have to really look. To start, choose something small, like this flower.'

He points to a small yellow flower in a vase on the table. I hadn't seen it earlier.

'Now you see the flower, but it's only a flower until the magic starts.'

I must be dreaming. Someone, please wake me! He pulls a drawer out of the side of the table and takes out a large sheet of paper filled with drawings.

'You don't really see something until its image has passed

through your eyes to your brain and your brain has made your hand copy it. When you look at something to draw, your brain slows down because it has to learn to do something new. You learn to think differently when you make an image of an object.'

He takes out a clean sheet of paper, picks up a black stick, breaks it and gives me a piece. Slowly he draws an outline of a petal in one corner of the sheet, then he pauses and points at a space near his drawing. 'Now your turn, you draw a petal.'

I knew he was going to say that! But I can't draw.

'You will be amazed at what you can do, especially when you let your brain try a new experience. Copy what I do. At first, don't try to draw a flower; draw the shape of the spaces that you see.'

I draw a loop for a petal on my side of the paper. He doesn't say anything but draws another petal. I copy him. We carry on till we finish the outside and the inside petals on our drawings. This is cool.

'Now we can show the light in the image by showing the darkness, and the shadows.'

He flicks a few diagonal dashes across his drawing, and then some more so I can see what he means. I do the same.

'Good, you have started. Keep drawing. Draw anything that makes you wonder why it's there or how it works. It's not the final sketch that's important, it's the act of drawing, because by drawing you learn to see; you start to look at the world and understand how it works.

'In my life I have had to paint and design, sometimes for weapons of war, which is the worst kind of madness. Drawing has helped me see the life in nature, and the chief gift of nature is freedom, freedom for everyone to enjoy life. I haven't finished my work yet but when it's your turn you will remember this, and you will do things to save the world from the madness of hate and war.'

The light fades, and the walls of the room wobble like jelly.

*

Then I was back in my own room, back to whatever normal used to be and back to school the next day. I wondered what

Leo meant about drawing, and how it would help me save the world. I started doodling.

What had happened was way too weird to explain to anyone except Mole. When I told him about the Virtual Exotransporter and meeting Leo, he was interested, but when I told him how drawing makes you look at the world differently, he made it seem like I was wrong to tell him. We could be friends as long as he explained the Web and stuff to me, but he went off when I tried to show him some drawings I had done. It wasn't just that he wasn't interested, he actually seemed to like me less because of it.

We started spending lunchtimes apart, and he stopped coming over to mine after school. Then he joined the gang at school. Why? Usually everyone tries to keep out of the gang's way.

It was after football, on the playing field at the back of the school beyond the car park, that I first saw him with the gang. I had stopped to tie a loose bootlace. Mole came over. He looked strange, like he was staring at me to make himself look hard. The gang crowded up behind him.

Mole spoke strangely, even for him. 'This is it. You are going down.' Like in a film. Now it was my turn to be beaten up and left for dead.

It took longer to get home afterwards but Mum didn't say anything, she probably didn't think anything was wrong. If she did, she must have thought it was from football – I usually get messy at that. And I didn't say anything, you don't. School policy is you're supposed to talk to someone, but we all know about the gang, except teachers and parents who couldn't do anything anyway. Is understanding about the world worth this? It was going to be hard enough staying out of the gang's way.

That night I had to write an essay on French peasant life for History homework so that's what I searched for. The results were scrolling up when a message appeared.

'For Help click OK.'

Help with what? I clicked OK anyway.

Whoosh! My room became the Virtual Exotransporter 4D

with flashing lights and that engine throbbing sound again. I tried to see from the console where I was going but it was too quick. Fifteen-something flashed on the clock dial so I expected to see Leo again, only it felt different to last time. The Exotransporter noise faded, everything became quiet and still. Spooky.

*

I am in a massive room. There is light from some windows but all I can see is shed-loads of books, zillions of them, all round the walls.

'Don't worry about all the books!'

This time my guide is a man in plain black, and the room is marvellous. Even in the roof there is all this weird writing. Why am I here? What is it with all these books?

'I will explain, oh, and my name is Michel. You must be visiting from the future world. I've not had many visitors recently.' He laughs. 'Well, the laws of the universe permit you to search for wisdom, but you have ended up here with me – never mind! Welcome to my small castle.'

Castle? I get a look out through a window and instead of a row of houses there is a forest in the distance.

'Tell me, do they still teach logic and Latin and Greek in your school? Or are there new facts and new languages to learn? Oh, it's all good, but it doesn't help with how to live, make friends, get on with others, and be true to yourself. What do you think?'

It is difficult to say anything when everything is so weird, so he goes on. 'For sure there will be evil, injustice, and wars too in your future world. So, everyone who wants to should learn how to live and be happy in an evil world.' He starts searching for something along one of his shelves. 'Let's listen to what those who have lived with evil say to help us.'

He stretches out to take a book, but he's too far away and doesn't grasp it properly. I see it's going to drop, so I jump across to catch it, and the floorboards creak just as they do in my room. Weird. I retrieve the book and hand it back to him and he fingers through until he finds something, and reads out loud, '"Courage in the unfortunate is respected even by an enemy, but cowardice, even if successful, is held in contempt," says Plutarch. He was a Greek.'

'One of the Ancient Greeks?'

'Ah, you know something of them then, but that's not important.'

What is? I wonder.

'Being brave gets you respected whoever your enemies are. Plutarch was writing about Roman soldiers who were trained to obey orders. Cowardice was punished by their commanding officer, in order to make Roman soldiers more afraid of their own officers than of the enemy.' He reads some more. '"True victory is battling bravely, it's about how you stand up in the fight, not about coming through safely." That's what the Romans themselves thought.'

He must know about the gang.

'But the Roman soldier was also loyal to other soldiers and would fight to save them if they were in danger. And that's another good principle. If you know someone who's in trouble from an enemy, you can help by joining with them. Even a few who agree together can resist someone who tries to rule over everyone.'

He begins to fade and the walls of the room race towards me.

Back in my room the console has become my PC again. This has been a different kind of experience from meeting Leo, and more training for something – but what? I still don't know what I have to do for my mission.

*

The gang had picked on others before me, like Stick. His name is short for Stick Insect because nobody could remember his real name, and we couldn't keep calling him Stick Insect, it was too long. Stick had arrived from somewhere else, he wouldn't say where. Although he can speak better English than any of us, I've been told he speaks a different language at home.

Stick was very surprised when I said the gang were getting me too. He was more surprised at what I said next, 'Together we can resist the gang, like the Romans against their enemies.'

'I agree that if we are together it will be harder for the gang to pick on either one of us. So I will join with you – on one condition.'

'OK, what?'

'You stop calling me Stick.'

But then we had the problem of what to call him, because he didn't like either of his real names which were Ivan and Stichovich. He didn't like Ivan because he knew he'd be called The Terrible, and calling him Itch would be worse. I told him he was stuck with Stick.

The way Mole had looked and spoken when the gang came after me that first time, I knew something had been wrong – like the gang had made him start on me because we had been friends before. I had to find a way to rescue him from the gang, even if he said he didn't want to be rescued. But things started going wrong when I tried to persuade Stick to help.

'If there's trouble we will have a fight, which we will lose and lose well.'

'Not helpful.'

I tried to think of a way to make it seem like the right thing to do, so I said, 'We need to form our own gang.'

'Then we'll have gang fights.'

'I want us to be different – to fight for freedom, we could be freedom fighters!'

'The freedom fighters of Hatchett School,' says Stick sarcastically.

That's how we started. At least calling ourselves freedom fighters meant we weren't wimps. Once we were known, and people knew we would stand up to the gang, more people wanted to join us. OK, not all new recruits added much, but it still felt like we were starting a resistance movement.

There was mega trouble because we had a name and the gang didn't, apart from 'The Gang', of course. It was like, who were we to be so clever we should have a name?

All we did was spread the word. Anyone, well, almost anyone, could join us, but you'd think it was a whole new era from the way things changed. First the teachers got spaced out, looking and acting stranger than usual. Then they told us there was to be a Wozza, a Whole School Assembly, the next day.

There was a bit of trouble having to sit in our core groups in the Performance Theatre. We nervously eyed members of the gang who were now sitting next to us or behind our backs. When things got settled, Dr Batteram stood up to announce, 'There will be no gangs in my school.'

That made it seem like we were real gangs, and that I was a gang leader.

Then she said, 'Staff will act,' which got a snigger and, 'Violence will be stamped out.'

We looked at the staff. They looked at the floor. I didn't think much of our chances. As soon as we got out of the Wozza we got into our gangs, huddling together as we walked down the corridor to our next class. You have to stay with your gang at all times; if you get split off, the others can get you.

That's how we rescued Mole.

*

One of our new recruits was Scarrot. He had fluorescent red hair so from day one you could always see him coming, and the first who did was legally bound to say, 'It's Carrot', but that got shortened to Scarrot. Also, because Scarrot stood for scary in a weird sort of way. Scarrot has this look of being scared the whole time, hair all sticking up, staring eyes, and white face. People moved away from him when they could. We said we'd let him join us if he helped in our plan to rescue Mole.

Stick and I psyched Scarrot up to go across the car park towards the gang, who always hung out there in breaks. He got half way and one of them shouted, 'Scarrot!' That distracted the gang. I hung back while Stick went round the edge by the wall. Stick called Mole over. At first Mole looked worried, but when he saw that Stick was going to help him, he realised this was his chance to get away from the gang.

The other members of the gang were all looking the other way, trying to decide what to do about the advancing Scarrot – no one was supposed to go near the gang unless they were one of them. So Mole slipped away towards Stick and they both edged back to the Break Arena. Then Big Miff, the gang leader, saw what was happening and ordered Mole to return or he would be got. The rest of the gang realised Mole was being taken, and so there was a chase as they ran after us across the

Arena. They caught up with us, of course.

We had to turn and face them. Then everyone looked at me as if I really was their leader. Everyone expected me to fight back, so I stepped forward. The gang included all the best fighters, and the tallest was Scrag. His name might have been Craig in the remote past but he never wanted to be called that or anything else. Miff only had to call on Scrag, give him an order, and Scrag would do it. So when Miff called, 'Scrag', he stepped forward to face me, or rather leer at me. He knew he had more practice at fighting, a lot more practice. As the 'Fight, fight, fight!' chant started up, I remembered about the Romans 'battling bravely'. I thought 'it's about how you stand up in the fight' just before I got knocked down.

The strange thing is, Michel was right. When I walked into Maths late, people round the class said stuff like 'Well done', 'You put up a good fight', and 'They won't treat us as rubbish anymore', even though I hadn't wound up victorious against Scrag.

I thought about that fight for weeks after, because even though I lost, things seemed different. First, everybody said I was a leader. More scary was the idea that just by being there I had changed things. Since I wanted to change the world, trying to make things better for people felt right. This is different to how I used to feel about school. Instead of just trying to survive, I could start to make changes.

So, the next time the PC became the Exotransporter I was ready for it, or so I thought. I concentrated hard on the console to see the number by the clock. It flipped over to 1500.

*

My room disappears; have I disappeared too? Everything is black, and it's freezing! What's that noise? I'm outside, it's a howling gale. Yuk! I'm standing in something squelchy.

'Come with me!'

A cold sharp voice. I can't see him, whoever or whatever is speaking – a chiller, this one.

Gradually I make out the black sky, slices of moon light up huge clouds being pushed along by the wind. I pull up my hood. When had I put my hoodie on?

'My name is Niccolo. That is all I shall tell you about myself.'

I begin to see him, tall and thin, almost covered by a dark cloak that keeps the weather out.

'You shall accompany me on my mission to serve my master. You will see what it takes to be a leader of men and how authority is imposed by force. And you will see things few people ever see in their lives.'

He's bad enough, whoever he is, so I don't want to meet his master.

I follow him until we are on the edge of a hill. There are lights from distant buildings and some towers, which are all packed close together. Over on the left there's movement. Somebody rides a horse from one place to another, stopping to check something, then there's a flame and a flash. The whole universe explodes with a roar and more lights. I see shapes of guns, which look like cannons. Small crumpling sounds come from where the buildings must be. A light in the town becomes bright red with flames and turns into a blazing fire. There's shouting and smoke, and a smell like fireworks on bonfire night gets in my throat.

'My master commanded the assault on the town. For the many to live in freedom and comfort it is necessary that the few who would destroy that freedom are eliminated as quickly as possible. But, more than that, they must also suffer in a way that deters all future destroyers of our liberty.'

I don't know why the town has to be attacked, but I can't bring myself to think the question. The wind and noise block out everything but this man.

'In our demon-possessed land, trust nobody. No one is true to each other, only to their greed, whether of the stomach or the purse.'

All these cannons. The town doesn't stand a chance. Everything is fading, the hill is turning to swamp, I'm sinking....

*

The console glowed.

'Thank you for connecting. The system has experienced a malfunction.'

Back again. What was it with these – whatever they are – who offer me vague advice and expect me to use it to change the world? I tried to talk to Dad about it, but he said I have to live in the real world. What does he know? – stuck in his car on his way to the office every day, polluting the planet.

Now school became weird. More than usual. It started with Stick, of course,

'It's not my fault, my father is in trouble at the station.'

'Police station? Bus station? Space station?' I ask.

He looked at me, ice-cold.

'They say my father has overstayed.'

'What does that mean?'

'He is to be classified as illegal. Now all of us have to return.'

'At last, I am talking to a real alien!'

He ignored my joke.

'First we go to a concentration camp while we wait for our appeal to be processed. Then, if we are unsuccessful, we are deported.'

This didn't sound fair. Word got round school pretty fast, and even the gang seemed to want Stick to stay. Big Miff said so, so the rest of the gang agreed. We all needed Stick around to make fun of, and so that he could make fun of the teachers: Stick read course books from back to front so he could take out the Teach with back-to-front questions. The number one priority was to stop Stick being taken. So we grouped up Stick, Mole, Scarrot, Big Miff, me, while Scrag glowered.

'Ideas?' said Stick.

'Take them out,' said someone.

'Take who out?'

'Protest.'

'Yeah.'

Up popped Mole. 'Stick a picture of Stick up in school, like a Wanted poster, make it scary.'

Scrag leered, 'Wanted – Ivan Stichovich dead or alive,' like the sound of it appealed to him. Stick's face started to collapse in on itself.

Mole ignored him and explained, 'No, I mean, it'll be ironic. We'll show them that it's not right he should be branded a criminal when he's not done anything wrong.' That stopped the chatter.

I thought of all those cannons and said, 'We need to print as many copies as we can and post them up all round the school.' Each poster would be a cannon and the school was the town – a co-ordinated attack.

We selected a digital image of Stick, and Mole printed enough for us to plaster them across the school buildings overnight.

As expected, the teachers all got spaced out, and there was another Wozza. The piranha stood up. 'Blah di government policy blah, need to accept democratic decision-making....'

Someone called out, 'We can protest, can't we?'

A giant hush cloud descended over us, as we all waited to see who would get the poisoned sting. Her X-ray vision scanned the theatre. Painful.

'No. There will be no protests. Not in school. Certainly not in public. This is something Parliament decides.'

So, our plan had failed. The hundreds of poster-cannons hadn't hit their mark. But Dr Batteram's words opened the next door: Parliament. How could we change their minds?

That was when Mole came to the rescue. Turns out his mother knew the local MP, Felicity Coleman. Mole had seen how things worked. He got us all to write letters to her, making a case for Stick. We even got Dr Batteram to write one, now that we were going about things in the right way. These were our cannonballs, hundreds of individual missives. The letters were all about how young Stick would be emotionally damaged by removal of himself and his family, how it would impair his life chances for him to be taken out of school, and how if his potential could be realised through continuous education he would be an asset to the school and, in time, to the country. We had to laugh, but it's called putting a spin on it.

Everything went quiet for a week, then things got real. A question was asked in Parliament, Hatchett's School was mentioned, and his family's appeal was granted. Now Stick is a national icon for freedom. Mission accomplished.

Instead of getting expelled, we got careers advice. Stick says he will go to uni, Mole is set for a job in IT, Miff wants to do social work, and, more scary, Scrag will apply to the Police! Scarrot thinks he wants to be a teacher.

Me? Now I know that anyone can change the world, and, if you can help a friend, maybe that's enough for starters.

Bridal Veil and Visions in Red

by Shirley Muir

Four days ago they bombarded him with a massive blast of chemotherapy.

It preceded the gruelling, life-threatening – yet potentially life-saving – stem cell transplant.

'Ass-till-bee,' Angus said last week, as he looked at the sumptuous red and white plumes of the perennials. 'That's how you pronounce it.'

He'd selected 'Visions in Red' and 'Bridal Veil' during his last visit to the flower nursery.

Then he'd planted the six Astilbes, three white and three red, on opposite edges of the lawn, as dusk fell on the night before his hospital admission. He'd carefully selected Astilbes: a colourful option for a shady back garden, easy to look after, the label said, provided they had enough water.

She'd promised to water them.

*

People didn't ask, 'Is he going to die?' or 'Will he be alright?'

Three months earlier she had been ready with optimistic phrases, 'I'm sure he'll be fine' or 'They're going to start treatment right away', trotted out with equivocation. Angus, on the other hand, struggled to find a response to people's concern and cautious enquiries.

She watched the facial expressions of the recipients at the awful news, and learned. Some muttered nervously things like, 'It's amazing what they can do nowadays.' She considered it banal, but wondered what the right reply was. Managing

---

First Published in *Insights: Fifteen Stories Exploring Disability* (Claret Press, 2018).

friends' reactions was going to be a challenge.

'Is there anything you need?' his cousin from Cheshire had asked.

'Yes,' she thought. 'I want this all to be a bad dream. I want to wake up.'

Instead she said, 'He loves crosswords, don't you, Angus? Perhaps a crossword book.'

She didn't say, 'Please don't give him novels about people with cancer,' which is what Auntie Jill had innocently done, bless her. Or worse still, books called 'Beat the big C'. Because if he dies then it will be his own fault.

She walked along the pathway by the dual carriageway in her smart belted raincoat, breathing in the toxic fumes belched out along the city's teeming ring road. A relentless thunder of cars and trucks sped past to oil company offices, to the city's conference centre or to catch a flight from the airport. Her hair was whipped up by the slipstream of the juggernauts that growled up the hill and down to the industrial estates or onwards to pollute the air of Peterhead and Fraserburgh.

At the red 'H' sign she pressed the pedestrian light and brought the vehicles to a purring, humming halt, venting their dirty discharge into a quietened atmosphere. Then she crossed four lanes of traffic. She could have walked blindfold to the main entrance of the massive teaching hospital.

The car park was always overwhelmed, with walkways blocked by cars and the aisles a constant stream of frustrated and complaining drivers, people who'd had to drop off their loved ones instead of trudging hand in hand with them to scary appointments, or to check in for surgery. Some had driven over a hundred miles for their consultation and surely deserved a parking space. So she walked from her house, and gathered her thoughts. She wondered if her walking pace slowed as she got nearer.

In the crowd that milled about in the hospital shop, dressing-gown clad patients mixed with those who were free to go home. She picked up a copy of The Times and browsed the magazines, chocolate bars, toothpaste and cheap children's toys. No crossword books.

The nurse greeted her warmly and said yes, he was well enough to have her visit today.

She had waited for the call. Only one visitor would be permitted to enter the isolation room during his indeterminate stay there. She was that person. For days she had suppressed her need to touch him, stroke his cheek, plant a kiss on his forehead, because he was untouchable and she was unsafe.

She had worried that she might fall ill with a cold or stomach trouble and then they wouldn't give permission for her to do more than see him through the glass panel in the door.

She panicked sometimes that he might never be well enough for a visitor and she'd miss the chance for any contact with him at all. Ever again.

Outside the door to his room she pulled on pungent, powdered, latex gloves and fastened the fiddly fabric ties of the obligatory face mask. Then the nurse helped her to cover her long, thick hair within the protective cap.

She knew that the chemo bombardment would almost kill him, then they'd embark on bringing him back from the brink, infusing his veins with life-giving stem cells. He would be given his own stem cells. They'd 'cleaned them up a bit', the consultant said, sounding colloquial yet indicating compromise. His six siblings were tested for compatibility and not one of them was a suitable match. Close sibling matches give the best result, the consultant said, not your own blood cells. But we're going to try it, he said.

Fighting his leukaemia meant Angus's immune system might let him down badly. He could die from a sore throat, today or in a year's time. And she could inadvertently infect him with something when she visited. He'd have to avoid crowds of people who exhaled bacteria and viruses, sneezed into the air that he must breathe, or even touched him with non-sterile hands. No supermarket trips, science fiction films at the cinema, tea and chocolate cake in John Lewis's café for a while.

Having been checked as safe by his nurse she turned the door handle and quietly entered the sterile room, as she'd seen through the glass that his eyes were shut. Imagining armies of powerful stem cells storming into his bloodstream through the narrow transparent plastic line that fed into his vein, she visualised them dashing to his rescue, although the infusion looked like an ordinary flow of blood. She encouraged them in whispers to hurtle through his veins, seek their new home, conquer the enemy and colonise his depleted bone marrow.

'I've brought you a newspaper,' she said through the mask, and his eyelids flickered.

A ghostly white figure on white sheets in a bright sterile room. She remembered the final scene of *2001: A Space Odyssey* with a frail body lying in a similar white room, dying. It was their favourite movie, they watched it when they first met.

Weak as a kitten, his face waxen and his head pink and hair-free, his attachment to life seemed no stronger than a thread. She prayed that the mask disguised her terror as well as it concealed her pallid countenance.

From the surreal blandness of the bed in the isolation room his azure eyes fluttered open. There's nothing pale or weak about the colour of his eyes, she thought. That blue gaze pierces my soul. It mirrors the colour of the Mediterranean where we snorkelled hand in hand through blizzards of silvery fish, the warmth of the sea caressing our bodies as we weaved through crowds of oblivious, rainbow-hued creatures. Some bold fish even stroked a leg or an arm, tickling our tanned skins.

That was only last year.

Through dry, flaking lips he croaked, 'Hello.'

She slid onto the hard upright hospital chair that someone had recently sterilised. Every item in this room was germ-free.

'I watered the Astilbes,' she murmured. 'They're doing well in this nice warm weather.'

She laid the newspaper on the bed, within reach of his motionless, skeletal hand with the white plastic tap delivering new life into a blood vessel.

'Sorry,' he mumbled, opening his eyes after a brief, unintended snooze, 'I can't concentrate. I can't read the headlines, but do leave the newspaper. You never know....'

His eyelids fell heavily as consciousness petered out. With one latex-gloved hand she picked up his hand, still brown from the June gardening stints in summer sunshine. It wasn't real touching, but she felt the warmth through the latex that signalled the life that trickled through his fragile body.

*

Each night, as twilight came, she conversed with the new occupants of the garden. She sluiced cool water onto their roots.

'Have a little drink, Astilbes,' she said. 'Grow strong and healthy.'

In the gloom she told them how he was. How he asked after them.

*

His face lit up each time she entered the white room.

During the hours she sat by him her heart stood still. Those times together were uneventful, but she knew they were precious like jewels. She collected the jewels in a box in her head, in case she needed them later.

'I did twelve across,' he said, huskily, one day. It was the same crossword from days ago, just after the transplant. The newspaper was dog-eared. She wondered why they didn't need to sterilise incoming newspapers.

'I'm sorry, I have no conversation, not in here with no connection to the outside world.' He slid back onto the soft pillow.

'I'm not interested in the Middle East or the price of milk or the train strike.' The smile was inside her mask, but she knew he could recognise a smile in her eyes. 'Just you.'

She waited for him to tell her to take note of current affairs, to be aware of the world around her, to care about the actions of statesmen, of politicians, of presidents. At his suggestion she'd learned, when they first married, about dictators ruling the nations of the Middle East, about countries applying desperately for acceptance into the European Union. She'd read about the goings-on in Parliament and about why the people of Scotland wanted independence.

Now she wanted him to ask her what was happening in the world outside, the place where she lived, where the Astilbes lived. The place that waited for him.

'Three more clues yesterday,' he said, 'in an hour.' His breathing was laboured, he wheezed, infection lurking behind each word he uttered.

'I got Sisyphus, the over-proud king who had to push a large boulder uphill forever as a punishment. Then I fell asleep.' His body was racked by a coughing fit.

Looking up at her, he said, 'Did you water...?'

'I did, and the flowers are out now, so pretty. The red ones on the left side of the garden are taller than the white ones on the right.'

'There used to be a compost heap there, that's why,' he panted, the effort straining his lungs. His eyes closed and the wheezing grew loud. It hurt her to listen, and be impotent.

He'd remembered about the compost heap and their hopes for Galapagos-dimension progress from the geraniums and fuchsias and begonias they'd planted last year. That was when they'd discovered extraordinarily fertile soil on the left side of the garden.

*

A week later the nurse said she could enter the room without gloves, that she could hold his hand.

Her fingers crept across the white sheet to meet his. Their skin touched, a spark of electricity across the void. The blue eyes gazed into her green ones.

His damaged lips had healed enough to allow sips of mushroom soup. The soup reminded him that the lining of his mouth was scored with deep, stinging ulcers.

'It rained torrentially in the night on Sunday,' she told him, 'so your Astilbes didn't need water. They've got big flowers now. Six inches, each one, Bridal Veils and Blood Red Visions.'

'I heard the rain splashing off these windows,' he rasped, and sank into the pillows. 'They prefer rain water, you know. It's better than tap water. What's the chemical in tap water?'

'Chlorine,' she said. He nodded.

She mopped a dribble of mushroom soup from his chin.

'I've done nearly half of that crossword,' he said, dazed by his own success.

She nodded.

'You mustn't do any, though,' he gasped with surprising energy. 'It's a barometer for my recovery.'

She smiled. Then he drifted away.

*

One day she was startled to find him sitting on the side of the bed in his outdoor clothes. A white paper bag sealed with a pharmacist's label stood beside him. It bulged with boxes and packets of life-saving medication. Antibiotics, mouthwashes, painkillers, anti-sickness, gut adjusters.

He handed her the crossword, then laid his hand over hers.

'Fifteen down,' he said. A smile cracked his dry, white lips.

'Bestial wild flower, seven letters.' She screwed up her nose. Then she grinned. 'Anagram,' she said, 'Astilbe!'

She stuffed the bulging bag of life-saving potions into his holdall along with the pyjamas, crossword book and unread old newspapers.

'No, I don't need a wheelchair,' he'd grumped. 'I'm not incapable, you know.'

Leaning heavily on her arm he walked like a frail, sick man. He raised her hand and brushed it with his scratchy, damaged lips. Tears trickled unexpectedly down her face. Together they shuffled towards the EXIT sign at the end of the corridor.

She realised that the comment, 'It's amazing what they can do nowadays' wasn't banal at all. During the cancer battles they'd fought over the last twenty years, he'd benefited from monoclonal antibodies, specialised radiotherapy treatment for his eye, and now this revolutionary stem cell procedure. Each new option was a miracle that had increased his grip on life.

'I never expected to walk under this sign again,' he puffed, and halted for a moment, drained by the physical effort of the very short stroll. She stifled her desire to call for that wheelchair.

'Well, the Astilbes are expecting you.'

Absent Friends and New Acquaintances

by David Perlmutter

It was pretty simple how we met, really. We were both at the costume party, and we hooked up based on our common interests.

Well, there *was* a little more to it than that, yes.

It's easy to spot people who aren't on Computron these days: it's anyone who looks like they know what planet they're on, and like they belong in this place. And they're a vanishing race. Me, I have no use for people with their heads in the clouds, so I avoid them.

And she looked like she had the same attitude.

I spotted her over by the punchbowl. You couldn't not see her – at least I couldn't. Tall, with bright red hair, red sweater, white skirt, and white shoes. The spitting image of who she was trying to be from TV. From a show long since gone, but well-remembered by those who saw it. At least, it would be if you're American, and you have a good working knowledge of early twenty-first century pop culture. You can't count on that anymore, because nobody pays attention to what's being made now, let alone what was made then.

I hoped that my similarly-designed outfit, based on another analogous character from another show of that era and type, was accurate enough for her to know a) who I was supposed to be and b) that I was tolerable enough to be thought of as a romantic figure, just like my TV role model hoped to be thought of vis-à-vis his particular crush. Thus far that night, strikeouts at both ends.

So I gathered myself up, cleared my throat and spoke to her.

'Shouldn't you be out busting your brothers?' I asked.

Fortunately, she smiled pretty wide, as if to say to me: *You know who I am!*

'I should be asking you the same thing about stopping all that weird supernatural crap that happens on your show. Or maybe just keeping your goofy twin sister in line, huh?'

I gave her the same smile she gave me, with the same meaning.

Then we hesitated as to what to say next. We clearly had something in common. Neither of us had that glassy-eyed look you get when you take Computron pills and can project the internet right in front of your face for hours and hours, just using your hands the way you used to use a mouse in the old days. We two were outsiders who refused to play by the rules of our time by following 'trends' and doing what was expected of us – just like those we impersonated. But was it enough to give us a connection beyond that?

Fortunately, she broke the silence.

'It must've really been hell coming down here in this weather, dressed in that getup,' she said. 'My damn legs are still freezing from walking down here. Stupid winter!'

'Yeah,' I responded. 'This is what happens when two fictional characters made for summer end up stuck in the middle of winter. But you took a bigger risk, since you've got longer legs to freeze.'

'I suppose,' she answered. 'Do you think anybody here knows who you are?'

'Not a clue,' I said. 'They figure me for some kind of twelve year-old.'

'Well, that's who he was.'

'Unlike me. It's not fun being a short guy, you have to look up to everybody.'

'Better than hitting your head on stuff all the time, and having to get things down from the shelf 'cause you're the only one who can reach them.'

'There are bad sides to everything.'

'You know something? I think the two of them could have made a good couple if there'd ever been a crossover between the shows.'

'You think?'

'Sure. He was real good at finding out the truth about stuff –

even if he didn't want to. She wanted to find a sure-fire way of making sure her mom saw what her brothers were doing, in an honest, no B.S. kind of way. Sounds like a good match.'

'Too bad it didn't happen.'

'Not in *their* worlds.' She extended her hand for me to take, as if she were an Elizabethan lady invited to dance. 'But that doesn't mean it can't happen in *ours*.'

'And with no Computron involved at all,' I said. 'Fabulous!'

And so, we got together and danced. And we decided to stay together after, from then right up until now.

And nobody had better tell us TV cartoons from way back in the twenty-first century, viewed and reviewed on ancient DVDs, aren't good for anything. Because we know better.

Gift of the Sky God

by Arthur Carey

Marshalling all the strength in his barrel-shaped body, Og leaned into the rock and pushed. Muscles and sinews rose in bold relief along his powerful shoulders and arms. At last the rock yielded, and a humid breeze swept away the musty air of the cave.

He stepped onto a rocky ledge and breathed in the familiar odours of decaying vegetation and carrion. Stretching to his full five feet, four inches, Og looked for potential danger. He feared a long-toothed cat, one of the sharp-clawed winged things that dive shrieking from above or, most dangerous of all, a creature like himself.

A silvery dot pulsed against threatening grey clouds, but he ignored it. The dot was only one more unknown in a world filled with unknowns. Who knew why light began and ended? Or why water vanished into scum-lined pools only to return in slashing torrents that flooded caves? Or why his mate, Mano, had died while birthing the silent, unmoving small one?

A far-off scream, cut off into silence, echoed beyond the woods. His eyes swivelled back to the sky and widened. The dot had mushroomed into a blazing object that grew larger and larger and seemed to be aimed directly at him. Terrified, he dashed back into the cave. The ground shook. Dust swirled and a hot wind swept across the cave's mouth.

Og brushed lank hair from his eyes. Acrid air burned his throat, just as it had during the dry time when the angry Thunder God stabbed the forest with brilliant darts, setting off dense clouds that rose from the wounded earth.

First published in *Writers' Journal* (US), May-June 2011.

He waited, squatting on stubby, muscular legs while peering through dark eyes masked by heavy, furrowed brows. To be quick was good, but to be rash could be fatal.

At last the dust settled. The shiny object that had smashed into the slope below stretched the length of two great fern trees but was only half as wide. Grey vapour like early morning mist trickled from gaping holes. A figure staggered out of the wreckage and collapsed.

Og picked his way down a well-worn path and approached the unmoving form warily, one hand on his sharp stone knife. He would have preferred his spear, but he had lost it hunting a red deer. He had hurled the spear wide of the mark, injuring the animal, but not killing it. Trailing blood, the deer had bolted, the shaft embedded in its side. With darkness falling, Og had not dared to follow. The price of failure had been the hard knot of hunger burning in his belly.

From a safe distance, still poised for flight, Og studied the smoking debris of the crumpled object. The impact had exposed jagged edges, reminding him of a splintered slab of rock fallen from a cliff during one of the shaking times. He edged closer to the unmoving figure, fear gradually yielding to curiosity. *Had the shiny, broken object expelled the thing on the ground while giving birth? Or was it some sort of movable cave in which the creature travelled, like the slow-moving animal that plodded along enclosed in a hard shell?* The shells were useful for holding nuts and berries.

The creature lying on scorched earth was colourless, pale as rainwater. Instead of arms, it had six slender tendrils, thin as vines on trees. A bulbous head, yellow liquid trickling from a deep cut, sat atop a plump frame that rose and fell with uneven, shallow contractions, unlike the rapid beating of Og's heart.

With a roar, the shiny object broke apart. Og flinched as yellow sparks swirled about him, stinging like bees. Ignoring the pain, he dragged the collapsed creature out of the fiery shower and watched the crushed silver tube flare and collapse inward.

Og waited, idly scratching an itch. What now? His vision

flickered and blurred, vanishing in a curtain of red mist. *Pain... pain...!* Thousands of sharp splinters pierced his mind. Howling, he dug broken fingernails into the sides of his head, shaking it violently to out drive the bad things.

The creature had awakened! Three slits blinked open in the gourd-like head. They focused on Og. The flow of yellow, viscous fluid draining from the creature's head had stopped.

He shuddered as something pushed and wrenched at his mind. Eyes shut in agony, he saw: images of the creature and others similar to it... luminous pinpricks, like those in the night sky when the Light God slept... the silver object, unbroken, floating against a velvet-black background as it approached a shimmering green and blue ball.

And then the creature's thoughts became his thoughts.

'You... you have saved me. I am the first of my kind to visit this planet. I shall reward you if you protect me until my... (unclear) come for me. Since you are primitive, my gifts must be limited to...'

Og pounded a side of his head, trying to drive out the unwanted thoughts.

'Fire... I can give you fire and the lever and the wheel!' the voice quavered.

Og watched in astonishment as the creature pointed a shaking limb at a green bush with tiny, desiccated berries. The bush burst into flames.

'Heat... light... protection!'

A second tendril encircled a slender tree and snapped it off at the base. The tree gyrated in the air, bark and leaves flying, until it had been shaped into a long, narrow pole. Purple light flowed over two rocks. The rocks spun and whirled and became smooth and round.

Og blinked. Now the rocks had holes in their centres!

Whipping two limbs through the air, the creature seized the pole and thrust it through the round stones. It pushed and pulled on the pole. The stones rolled forward and backward. Og watched as one end of the pole was placed over the round stones and the other end under a stump. Three limbs wrapped about the pole and forced it downward. The stump rose, tearing loose from the earth.

Reluctantly, he tore his eyes away and fastened them in awe on the mysterious visitor. *What gifts!* he thought. He would make use of all of them.

That night, shivering in the dank cave despite the scratchy, flea-infested skin of a giant rat drawn about his shoulders, Og thought of what he had seen. The hot, flickering light that consumed the bush had been interesting, but he had hurt his hand touching it. Eventually, the light had shrivelled and died.

The pole, he had decided, would make a suitable replacement spear once he added a sharp flint point and bound it with tightly-drawn wet strips of skin baked in the hot sun.

Best of all were the strange stones through which he could thrust his hand. One at a time, he carried them back to the cave, staggering under their weight. His back hurt. But by setting the stones flat, one atop the other, he created a hard, raised surface on which to work spear points more efficiently.

Og twisted his flint knife back and forth in the gritty sand to remove the hardened yellow film coating it. He burped and rubbed his stomach. Perhaps the Sky God would provide more of the entertaining pale things. The first one had been tasty.

Home Improvements

by Georgia Hilton

It was a cold tumble-down sort of house I grew up in. One that had bare floorboards with gaps in them, one that teemed with spiders. The paintwork needed attention – it had long since turned yellow, and even grey in places. The whole place felt unloved and worn out.

Coming back from school was always a bit of a letdown, especially on bleak winter days. I wanted to come home to twinkling lights and a cosy fire, but usually it was gloomy and dark, apart from the flickering light of the TV. I was yearning for something intangible, something like security, and it felt like the whole house was yearning with me.

One particular day – I was about fourteen and had just trudged the half-hour journey home – I noticed something was different about the place. The outside looked cleaner somehow. I let myself in, to find my mother beaming in the kitchen. This was most unusual, as she didn't often smile at all, let alone grin. She was bursting to tell me something.

'So, a young fella knocked on the door and says he's here to paint the front of the house. So I says to him, "Well, I haven't the money to pay you," and he says "It's OK, that's all taken care of." So I says to him, "Who's paying for it?" and he says, "I don't know, the boss is just after telling me to paint your house." Can you believe it, Ciara?'

Actually, I could believe it. I had been reading the predictions of Nostradamus and believed that one day an alien race would come to Earth and take me back with them to their home planet – so an anonymous well-wisher painting our house for us was not such a stretch for me. My mother, on the other hand, had long lived in a world where Only Bad Things Happened. She would not be surprised, for example, by an aeroplane crashing into the house, but a random act of kindness was unfathomable. I just shrugged my shoulders and went upstairs to my room to do my homework.

The following day was Friday, and there was nothing unusual going on when I got back from school, but that night there was a phone call. I ran down the stairs and breathlessly answered. I thought it would be one of my school friends, it usually was.

Instead a man said, 'Hello, is that you, Maureen?'

I don't know what took hold of me but instead of apologising and telling him he had the wrong number, I said, 'Yes, it is, who is this, please?'

'Oh, Maureen, do you not recognise my voice? It's your daddy. I know I haven't seen you for so many years, sweetheart, but I still love you, you know that, darling?'

'Um, yes, I do, Dad,' I replied. My heart had almost stopped beating with the enormity of the lie I was telling, and I was scared even to breathe.

He went on, 'I know I've neglected you all these years, darling. I got word about the state of the house, how you're living. Listen, I can't leave here, I can't come home, not now. I'll never get back into the country if I leave. But I'm going to make things better for you, darling, I promise. And then when you're eighteen I'll buy you a plane ticket, and you can come out to me. Would you like that, Maureen?'

'I would, Dad, I would,' I said in a whisper. My mother was in the front room watching Coronation Street; she could be eavesdropping on the call, as she often did.

'Good, good,' the man said. He sounded relieved, and then awkward, like he had run out of things to say.

'So… Maureen, be a good girl for your mother, and uh, there'll be some more things coming for the house, and for you, love. I love you, bye.'

'Bye,' I said.

'Who was that, Ciara?' my mother called from the sofa.

'Oh, just a wrong number,' I answered, as truthfully as I could.

In the next few weeks the following transformations occurred around the house: a new bathroom and kitchen were put in, new carpeting was laid throughout, a new suite of furniture arrived for the front room, a new set of bedroom furniture was delivered for my room, all the curtains were replaced, and a fresh coat of paint was applied everywhere.

My mother alternated between extremes of joy and fear. Who was the anonymous benefactor? What was their motive? Was all this generosity even meant for us? I had read Great Expectations only recently, so I thought this kind of thing must be fairly common. But even though I had a more sanguine attitude, the sense of mystery and excitement infected me also.

My mother speculated endlessly about the identity of the generous person who was transforming our lives. Perhaps it was her mother's sister Kathleen out in South Africa? It was said she had married a banker. Perhaps it was a secret admirer who had loved her from afar for years. In her darker moments my mother cried and said that maybe it wasn't meant for us at all, and we'd get into trouble for accepting such largesse. Or, even darker still, someone was trying to buy us for their own nefarious purposes, though what these might be she couldn't say.

The neighbours speculated too, though their conclusions were unflattering to say the least. My mother must have a gentleman 'friend' who was rewarding her for services provided, some of them said. My mother had had a lot of money all along, and was being greedy claiming benefits, said others. Still others said she had carried out an insurance scam, and this was generally considered to be the most plausible explanation up and down the road. My mother was not unpopular, but as a single woman with a child she had always aroused suspicion. She could never really be considered of good character.

Meanwhile, I was keeping a secret of my own, for I obviously knew more about our anonymous benefactor than anyone else. I knew that he thought I was a girl called Maureen. I knew that he lived overseas. But that was about it. I had mixed feelings about the situation. I felt I deserved some good fortune, at last. For hadn't my own father deserted us when I was very little? Hadn't I grown up feeling second best all my life? On the other hand I felt some guilt that I was accepting all this stuff that was meant for someone else. Who was Maureen? And why did this man think I was her? There were a lot of questions to answer, and nobody that could answer them for me, so I decided to keep quiet and enjoy the bounty while it lasted.

Eventually, feeling bad about usurping Maureen's birthright, I alighted on a fanciful explanation that could assuage my guilt. I decided that this man really was my dad. He really was going to send me a plane ticket to God knows where when I was eighteen. My mother had obviously changed my name to Ciara after he left, just to spite him. I knew deep down that this was untrue, but I chose to believe it anyhow. I repeated it to myself over and over, even jotting down the particulars in a notebook to make it seem more real.

And then, just as suddenly as it started, it stopped. There were no more tradesmen turning up, no more furniture deliveries. By this stage our house was unrecognisable from the slightly dilapidated building it had once been. It was now a smart looking townhouse. Quite plain and unpretentious, but smart all the same. Good enough for anyone, as my mother liked to say. Her only disappointment was that the anonymous benefactor hadn't turned their attention to the garden. That was still a jumble of nettles and rusting bikes, with a roofless dog kennel thrown in for good measure.

'It would have been so nice to have a lawn laid down,' my mother said wistfully, looking out of the kitchen window.

Some years went by, during which life progressed much as it always had. I was older now, almost eighteen, and looking forward to some independence. I was only a few short weeks away from the end of school and impatience was already setting in.

One day I came back from school a little late. I had lingered over the walk home, enjoying the late spring sunshine and the smell of apple blossom. I had a boyfriend, Vincent. I kept this fact a secret from my mother, though she must have known and kept a tactful silence. I was always crouched over the telephone of an evening, playing a game of 'hang up, no, you hang up first'. Anyway, he had walked me home, stopping at the lamp post just before our neighbour's house, as he always did.

'There's a car outside your house, Ci,' he said. This was remarkable because we didn't own a car and my mother never had visitors. For a moment I thought about not going in, but my curiosity got the better of me. I said a quick goodbye to Vincent – no kissing, my elderly neighbour Mrs Murphy would almost certainly be watching from her porch – and walked into the house as casually as I could.

Sitting in my mother's best chair in the front room was a young woman with a long fair plait and a smattering of freckles on her nose. She was tall, her long legs extended like a telescope as she stood up to greet me. My mother was buzzing around with excitement, bringing plates of biscuits and glasses of water, pots of tea and slices of buttered toast to our unexpected guest.

Our guest's eyes were alight with interest. I knew her name before she spoke.

'I'm Maureen, I used to live here when I was little, I even had your bedroom! I was in the area, well, I'm here for college, and I thought I'd drop in to see the old place, see how it's changed'.

'Where are you staying, love?' asked my mother.

'I'm in digs right now, but it costs a fortune and it's disgusting, to be honest. I think I'll look for lodgings for September.'

My mother and I exchanged a Meaningful Look. I was due to go away in the summer. I had a job lined up as a nanny in New York. The plan was to spend a few weeks bumming around in Greece with Vincent and then head over there. Vincent hoped to follow me. His uncle had apparently worked in construction in New York for the best part of two decades and had promised Vincent he could get him a job. Illegally, of course, but the pay was good and it was cash in hand.

'You can have my room!' I blurted out.

'Oh, I couldn't, I mean, I didn't mean, I wasn't asking,' said Maureen, looking flustered and embarrassed.

'Well, I suppose you could,' my mother said slowly. 'Ciara will be gone at least a year, and this is your old home after all.'

I knew my mother would love the idea – she was dreading

evenings at home alone, with nobody to cook for, talking only to the TV.

'What would your parents think?' my mother asked gently.

Maureen coloured slightly. 'Well, Mam might be surprised, but she'll be happy I'm living with a nice family, and Dad, well, he vanished when I was three so I couldn't care less what he thinks about anything.' This was said with some feeling, a sort of pouting defiance that made her look very young, a little girl.

'Typical, that's men for you,' opined my mother sagely. 'I'm always tellin' Ciara, you're better off without them. Useless wastes of space.'

I sighed deeply. 'Any idea where he went?' I asked.

The telephone was ringing.

'I'll get it,' said my mother. 'You girls sit and have a nice chat.'

'He never said, but he always talked about America…'

Just then my mother came back into the room, looking strangely animated – 'Maureen, it's for you!'

Seeing is believing

by David Binelli

What a lovely day.

It's about 5pm on a beautiful Sunday evening and I've been sitting on a wooden bench in the middle of York for the last hour or so, enjoying just being out and about. I've lived in the city centre for about three years now and I love it. Everything is on my doorstep: shops, cafés, bars and restaurants. What more could a middle-aged single guy want?

The sun is shining and it's about twenty-seven degrees. A perfect evening for sitting here in my cargo shorts, displaying my lily-white legs, my eyes hidden behind some mirrored sunglasses I bought in the market for a fiver, and doing some people watching.

Tourists. Loads of them.

Whenever I'm sitting alone watching the world go by, I play a little game with myself called *Guess where they're from*. I try to guess what nationality people are by the way they're dressed, or how many cameras they have suspended round their necks. Sometimes it's easy because I can hear them chatting to each as they saunter past, other times it's damn near impossible. German, Polish, French, Chinese, Japanese, Thai… or Indonesian at least. And very occasionally, English. Who would have thought it, in the middle of Yorkshire's county town? An Englishman… or a couple of them. Amazing.

Wait a minute.

She looks lovely. Blonde hair. Slim build.

She has my full attention now. I sit up and rest my elbows on my knees, trying not to make it obvious I'm looking at her.

Slowly, she walks across the paved open area in front of me probably no more than a couple of yards away.

I can almost smell her.

I lean back and stretch my arms along the back of the bench, trying to be as cool as a middle-aged man showing off his hairy legs in shorts can be, as she ambles past.

She is about 5' 6", her hair held back by her sunglasses. She has piercing blue eyes. She is wearing a loose-fitting white blouse, which billows slightly as she walks. She has on pink knee-length shorts and white sandals.

Beautiful.

As my eyes, hidden by my sunglasses, study her slow and deliberate steps, she glances sideways, and I swear she smiles at me.

I immediately turn my head away, like a child who's been caught doing something he shouldn't. I feel my face blush with colour, embarrassed at being caught watching her, admiring her.

Love at first sight. Is that a real thing?

When I turn back, she is already about ten yards further on and halfway across a narrow bus lane that the council have carved through the pedestrianised centre of York. Once across, she sits gently down on a bench similar to the one I'm sitting on, and faces me. She looks straight at me and this time I don't turn away. I keep my eyes fixed on her, hoping that my sunglasses make it impossible for her to see what my eyes are doing: watching her.

She looks at me for a couple of seconds before searching in her brown leather handbag for something. She pulls out a mobile phone and makes a call. At first it looks like a normal chat: she smiles several times, a wonderful smile that would light anyone's day, sometimes breaking into a full-blown laugh. Already I feel a tinge of jealousy of whoever is on the other end of the call.

Suddenly, the call seems to take a darker turn and her delightful smile fades into a scowl, with tears forming in her eyes. Even from where I'm sitting I can see her eyes glistening in the evening sun, and then tears cascade down the almost-perfect skin of her cheeks. She swaps her mobile phone to her other hand and thumps it against her ear, while frantically waving her free hand around in front of her.

She's upset and appears to be arguing with the person on the other end of the line. She sits bolt upright and throws her head back, running her hand through her hair again and again. I can't take my eyes off her. She's beautiful.

Abruptly she takes the phone from her ear, stabbing her finger at its screen and then slamming it down on the bench beside her.

I can see her eyes are clenched tight. Her arms are shoved rigidly down either side of her body, grasping the slats of the bench. She begins to rock slowly back and forth in distress.

York city centre is full of people milling about but they are oblivious to her, completely unaware of the drama playing out in front of them.

She is in pain.

Should I go across and talk to her? No. Definitely not. She will think I'm a weirdo. She has seen me watching her so she will think I'm hassling her, at the very least.

But I feel I have to do something. What? And why?

I don't even know this woman. For all I know she's just been arguing with her bank about an overdraft, or she's just been sacked from her job for stealing stationery.

No. It's a lover. I can tell. Definitely the husband, or a boyfriend.

I *want* to do something. I *have* to do something.

Any minute now she could stand up and walk away and that would be it. I would never see her again.

I can see she is upset and confused. She keeps turning her head one way and then the other, looking up and down the street as if she is looking for something, or someone.

I lean forward slightly and pull my sunglasses down, resting them on my nose, so I can get a better look at her. Then, completely unintentionally, my eyes catch hers. She stares directly at me for what seems an eternity, but in reality is only a few seconds. I hold my nerve and keep my eyes fixed on hers.

This is it. The moment I've been waiting for.

I take a deep breath and puff out my chest, but just as I'm about to stand up, she grabs her phone from the bench and throws it into her bag. She leaps to her feet, still looking straight at me. Is she going to come over?

Shocked, without looking away from her, I jump up too, scaring a few pigeons that had been scavenging for crumbs on the pavement in front of me.

I move towards her, I can see she is already at the kerb's edge.

But wait. There's something coming along the road. Fast. Much too fast. It's a bus.

I can tell she hasn't seen it. She steps off the pavement into the path of the oncoming bus. At that heart-stopping moment everything seems to flow in slow motion. I try to call out to her but my throat is dry. I cough and try again.

'WATCH OUT!' I yell at the top of my voice. 'STOP!'

She doesn't hear me, and takes another step, blind to the impending impact.

I freeze on the spot and close my eyes as the bus hits her head on.

Except.

There is no screeching of brakes. No bone-crunching thud or scream. No reaction from passers-by. Nothing.

I spin round in utter disbelief that no one else saw the accident and that the bus didn't stop.

Everyone and everything continues as if nothing happened.

What's going on?

I turn back to see her calmly walking across the remainder of the road and directly towards me. I'm utterly confused, and stand motionless with my mouth wide open as she approaches me.

'How– Didn't you see the bus?' I splutter.

She doesn't reply. In fact she doesn't even acknowledge me. It's as if I don't exist.

'Excuse me but...' I begin, as something happens that only happens in horror films.

She walks straight through me.

I mean she walks through my body as if I'm not even there. I whirl round just in time to see her walking across the pedestrian area, but instead of bumping into people she walks through them, just as she had done to me. My shoulders droop as every piece of reality I have come to believe swirls around in my head.

What have I just witnessed?

I feel a slight push on my shoulder. And then again.

'Excuse me.' I hear faintly. 'Excuse me. Are you alright?' says an elderly lady standing next to me. 'Did you drop these sunglasses?'

'Oh… Yes… Thank you,' I reply, still in shock, holding out a hand for the glasses.

'You look like you've seen a ghost,' she says handing them to me.

'Well, yes. I think I have.'

'Was she blonde?' she says, looking at me with a twinkle in her eye.

'Yes. Yes, she was. Blonde and beautiful.'

'That'll be the lady that was knocked down by a bus a few years ago. She shows up from time to time. No one knows why. They never found out why she didn't see it coming. Poor thing,' says the old lady, taking an orange from her bag and sitting down on the bench where I had been. 'Come and talk to me for a while. It's such a lovely evening.'

'Oh, alright. You know what… I have an idea as to why she didn't see the bus,' I say, slowly sitting down beside her.

'Really, dear? Tell me all about it.'

La Petite France

by Mike Evis

Anna felt a nudge from Stella.

'Oh God – isn't that Daniel walking across the square? It is. He's not coming in here, is he? Oh Christ, he must be. How did he find out about tonight?'

'I invited him,' said Anna. 'That's how he found out.'

They sat in the centre of the long, half-empty table, the candlelight appearing gradually brighter as the day faded into evening. A solitary street light came on across the road. They watched a man in his early fifties, perhaps older, striding across the cobblestones towards the restaurant.

'What were you thinking?' Stella demanded.

Anna stared coolly at her friend, as if taking in for the first time the thin face, the pinched nose, the mean twist of her mouth, and the restless eyes that even now scanned the room, as if seeking prey. Had she got worse, thought Anna, or was she always like this?

'You invited him tonight? Here, to La Petite France?'

'Yes,' Anna said.

'Hello? This is your birthday. Why?'

Anna sighed.

'You know perfectly well why: he's an old friend.'

'He gives me the creeps.'

'Come on, Stella, don't be so silly. Sometimes I really–'

'It's the way he looks at you sometimes. You don't notice it, but I do.'

'He's alright. Really. He's harmless.'

'They're the worst, believe me, they lull you–'

'Shush, he's coming in.'

'I'm telling you–'

The door opened, and they felt a cooling blast of evening air come in with him.

'And why,' Stella whispered, 'has he never married or anything? No girlfriend, no–'

'Stella–'

'Oh.'

He was there.

'Anna, Stella, lovely to see you again.'

Did Anna imagine it, or was there a brief grimace as Stella's name passed his lips?

He kissed Anna on both cheeks, his delicate hands lingering for an instant on her shoulder.

Stella pulled back as he leaned towards her.

'Remember, Daniel–'

'Oh,' he said, looking confused.

'We don't do that. Not after…'

'Yes, I know. Sorry.'

'I had to disinfect myself for a month.'

He looked down at the table, before Anna broke in.

'Stop it, you two. Daniel, it's lovely to see you again. Thanks ever so much for coming.'

He sat down in the chair right next to her, leaning in close. Stella was on the other side.

'I haven't seen you in ages,' Anna continued. 'Must be at least two or three months.'

A strange half-smile played across his face and was gone. Stella leaned over, behind Anna's back, and prodded him heavily.

'You can't sit there. That's her husband's seat.'

'Oh, Stella,' said Anna, 'stop being so silly. You know I haven't seen Daniel for a while' – and again that strange look came onto his face – 'but I see Gerry every single day. I don't need to sit next to him tonight as well.'

'I'm just saying it looks odd.'

'Stella, this is my special birthday.'

Stella slumped back in her seat, looking sullen.

*

The hall was vast, overwhelming to Daniel at first sight, crammed with stalls, the passages between thronged with students as confused as he was. The noise too, echoing off the high roof above, made it hard to think. How was he to make sense of it all? Some of the stalls were easy to discount – the Sailing Club, Gay Soc, the African Students Society, the Young Conservatives, the Socialist Workers Party. But others needed more thought, like the Film Society, the Writers Club, the Literary Society. How did you choose? How did all these people define exactly what they were, or wanted to be? It was confusing. He'd thought all his choices were over once he'd decided which university to go to, and which course to take. But it seemed it just went on and on.

Amid the bewildering choice of stalls, set out like a market square in a busy town or at some bazaar. He wandered listlessly, driven on by a restless crowd unsure where it was going, drifting with no clear purpose. The Christian Union, the Oriental Society, the Labour Party, he walked past them all. It'd been simpler at school, there were only a few clubs to pick from. But here....

*

Anna was aimlessly wandering around the stalls, waiting for Stella to turn up, when she saw him standing right in the middle of a busy crossroads, next to the Jewish Society stand. He looked lost, his face a boyish mix of confusion and innocence, his duffel coat marking him out as a first year like her. But something wasn't right. As she got closer she realised it was the way he was so completely motionless. He wasn't absorbed, it was if he wasn't there at all, wasn't seeing anything, not even her peering at him. His eyes were empty, unfocussed, he was frozen. She frowned.

'Are you alright?' she asked, and when he didn't reply, she tugged his sleeve.

*

The girl in front of him was beautiful, her freckled face like a fresh page in a book, standing out in contrast to the cynical expressions of the other students. As she stood in front of him, the ponytail that neatly tied up her dark hair swayed ever so slightly behind her. Was it her tentative smile that made him instantly fall in love? He knew this frail, pale looking creature in a long dress could rescue him. Yet he also knew she would rebuff him, as they all did.

'Hard… hard to know which one to go for, isn't it? I can't decide,' he said.

He saw doubt, perhaps even fright, flicker through her eyes as he spoke. She realised she'd left it too late to escape, he thought.

'I mean, there are so many, aren't there?' he added.

But she stayed standing there, simply giving an embarrassed cough.

'Is that what you were doing standing there? Trying to decide?'

'Yes,' he said. He'd learned to be careful about these episodes. 'I've given up. I don't want to choose any of them. I'm just hanging around until my friend gets here.' She laughed, a soft tinkling sound, as a smile lit up her entire face.

*

'So, you got chatted up by some bloke at the clubs and societies fair?'

'It wasn't quite like that.'

'No? Sounds like it to me. Some strange bloke–'

'Daniel. His name's Daniel.'

Stella sniggered.

'What's so funny?'

'Bit pretentious, isn't it? Daniel. Not Dan, Daniel.' She sniggered again. 'Hello,' she said, in a deep, mocking voice, 'I'm Daniel,' then dissolved into giggles.

She slapped Anna playfully and the bar table shook, rattling their drinks.

'Shush, he'll be here in a minute. Stop being so sarky. Why did I ever ask you along?'

'I can't believe you'd let yourself be propositioned so easily this time.'

'Stella–'

'He was just lonely, I think.'

'Right, and Mark's like a hundred miles away.'

'Why do you have to twist everything? I only agreed to meet him out of politeness.'

'Oh Christ, Anna. Politeness! You're like, so totally middle class sometimes. You're so nice. Too nice. It can get you into a lot of trouble, trust me.'

'I'm not blunt like you.'

'Look, I say it how it is. People know where they stand. I don't take bull from anyone. And how are things with Mark?'

Anna grimaced.

'That bad?'

'I don't know. We haven't spoken much. And he was really odd before I left for uni. I don't think he wanted me to come.'

Stella snorted. 'He knew you were going to university. If he can't deal with it, then, look, you can't put your studies, your life, on hold. Not for any bloke.'

'I know, but–'

'But what? There is no but.'

'You're so cynical about people.'

'I'm realistic. That's how blokes are.'

'It's different with me and Mark.'

'Hello.' Daniel had arrived. He looked like he was about to bend down and kiss Anna on the cheek, before realising she wasn't alone. He stood, looking flustered, before stuttering, 'Anna, I didn't realise you were bringing a friend. So, what's this? Two beautiful girls, not just one. Who–'

'Is this guy for real, Anna?' Stella said incredulously. She stood up as if she might be about to storm out, but seeing that Anna hadn't moved, she turned to Daniel. 'I'm Stella, and I'm not just some beautiful girl, mate, for you to patronise and look down on. I'm an adult human being, like Anna, so treat us like it.'

'Oh. I'm sorry.'

'Stella–'

'Anna, I won't put up with this sort of male chauvinist crap.'

'I'm sure Daniel was just trying to be nice.'

'Right.'

'Can I... can I get you two a drink?' Daniel stuttered.

'I'll have a pint,' said Stella. She sat back down and crossed her arms.

'A pint?'

'Of beer. You got a problem with that?'

'Stella–'

'No, no,' Daniel said defensively, 'it's just–'

'Unusual? Get used to it.'

'I'd like a vodka and lime,' said Anna.

As he quickly walked to the bar, Stella barely suppressed her giggles.

'You've got a right one there.'

Anna frowned. 'Can't you just be nice for a minute? It's not much to ask, is it?'

'Now you sound like my gran. Sometimes you're so uncool.'

'I just think it wouldn't hurt, that's all.'

'So you do fancy him? God knows why.'

'Must you always be so difficult?'

'You've got to admit, he's, like, a total prat.'

'Stella,' Anna protested, then she caught her friend's eye and they both dissolved into giggles.

'And fancy saying "two beautiful girls" – how uncool is that?'

They controlled their laughter, then looked round, expecting him to be back. But he wasn't.

'He's taking his time,' said Stella.

'I'll go up. The bar doesn't look that busy, does it? I can see him standing there, maybe he needs a hand,' Anna said.

His face was vacant, as if no one were there. He stood as motionless as a marble statue. It was just like at the clubs and societies fair. What looked like their drinks were on the counter in front of him.

The barman shrugged.

'Been like that for a few minutes. Has he taken something?'

'No. I mean, I don't think so.' She tapped Daniel's shoulder. 'Daniel?'

'Oh.' He was like a clockwork toy that had just been wound up. Confusion showed in his eyes until he focussed on Anna.

'Daniel, are you alright?'

'I'm fine.' He picked up the drinks, his hands shaking slightly.

Reaching the table, he set Anna's glass down with exquisite care but spilled Stella's pint. As well as the spreading pool of beer on the table top, there was a trail of drips leading all the way across the floor towards the bar. Stella stared at it, but said nothing.

'So, Dan,' Stella began.

He cringed.

'Did you have someone special back there?'

'At the bar?' He looked round.

Stella sighed loudly, too loudly.

'Don't be stupid.'

'Stella–'

'Where you came from, I mean.'

'Yes,' he said. 'Her name was Rebecca. She was head girl at school. We were childhood sweethearts. But we broke up to go to uni.'

'Aah,' Stella said. It wasn't clear whether she was mocking him or not.

'And you're studying?'

'Physics.'

'Yeah, it would have to be.'

'Stella, can't we just have a normal conversation,' Anna said, looking pleadingly at her friend.

'I'm just asking Dan a few questions, that's all. He doesn't mind, do you? Do you have your own transport, Dan?'

'I've got a car. A Cortina.'

'I suppose you think that'll impress us?'

'Stella,' said Anna. 'Sorry, Daniel, she can't help–'

'Don't make excuses for other people, Anna. So, Dan, where's this car of yours? Can we see it?'

'Er, I had to leave it behind.'

'So we can't see it.'

'No.'

'I bet it doesn't go. I know your type. You've got some old banger that never starts.'

'Of course it goes alright. You should see it when I put my foot down, it goes like the wind. You get solid workmanship in a Vauxhall.'

'Thought you said it was a Cortina?'

'I–'

'Stella, stop having a go at Daniel.'

'One minute he says it's a Cortina and the next minute he says it's a Vauxhall. A Cortina's a Ford.'

'You're probably flustering him with all the questions you keep firing off.'

'I couldn't bring it, I had to leave the car up at my parents', there's not much parking here.'

'That's a shame. You could have taken us beautiful girls out in it, couldn't you, Dan?'

'That's enough, Stella.'

*

Nothing before or since would ever compare with the sumptuous memory of that first encounter at the clubs and societies fair. It had stayed vivid in his mind all these years. Every now and again he would bring it out, like a fine wine, simply to taste and savour, before carefully putting it away again. His first sight of that young, fresh face, the freckles on her cheeks, and that innocent smile, all of it was etched into his memory, becoming richer and more luminous every time he revisited it.

'Do you fancy a coffee or something?' he had asked her.

He didn't realise then that this would be one of the formative experiences of his whole life.

Anna's smile had narrowed. Doubt and bewilderment flickered over her face as she looked from side to side for someone to rescue her. But no one did.

'Oh. No, not right now.'

'When? Tonight, perhaps?'

'Not tonight. I'm meeting a friend.'

'Tomorrow night then?'

'Alright. Yes. Tomorrow night.'

'At the union bar?'

And then to find that other girl, that dreadful friend of hers, was there too, glaring at him, asking all those questions. And why had he said Rebecca, the ice-cold blonde from the school hockey team, had been his girlfriend, when she wouldn't even give him a second glance? And why had he told them he had a car? Luckily he'd got away with it.

And it hadn't prevented his friendship with Anna. He'd been

there for her, over the years – like when she finally broke up with that waster Mark. Why did she always fall for those complete losers when there was him at hand, who knew her better than anyone?

He hadn't seen her for weeks on end while she was going out with Mark. Then, one night, her pounding on his door woke him from a deep sleep, and it took him a good minute or two to come to. When he realised it was his door that was being banged on, he quickly leapt out of bed – was this another fire alarm? Some drunken idiot was always breaking the glass to set it off on a Friday night – but you never knew. He fumbled with the lock, unable to co-ordinate fingers, thumbs and keys – it was twenty to two in the morning – and finally flung the door open to find, not one of his corridor mates, but a tearful Anna in her dressing gown, her face screwed up and wretched.

'He's dumped me,' she wailed, stumbling into his room like a toddler learning to walk. She paced unevenly up and down, her arms flailing, while he longed to hold her, to comfort her – purely as a friend, of course.

'Why?' she demanded, banging his flimsy desk, shaking the mug he was about to rinse so she could have a cup of tea. 'Why? Why would he do that, after all this time? Why?'

Because he doesn't deserve you, he wanted to say. Because he can't look after you properly. Don't you see, he screamed in his mind, don't you see how... but instead, other words came to the surface as he spoke. They came automatically, without conscious thought; perhaps he'd read them somewhere.

'These things happen,' he said. 'Maybe it simply wasn't meant to be.' His mind raced ahead. With Mark out of the way, suddenly there was hope. Suddenly he had a chance with Anna.

'No,' she said. 'It was so perfect. How could he ruin it like that? With her, of all people?' Her face looked wild, as if she were possessed.

Finally, when she stopped pacing in front of the wardrobe, he put his arms clumsily around her shoulders and hugged her. Her face was wet, her eyes puffy, and every now and again she would shudder. But touching her, it was like an electric shock went right through his body. This was contact of another kind, on a different level entirely from the first time he saw her. He'd waited so long for this. It felt warm, soft and safe, like a cocoon. Still the occasional sniffle escaped her lips, still she shook with tears, but the storm was subsiding. He patted her back. That Mark was a fool, but Mark's loss was his gain.

Suddenly she pulled away, her eyes for an instant locking onto his, looking perplexed and uncertain.

'It's confusing,' she said. 'I should have gone to see Stella, but she's gone back home for a few days. And then I thought of you.'

That was fortunate, he thought.

'Can I stay?' she said, and his heart leapt. 'I mean, I'll sleep on the sofa.'

'Yes,' he said quickly, only realising too late he could have given her the bed and taken the sofa, but she was already curling up on it.

He hardly slept that night, listening out for the sound of her breathing, the occasional sniffle. She was sleeping, there, in his room, only a few feet away. His heart pounded.

*

'I'm going to give you an experience you've never had before,' Anna said as they walked up the High Street. A frisson of excitement, mingled with curiosity, went through him. He tried not to imagine what it could be, his mind racing while he tried to hold it back. He had to experience whatever it was at her pace.

'Here we are,' she said, turning in through the door of Laura Ashley. 'I bet you've never been in here before.'

She laughed, and he echoed her laughter, even though it sounded hollow in his ears, like he'd betrayed himself.

'Now I'm working I've developed this bad habit. I have to go into Laura Ashley at least once a month.'

Afterwards, in the café down the street, with the Saturday afternoon shoppers trudging past the window, she suddenly leaned forward, chin resting on her hands, a serious expression on her face. He loved it when she looked at him like that.

'What is it you want?' she asked, and he hesitated, his heart thumping hard, feeling himself about to make that step and declare himself. Was this the moment? His hand crept over the sticky surface of the table, inching towards hers. The grey winter's day was suddenly far away, shoved into irrelevance. How should he begin? The words were like tenuous foot-holds on a steep, slippery mountainside.

'What do I want? I suppose I thought we–'

'Sorry, what I meant was: what is it you men want? I didn't word it very well.'

Now his hand lay limp and useless on the table top.

'I suppose what we want...' he stumbled, picking his way across a minefield of words, '...is just the same as you.'

'Then why,' she turned to him with vivid eyes, eyes he wished were always so bright when she was with him. 'Then why is it so difficult?'

Hope, which had flared up like a fiery beacon only a moment ago was now extinguished. The films they went to see, the cafés, the shopping trips, he could see it all clearly now. He was the stand-in, until the next useless boyfriend came along. 'Always the bridesmaid, never the bride.' He had to face it, he'd drifted firmly into the friend zone. And once you were in there, there was no way out.

'Oh God, was Laura Ashley really that terrible?'

He looked at her, broken-hearted.

'Your face! I'm sorry – I promise I won't ever subject you to that again.'

Yes, he'd spent years and years hoping, but nothing was ever going to develop between them, was it? Would he ever feel satisfied without her?

*

'You're gorgeous, aren't you, darling? Oh, did I make your sister jealous?'

Stella dangled one of Anna's toddlers on her lap, as Anna sipped her coffee with the other twin sitting next to her in a high chair.

'Feeling broody?' Anna asked Stella with a wink.

'What? Not bloody likely.'

'It'll happen. You know, once I thought – you'll laugh at this

– you and Daniel…. Sometimes I wondered if your total disdain was just your way of flirting.'

'Don't.' Lifting the girl in her lap she said, 'Your mummy's got some wicked ideas, hasn't she?'

'I just thought – you were my best friends and it would have been nice….'

'Nice? Nice for who exactly?'

'You know,' Anna said, and changed the subject. 'I hardly ever get out these days. I never go anywhere, not now I've got the twins.'

'You're making a good case for not having kids.'

'It's so precious for me to get out to a café like this. La Petite France. How long has this place been here? I didn't know it even existed.'

'You really don't get out much, do you? Couple of years, I think,' Stella said.

'I bet it's nice in the evenings too. Wine and candlelight.' Anna went quiet for a moment, then returned to her previous train of thought. 'You know, I haven't seen Daniel in ages. It's like he's avoiding me, or lost interest.'

'Anna, get real. You're married, you've got kids, your life is different.'

'But we were friends.'

Stella shrugged.

'People change. Does he still do that thing where he freezes?'

'I suppose.'

'He never got treatment for it?'

'I don't suppose he did. He never mentioned it so I never brought it up. Anyway, why are you asking? If you really don't like him.'

'Got to know your enemy, Anna.'

*

When Anna turned up at his flat one night, it was a couple of years since he'd seen her. He'd not seen her since her wedding, in fact. She'd married some bloke called Gerald – an accountant, for God's sake.

Standing on his doorstep, her mascara running and her hair tangled like a bird's nest, she wailed, 'Why is Stella never in when I need her!'

'What's happened?' he asked. 'What is it?' Somewhere deep inside he felt a small flame light. Was there hope?

'He says he'll leave me. He says it's all over.'

Careful, he thought. Don't leap in too obviously. 'People say that in the heat of the moment. It doesn't mean anything.'

'You don't understand. This isn't the first time. He means it, I know. I wish Stella was home.'

There were other words he wanted to use, but he had to choose what he said carefully. He had a role to play and he couldn't be too clumsy about this. It had to be done stealthily. 'Look, give it a few days. Sleep on it. He'll see sense.' Every word false, every phrase the opposite of what he longed to say, like a sharp knife in his guts. Always the bridesmaid, never the bride.

But a few days later, she rang him up: 'Meet me at La Petite France.'

'That's the bistro by the square, isn't it? Yes, but what's the occasion?'

'Just meet me there. One o'clock. I'll explain.'

Lunch was quite innocent, like it had been at university. She talked and talked, about how kids changed you, about her responsibilities, about staying with Gerry. Nothing more, just everyday conversation. Until, 'I wish I could leave him.'

'Then do,' he said, too quickly.

'It's not so easy. There's the girls. I can't do that to them. It would be so awful. They're so young still. They need a family.' She drained her wine glass as soon as the waiter refilled it.

'You didn't drive here?'

'Daniel, I need something more than – this.'

Heart pounding, yet cautious after the long years of waiting, he hardly dared hope for what she might say next. It had always struck him these things were like landing a big fish. You took it slowly, carefully: you had to hook it first, then you could reel it in. But was this it at last?

He contented himself with reaching out across the table. Her fingers wrapped themselves around his like a vice. He began to imagine those same hands caressing his chest, he imagined the two of them alone in his flat....

It was the following week that things really developed. A Thursday, the same time, and the same café again.

'It's no better,' she said. 'I'm so unhappy. Do you understand? I need more than this.'

This opening up, deepening the trust between them, was what he'd dreamed of since the first time he saw her. For a moment he could hardly breathe, his chest felt so tight. He remembered his own internal advice. Slowly, slowly. 'You have to give it time.'

'All these years I've never really seen you,' she said, her eyes suddenly vibrant. 'You've just always been there. But I never saw you. Not till now. Now my eyes are open.'

'I – never imagined,' he lied.

Afterwards, lying together, her small body pressed up close to his, she uttered a deep sigh of contentment.

'That wasn't wrong, was it?' she whispered, rubbing her leg absently against his.

'No,' he said, every fibre of his body at fever pitch.

'Am I a terrible person if I say–' her eyes suddenly wide open, their gaze lingering on his face 'if you wanted – I mean, we could make this a regular...? Oh God, am I really saying this? What am I, some sort of hussy?'

His arm crept up to smooth her cheek. 'Of course you're not.'

She laughed. 'I know.'

'You're not... you won't tell Stella, will you?' he said tentatively.

She snorted. 'Christ, no. Imagine that.'

'Yeah, I'm trying not to.'

How long had their weekly liaisons been going on? Years. The weeks filled with meaningless days, all empty as each other, waiting for Monday, Tuesday and Wednesday to go past, until Thursday arrived. Thursdays were all he lived for: lunch at La Petite France, followed by blissful afternoons spent at his flat.

Their time always ended too soon.

'I'd better be going.'

'Already? Come on, just a few minutes more.'

'I'd love to but Gerry and the girls will miss me if I don't get back soon. They think I'm with an old friend.'

Stroking the upper part of her thigh, he murmured, 'Well, you are.'

The meal, the words, the actions, the touching had become ritualistic, almost choreographed. After all this time, every week, for years, the same time, the same place, the same words, the same actions, over and over… it had become cosy and comfortable. Sometimes, in odd moments, he had the strange thought that his life had turned into one big lie. No one knew, except him and Anna.

So it was odd that she'd arranged her party for the very same day they always had their weekly liaison, and at the same restaurant. Thursday was their day – why have her party then?

*

'Is your friend alright?' said the woman sitting next to Daniel.

'Oh God,' said Stella. 'Dan's ruddy zoned out – and at your party too, Anna! Christ, he picks his times.'

'Just leave him, he'll come to. It's just something that happens. If he doesn't come back in five minutes or so, I'll give him a nudge,' Anna said.

'Have you and Dan always been friends then?' the woman asked.

'Since the first week at university,' said Anna.

'And was there ever a time when you might have been more than friends? I mean, did you ever…?'

'No, no, we've never been anything more than friends.'

*

He had this ability, but he didn't realise when he was growing up that there was anything different about him. He thought everyone could do this. It only slowly dawned on him that they couldn't, that it was a unique talent only he had.

He could conjure up… not daydreams, but visions far beyond that, so vivid they were almost real: imaginary toys you could touch, playmates to talk to when he was lonely, magical lands, and mythical creatures. At first the visions weren't easily controllable, it was random, hard to summon when you wanted it; but as a teenager he learned how to control and shape his thoughts, and soon he could conjure up almost anything he wanted.

True, it was never quite the same as real life, but it was close. You might be able to tell the difference if you paid attention, but it was good enough to feel real at the time.

The concentration it demanded was mentally enervating. He couldn't kept it up for too long, and eventually the pictures would fade. But if he was careful, he could return, time and time again, pick up where he left off.

When you can imagine your own version of the world, suddenly it no longer matters that your life hasn't worked out how you wanted. You have your own reality, but the further it is from how things actually are, the more effort it takes.

So, as he got older, and her life developed, he found it harder to accommodate reality in his imagination. When she married, he had been able to conjure up images of him by her side in the church, at their own wedding, rather than her marrying that Gerald jerk. But it was hard to hold onto after a few years, especially after the twins arrived. The mental exertion of conjuring up a scenario so at odds with real life was too great.

And then he thought of something more straightforward: they didn't have to be married. She could still be married to Gerald, but what if the two of them had an affair? That didn't require such a vast deviation. It was simpler and more plausible.

But lately he was finding it harder and harder to distinguish between reality and what he'd invented. Had he been trying too hard? Had he been living in these fantasy worlds for too long? Was he now incapable of distinguishing between what was real and what wasn't? And did it matter?

Lying on the bed, he gently caressed Anna's back, feeling a huge wave of contentment wash over him. This is what I've always wanted, he thought.

*

'What do you think goes on in his mind when he zones out like that?' the woman asked.

'God knows. I don't want to imagine,' said Stella.

About the Authors

David Binelli: I am fifty-seven years old and have been writing as a hobby for approximately five years. I have written five novels and one book of children's short stories which I have self-published on Amazon.

Angus Broadbent is a full-time creative writing student and a part-time bookseller based around Oxford. His life seems to revolve entirely around books. He enjoys writing and reading science fiction and fantasy.

Oliver Bussell left graphic design and copywriting to pursue writing full time, travelling the world in search of inspiration. With roots in literary fiction, his stories cross genres, united by a fascination in the human condition. Follow his journey @byOliverBussell

Sarah Byrne is a writer of fiction for both adults and young adults. By day she is a film and theatre researcher and you can find her talking about all of that on twitter @sarahbyrnesays.

Arthur Carey is a former newspaper reporter, editor, and journalism instructor who lives in the San Francisco Bay Area. He is a member of the California Writers Club. His short stories have been published in the US, the UK, Canada, and Australia.

Zoe Chater is a physics teacher with a background in experimental particle physics. She writes fiction for fun.

Emma Crees is a writer and blogger from Didcot who talks about writing much more than she actually writes but is rediscovering a love of fiction writing. Find her blog at writerinawheelchair.co.uk.

James Debenham is an English writer who started his professional writing career in television as a creative copywriter, writing everything from promos and branding to comedy sketches. Despite being an experienced screenwriter and director, nothing gives him more pleasure than when he's writing short fiction. 'Swarmer' forms part of a collection of his London short stories all centred on women.

Mike Evis lives in Abingdon, and has had a lifelong passion for writing, He mainly reads modern literary fiction or science fiction; both genres are reflected in his short stories, of which he has had fourteen published in various anthologies to date (including a novelette-length piece of fiction).

Marina Favila is an English professor at James Madison University in Virginia. She has published essays on Shakespeare, poetry, and film in various academic journals. Her published creative work includes pieces in the journals Jersey Devil Press and Wraparound South, and in the anthologies *Seven Deadly Sins* (Harvardwood) and *Haunted House* (Flame Tree Press).

Deborah Freeman is a playwright who also writes short stories and occasional poetry. In 2018 her stories were published in Stand Magazine, on the website called 'Words for the Wild', and in the USA-published Momaya Press 2018 Anthology of Short Stories. For contact see www.deborahfreeman.co.uk.

David McVey lectures in Communication at New College Lanarkshire. He has published over 120 short stories and a great deal of non-fiction that focuses on history and the outdoors. He enjoys hillwalking, visiting historic sites, reading, watching telly, and supporting his home-town football team, Kirkintilloch Rob Roy FC.

Margaret Gallop: I have always loved writing and value my travels and experiences to dip into for ideas. When writing short stories I enjoy entering a world I can barely imagine and attempting to bring it to life.

Stewart Greene: thirty-nine years old, a detective. Took up writing a short time ago. I'm writing because I want to pick at the threads. We're all woven together, an exultant mixture of blood, bones, and fibres. I want to strum the threads that course from heart to soul like violin strings – make them sing.

Georgia Hilton is a poet and fiction writer. Her debut poetry pamphlet was published by Dempsey and Windle in 2018 and she won the Brian Dempsey Memorial Prize in the same year. Georgia loves writing stories with an unexpected twist. She lives in Winchester with her husband and three children.

Tony Lawrence: I am a recently-retired businessman, married and living in North Yorkshire. I'm new to writing and spend my newly-found leisure time writing short stories, playing my drums and enjoying nice holidays in the sunshine.

MM Lewis has had over twenty-five short stories published in themed anthologies, journals and eZines, including BFS Horizons, Another Place, and Full Fathom Forty. He has also been running Creative Writing workshops since 2008. If you want to know more, check out the blogsyntheticscribe.wordpress.com or Facebook page @mmlewiswriter.

Alice Little's writing is inspired by literary fiction of the early twentieth century and real life moral dilemmas. She had had sixteen short stories published since 2016, alongside four anthologies, and has edited three collections of short stories by others. Find out more at alicelittle.co.uk/fiction, and find her on Instagram and Twitter at @littleamiss.

Rose Little: I am busy writing a longer work using experiences from teaching in Kenya in the '70s. It is fun bringing these scenes back to mind and making up characters to people a well-defined place. I find writing in a group with a shared goal a great incentive

John Ludlam: A career that spans the IT revolution and social care made me a witness to the impacts of telecoms, high finance, the credit economy, childcare issues and data regulation. Story (reading/writing) for me is more than therapy, it is through character that I comprehend our changing world.

Shirley Muir writes poems, short stories and creative non-fiction. A molecular biologist, she is a medieval re-enactor, tarot reader and makes costumes to wear at the Venice Carnival. She won the 2015 Crediton short story competition. Her work has been published in *The Eildon Tree, Fifty Flashes, Insights: Fifteen Stories Exploring Disability*, and the inaugural *Henshaw Anthology*, and can be read online at InfectiveInk, Caesura, and Bunbury.

Clare Marsh lives in the Weald of Kent and works as an international adoption social worker. An active member of local writers' groups, she recently completed MA Creative Writing at the University of Kent. She has enjoyed many successes in writing competitions and is currently assembling her first poetry collection.

David Perlmutter is a freelance writer based in Winnipeg, Manitoba, Canada. He is the author of *America Toons In: A History of Television Animation* (McFarland and Co.), *The Singular Adventures Of Jefferson Ball* (Amazon Kindle/Smashwords), and other works. His short stories can be read on *Curious Fictions*; he can be reached on Twitter at @DKPLJW1.

Thomas Redjeb was born in 1995 and raised in Berkshire. He completed an Undergraduate Degree in English at Bath Spa University before attaining a Master's Degree from the University of Reading.

Lavonne Roberts, the author of stories and personal essays, is completing her memoir and creative writing MFA at The New School. Lavonne founded WRITE ON!, which provides free creative writing workshops for marginalized voices. She's an aggressively-optimistic Texan who plans road trips around culinary adventures, coastlines, and independent cinemas.

Dr David Rudd is an Emeritus Professor of Children's Literature at the University of Bolton, UK. He has published extensively in the academic field but has only recently turned to creative writing. He also enjoys playing folk and blues music and travelling.

Abigail B Vint has spent over twenty years playing with words professionally and has come back to fiction after a post-elementary school hiatus. She uses writing to explore our deepest and closest relationships. Her short stories have been published in anthologies by the Oxford Writing Circle. A dual Canadian-Irish citizen, she lives in Oxford with her partner, David.

Grant Waters is a portrait painter based in Oxfordshire. When not painting he is a college lecturer. He has been spinning yarns for his children at bedtime for a good few years and has latterly tried his hand at writing more adult fare.

Rachel Waters studied English Language and Literature at the University of Manchester. She is married to the artist, Grant Waters, and they have two children. She works at a primary school after-school club and enjoys being in a book group and writing in her spare time.

Kathryn Wills is currently researching a PhD on Theology and English and French poetry at Glasgow University, and has an open mind about her next job; she is also a freelance teacher of English. She writes poetry, short stories and parts of longer works of fiction in her somewhat limited free time.

Other Books

The Most Normal Town in England, launched in December 2018, was Didcot Writers' second collection, and its first in print. In this anthology authors were challenged to consider what makes a town normal – or not: who lives there, who never leaves, what skeletons are lurking in the closets? From sci-fi to romance, from horror to literary fiction, this book contains 42 stories by 40 authors detailing the happenings in a range of apparently normal English towns, villages and cities.

Compositions: a collection of short stories on the theme of music, was launched in December 2018. The stories in this book were selected from among the submissions to Didcot Writers' summer competition. You can read some of the stories at didcotwriters.wordpress.com, where you can also find out about new opportunities. From musicians to collectors, instruments to electronics, this book approaches the theme of music from a range of directions.

Printed in Great
Britain
by Amazon